TOM SAWYER RETURNS

THE NEW ADVENTURES

E.E. BURKE

Tom Sawyer Returns is a work of fiction. All characters and events
in this publication, other than those clearly in the public domain,
are fictitious and any resemblance to real persons, living or dead,
is purely coincidental.

Cover Design by Erin Dameron-Hill

Cover image (painting) by Gary R. Lucy: MISSISSIPPI RIVER
LANDING: Loading Cypress Lumber at Caruthersviees Landing,
1857. Courtesy of the Gary R. Lucy Gallery Inc., Washington, MO

Published by E.E. Burke
eBook ISBN: 978-0-9985382-6-6
Print book ISBN: 978-0-9985382-7-3
www.eeburke.com

This book is dedicated to the gifted storyteller who brought Tom and Becky to life, and to the dear friends who encouraged me to tell the rest of their story.

AUTHOR'S NOTE

From an early age, I've been afflicted with a fondness for two precocious Missouri-bred boys introduced to me by Mark Twain. As I read (and reread) Tom and Huck's adventures, I hated to bid them farewell at a point where their stories were just taking off. What happened to them when they grew up?

Tom Sawyer Returns picks up more than a decade after we left him as a carefree lad in a sleepy town on the Mississippi River. It made sense that Tom would eventually leave to seek adventures. History provided a desperate event that would bring him home, determined to be a hero.

Numerous incidents in this book are based on historic reports, one of which alludes to a shadowy conspiracy by Confederate sympathizers. Put Tom in the middle of a deadly scheme, having to solve a mystery without crucial memories, and you have an exciting plot. But a love story requires more.

In Twain's book, the character of Becky Thatcher fits the traditional stereotype of the Victorian female: beautiful, helpless, idealized, and, quite frankly, boring. I wondered what a girl like that might do when faced with adversity if she were made of more than fluff? The Becky Thatcher who sprang to life onto these pages surprised me with her cleverness, compassion, courage and sense of adventure. She'd shown something of her spunk in choosing Tom in the first place. Seeing her develop into a multi-faceted, independent woman, was pure delight.

After you finish *Tom Sawyer Returns*, be sure to pick up *Taming Huck Finn*.

Enjoy the New Adventures!

E.E. Burke

Better a broken promise than none at all.
~ *Mark Twain*

CHAPTER ONE

AUGUST 15, 1864, ST. PETERSBURG, MISSOURI

Poets and dreamers possessed the right words to explain love. Ordinary people were left to work it out one difficult decision at a time. Becky Thatcher considered herself quite ordinary, despite what she'd been led to believe as a petted and pampered child.

She stirred a pot of beans on the stovetop, mulling over the only marriage proposal she had ever received. Rather, the only one that counted because the man who'd issued it could be depended on to honor his word.

Was she in love with Alfred? The right question might be, did it matter? Passion, ardor, *amour*, or whatever one might call that fleeting, ephemeral force, had given her nothing more than a broken heart. Alfred offered her a path to safety and security, which would prove far more useful than anything her previous beau had ever promised, much less delivered.

In present circumstances, she should count herself fortunate that a childhood friend wished to honor her with marriage. Other women in her situation would simply end up on the trash heap of failed dreams as embittered old maids—or worse.

A faint scratching sounded at the kitchen door.

Becky stopped stirring and held motionless. Surely her cousin knew better than to come around for handouts and risk being seen by the commander of the military police.

More scratching, followed by a faint yowl.

Jeff wouldn't carry on like that. It had to be the old stray that turned up with some regularity.

Setting aside the spoon, she went to the door and opened it. A scruffy tabby sat on the stoop, regarding her with a green-eyed stare that bespoke expectations.

"So, it's you again. Is the army rationing mice now?"

The rangy tom flicked its torn ear then stepped over the threshold and wound around her ankles, purring loudly.

She relented and returned to the stove to spoon out a fragrant bit of pork from the bone she'd used to season the beans. "Here you go," she said, bending down to offer the treat to her uninvited guest. "That's all I can spare."

The cat sniffed at the offering before taking it.

"You do know we're in the midst of a war? Beggars can't be picky." Becky wiped her fingers on her apron and waited for the cat to finish eating.

"All right. Now you need to leave." She opened the back door. "I happen to know there are vermin aplenty in the carriage house."

Upon hearing the news, the predator raced into the dusky eve across the back yard toward a building that had once housed a pair of fine horses, confiscated by Union soldiers over a year ago.

Standing on the stoop, she gazed up at the first faint twinkles in the sky. Later in the night, the Little Dipper might be visible and she could find the North Star. That is, if she went back out to look for it, which she wouldn't do because civilians weren't allowed outside after dark. Even if she could locate the right star, she wouldn't make a wish on it. Wishes were for dreamers, and she could no longer afford to be one.

Once upon a time, she had fancied herself in love. But Tom, like that unpredictable stray, could never settle for permanence. When adventure beckoned, he'd left her behind with nothing more than lofty promises, which turned out to be as worthless as Confederate currency.

No one in town had a clue about what happened to him. Most believed, for good reason, that he'd come to a bad end. After clinging to hope for seven long years, she had finally accepted reality. She would never meet Tom Sawyer again this side of eternity. Not even long enough to dispatch him to the next world by putting a bullet through his worthless hide.

Becky put her hand into the apron pocket where she'd tucked Alfred's letter. His ardent proposal held far more value than Tom's useless vows.

She sniffed. *Something's burning...*

"Oh no! She rushed inside and opened the oven door, nearly crying when she pulled out the scorched cornbread. They'd have to eat it anyway. Given her father's unemployed situation, they couldn't afford to waste food.

She set the bread and beans on the table and called down the hall. "Papa, dinner's ready!"

No response came from the front of the house. The judge must not have heard her or perhaps he had gotten absorbed in a book.

Taking a lit tallow lamp, she made her way down the hall without stopping to light the candle in the wall sconce. *Waste not, want not.*

"Papa? Time to wash up." Becky paused at the entrance to the study and frowned at the empty chair behind the desk, where he typically sat this time of day, reading a book or the newspaper.

He hadn't come home yet. What could be keeping him this late?

A brisk wind swirled through the room and sent a pile of newspapers stacked on the desk fluttering to the floor. She crossed to the open window, but before closing it leaned outside, peering the direction her father usually took home.

In the soft twilight, a dark figure, his shape as familiar as his methodical pace, made his way up the cobbled street.

"Hurry!" she whispered, despite knowing he couldn't hear her. Calling out would draw too much attention. The provost marshal lived right across from them in the same house where he and Tom had grown up. Stodgy Sid wouldn't hesitate to lock up a civilian who violated the curfew.

Her father strode past their picket fence. When he opened the gate, the rusty hinge squeaked, causing her to heart to trip.

She rushed to the front door and flung it open. As soon as he stepped onto the porch, she grabbed his arm and hauled him inside. "What on earth! Did you forget the curfew?"

"There's nothing wrong with my memory," her father grumbled. "We had to finish putting out the newspaper."

Granted, the hours he spent helping his friend, the publisher, kept his mind off his own troubles.

"Mr. Stearns ought to be mindful of the time and not take advantage," she scolded.

"My tardiness isn't his fault." Her father hung his hat on the hall tree. The light she held reflected off his white hair, which not that long ago had been flaxen. On his face were grief lines carved by loss upon loss. His beloved wife, his brother, his position, his reputation—everything had been taken from him. If that weren't bad enough, his only nephew had cast his lot with rebels and would be hunted down like an animal.

Come to think of it, perhaps the newspaper was only an excuse for a more dangerous errand.

"After you put the paper to bed, did you stop off on another errand?"

"I don't know what you're talking about." The judge brushed past her on his way into the study. He stopped to pick up one of the newspapers that had been blown onto the floor.

Becky followed, collecting loose pages along the way. "You know precisely what I'm talking about. You left something else for Jeff, didn't you? The brand-new quilt our sewing circle just finished is missing."

"I don't know what you're talking about. Jeff is gone.

"That's what we tell everyone. You and I know better." She folded the gathered pages and placed them on the corner of the desk.

Her father arranged it into a neat stack before retrieving his pipe from its stand. As he lit it, the bowl glowed and the room filled with fragrant smoke, a smell she had once associated with comfort and security, but tonight it made her eyes water.

"Papa, I understand why you want to help him and I sympathize, I do. But you cannot continue to supply Jeff with food or bedding or anything. It only encourages him to remain here. You know Sid is itching to arrest you after you refused to declare your loyalty to the Union."

Her father straightened to his full height, looking every inch *the judge*, which was what everyone still called him even though he no longer presided over the county court. "I *have* declared my loyalty."

God give her patience. How many times had they argued about this?

"Verbal declarations mean nothing until you sign that piece of paper. Why won't you just put your name to the blessed oath and be done with it?"

"My principles won't allow me to sign a vow I can't uphold."

"Principles will do you little good should they put a rope around your neck."

5

"A man who acts without honor isn't worthy to be called a man."

"If that's true then this country is populated by animals."

"Rebecca..." The judge only used her full name when he rebuked her or wanted to hug her. He opened his arms.

If only she could run to his embrace, regress to the little girl whose father could fix anything. "Please don't lecture me on honor and family loyalty."

"I won't lecture you on something you understand as well as I do."

The judge set his pipe aside and pulled her into his arms. The soothing back rub might work if she was ten. "I know you're frightened, my dear," he murmured. "You don't have to remain here. Go to Illinois and stay with your cousins."

Another ploy to prevent her from doing something that might actually help.

She broke away to remain stalwart against his tender attack. "My plans don't include a trip to Illinois. You know that. Alfred has asked me to move to St. Louis and marry him. I want you to come along."

"He hasn't proposed to me," came the glib reply.

"Don't be silly. He wants you to be safe." She gripped the loose sides of her father's coat with dismay. "Look at you! You don't eat enough as it is. If I leave, who will fix your meals? Come with me to St. Louis and you won't have to fend for yourself."

He gathered her hands with a paternal smile. "I will manage fine on my own."

"Will you? If you insist on staying here to sneak food to Jeff, you'll end up in jail, and Alfred can't help you."

The softness in her father's expression vanished behind the judge's stern demeanor. "Is that why you're so anxious to tie the knot? For my sake?

Pride wouldn't allow him to accept such an arrangement and it wasn't the only reason. Ever since she had reconnected with Alfred, quite by accident. He had written to her without fail every week.

"Of course not. Alfred is devoted and very attentive."

"So is a dog."

Becky clamped down on her exasperation. This was precisely his intention, to fluster her and make her doubt her judgment. "Why on earth would you object to Captain Temple? He's wealthy, well educated, from a distinguished family. He's everything you could want in a son-in-law. You know how Mama prayed for the day I'd chose a man like him."

"Is that why you want to marry him? Because your mother would approve?"

He had switched to fighting dirty by attempting to stir up resentment at her overprotective mother, who had been dead for four years and had nothing to do with this decision.

"I'm only pointing out that she would be happy for me, as you should be."

"And I would be, if Alfred Temple were the right man for you." Her father sank into his desk chair, regarding her with that infuriating matter-of-fact expression.

Was it any wonder she remained unmarried? No man could be the paragon her father sought for his only daughter. Tom had left rather than try.

She propped her hands on her hips in a gesture her mother had used successfully to face down the judge. "Alfred is a Union captain, and he has the influence and means, not to mention the desire, to protect and provide for me. Who can meet your high standards if not someone like him? Pray tell, who can be *right* enough?"

The judge lifted the pipe to his lips, cradling the meerschaum bowl between thumb and forefinger, puffing placidly. "Are you in love with Captain Temple?

The question put a knot in her throat. What did *love* have to do with this? It had taken her seven years to purge the malady from her system and the process had nearly killed her. She wasn't even certain it was unrequited love. Perhaps her suffering had more to do with an unquenchable thirst for meaning and significance. Regardless, it was a distraction she could little afford in the midst of the chaos that had descended on them over the past three years. Her only concern was survival—hers and her father's.

"Rest assured, I have a deep affection for Alfred. He and I are well suited. You'll see. Once you get to know him, I am sure you will come to appreciate his finer qualities."

"Which are, other than penning romantic letters?"

A crash resounded from the back of the house.

She whirled around. "What was that?"

"The wind blew open the kitchen door."

"And heaved a boulder through it?"

Her father stood and retrieved a pistol from a drawer. He clearly didn't believe it was the wind and only said as much to avoid sending her into a panic.

"It might be Sid's men," she whispered. "Don't let them see your gun. They'll shoot without giving you a chance to explain."

She crept after him down the hall to the doorway leading into the kitchen. When he came to a stop, she had to jerk to a halt to avoid running into him. "What is it?"

He gestured with the pistol.

Just inside the back door, a man sprawled face down on the floor. He had his right arm stretched out, as if pleading for help. Or had he been reaching for the sack and rifle he'd dropped? He didn't wear a uniform, which meant he could be anyone, a robber or a raider, or possibly one of Jeff's unsavory friends.

The judge approached the still figure, whose lean, powerful body reminded her of a panther, and nudged the larger man with the toe of his shoe.

She ventured closer. "Is he—?" Her mouth went dry and she had to wet her lips. "Dead?"

"Hard to tell." The judge knelt and rolled the unconscious intruder onto his back.

Beneath a crisscrossed ammunition belt, the rise and fall of the stranger's broad chest confirmed he still breathed—for the time being. Blood matted his dark, tousled hair and collected in the curve of his ear and in a thick, black beard. Even senseless and wounded, he appeared fierce, dangerous.

As she bent to peer at his face, her heart pounded. His eyes remained closed. But a small, worried voice whispered that if he opened them, they would be forest brown with flecks of green and gold.

No, it wasn't possible. It couldn't be...

"Tom?"

CHAPTER TWO

Becky and her father managed to haul the unconscious man upstairs to the closest bedroom. Her heart insisted it must be Tom while her head argued against the probability. Then again, it would be just like Tom to show up at her doorstep the day she'd decided to marry someone else. He always did have the worst timing.

After stitching up the man's wound and bandaging his head, she roused him enough to spoon a little water and broth down his throat.

Shortly before dawn, she crossed her arms on the edge of the bed and rested her head. No physician could have provided more tender care. He would improve. She wouldn't allow him to die on her watch.

He moaned and muttered something unintelligible.

"Yes, what is it?" She peered at him, praying he would awaken and clear up her confusion.

His black lashes formed dark crescents above high cheek-bones. A white scar bisected his left eyebrow, lifting it in a devilish arch. The bristly beard made him look like a pirate. While it fit what she knew of Tom's character, it revealed nothing about his motivations for returning.

If indeed this man was Tom.

"Can you wake up?" She would know for certain once he opened his eyes. "Tom?" she ventured, her voice wavering.

"Miss Mamie," he murmured.

Becky fisted the bed sheets to keep from striking him. "Who is...? Oh, never mind. I don't want to know. Why are you here?"

He gave a soft snore.

The door to the bedroom creaked and her father poked his head in. "How's Rip Van Winkle this morning?"

"Talking in his sleep." She stood and stretched, then reached for the empty bowl on the table next to the bed.

"Has he said anything helpful?"

"Not in the least."

"Come downstairs and eat before *you* collapse," her father suggested.

Indeed. She needed a respite from worrying over a bounder.

"Becky," Tom rasped.

"Yes?" She was by the bed in an instant. The black-haired man squinted at her. Hard to tell the color of his eyes.

"Is he awake?" The judge held up a candle, casting light into the man's face.

With a groan, he screwed his eyes shut and raised his arm.

"Move back. The light bothers him." She rested her hip on the edge of the bed and the judge repositioned himself behind her.

"There. How's that?"

"Better." Becky leaned over and kept her voice low. "Tom, open your eyes."

With an obvious effort he pried his eyelids open enough to look through slits. "Are you...an angel?"

His voice sounded familiar, but rougher, deeper. Of course, it would've changed, like the rest of him. No matter, it was Tom. She could no longer argue against the miracle.

"Me, an angel?" she laughed. "I scarcely feel human." She brushed away a strand of hair stuck to her cheek. Having been so busy caring for him she hadn't even had time to change her soiled apron. "What makes you think I'm an angel?"

"Your halo."

Becky glanced at her father. "The judge is standing behind me holding a candle. The light or your fevered mind could be creating that effect."

She smoothed a tangle of damp curls away from the man's forehead. His skin felt cooler. Lord, he was a handsome womanizer, even scruffy and ill. "You don't think you'd end up in a place with angels, do you?"

"Not likely." He heaved a long sigh and let his eyelids drift shut as if the effort to hold them open taxed him. His malaise frightened her.

"No, don't go back to sleep. You have to stay awake and talk to us."

He kept his eyes closed. "Where am I?"

"You are at our house. In the guest bedroom, to be precise."

After a few slow blinks, he propped his eyes open. The warm light reflected in the dark irises, making them gleam. After gazing at her for a long moment, he scrunched his forehead in confusion.

"Do you recognize me?"

"Well, you look like Becky, only tired, and older. But you aren't real and I can't be in your house. Not unless it floated down the Mississippi."

Tired? Old? Her pride took a beating. The rest of what he said made no sense. "Pray tell, where should you be?"

He rubbed his eyes with his thumb and forefinger, drawing her attention to lines etched at the corners. She wasn't the only one who look *older*. "Vicksburg," he said wearily. "Did he surrender?"

"Who?"

"Pemberton."

More nonsense.

"He's talking about what happened over a year ago. When the Confederate commander at Vicksburg surrendered to Grant," her father whispered.

Something she'd rarely seen in Tom's eyes—fear—flickered in the dark depths. "A *year* ago? That's not possible. He just told me yesterday."

Dread settled in an icy pool at the pit of her stomach.

Dear Lord. Tom had lost his marbles.

She grasped his hand and squeezed comfortingly. "Nonsense You've had a bad dream. Where were you before you came here?"

He returned a blank stare.

"You arrived with a burlap sack that held a federal officer's uniform, ammunition, guns. Does that jog your memory?" the judge asked.

Tom's lips parted as if he might speak, then he sighed deeply. "No."

"What about that blow to the head?" she asked. "Were you attacked? Robbed?"

"I don't...can't remember..." his voice trailed off.

Becky released his hand and stood. Was he lying to cover up his true purpose for appearing out of the blue? As a boy, he'd earned a well-deserved reputation for twisting the truth. She had foolishly contended he would always be honest with her—until he wasn't. "You want us to believe you can't recall anything that happened over the past year?"

Another blank stare.

Her father rubbed his chin. "A concussive blow can result in amnesia. It's usually temporary, from what I've read."

What if it wasn't amnesia, but something worse? A local man who'd been sent home after suffering a severe head injury still slobbered like a crazed dog and couldn't remember his name. Becky leaned over to look at Tom's mouth and make sure he wasn't drooling.

"Water..." he rasped. "Dry as a desert."

She snagged a pitcher from the bedside table and poured a glass, holding it as he drank.

After draining the glass, he sank back onto the pillows and closed his eyes. "Thank you, Becky."

The simple expression of gratitude jerked at her heartstrings. And that was exactly what he was counting on. How many times had Tom faked illness? He'd even staged his death to get attention. Young, naive Becky might've fallen for it, but not the *older* one.

"It appears Tom has fallen asleep again." Faking it is what she'd bet. The fact that he made up that ridiculous story about losing his memory only confirmed her suspicions.

Tom was in some kind of trouble. Why else would he show up unannounced and injured?

Becky arranged a quilt over him, which reminded her about the loss of the other quilt. She should've told her father it was a gift from the sewing circle for the Union soldier's hospital. He wouldn't have given it away. Although some of the ladies, like Mrs. Bent, wouldn't care if it ended up in a rebel's hands. Nevertheless, the old lady had contributed her time to making other quilts for those who considered her family enemies. It was such a pity what had happened...

"I have to go check on Mrs. Bent," she told her father. "Will you sit with Tom?

"Certainly." The judge followed her into the hall. "You are good to keep an eye on the widow."

"Someone needs to. She's all alone." Becky pulled the bedroom door closed so their voices wouldn't be overheard. She didn't trust Tom not to eavesdrop. "Don't answer any knocks or let in any visitors. We have to be careful."

Heaven forbid Alfred discover her former beau under her roof. As boys, the two were fierce contenders for her affection, and she didn't expect they'd like each other much better as men.

"You go on. We'll be fine." The judge held up a book. "If he wakes, I'll read to him from Homer's *Odyssey*. As I recall, he liked that story."

"What he liked was to compare himself to the hero," Becky reminded her father.

"He did, didn't he?' her father answered with an amused gleam in his eyes. "Who knows? Tom might've overcome impossible obstacles to return home."

No one could doubt Tom's adventurous nature or even his occasional good intentions, but he certainly wasn't her Odysseus.

"I doubt anyone has been holding Tom hostage. Then again, it would be just like him to get kidnapped, break free, then drag me into the middle of his mess."

After eating a quick bite, Becky set off down the back alley, a route that had the advantage of keeping her off the main road and away from the patrols. Thus far, no one had come looking for Tom. But why take the chance she might be questioned? Her ability to lie wasn't nearly as well developed as his.

She made her way over to Widow Bent's tidy cottage, tucked in between two larger houses that had been vacated by the owners after the federals declared martial law. Weeds overgrew the yard, including what once had been a lovely flower garden that Becky's friend tended for her aging mother.

Poor Anne. She hadn't hurt anyone or done anything a person who possessed a heart wouldn't do. She hadn't deserved to be jailed, much less prohibited from communicating with her only family. It was ridiculous, and Alfred agreed, one more mark in his favor.

Becky knocked on the widow's back door and waited. She knocked again. This time harder. "Hello? Mrs. Bent? It's your neighbor, Becky."

The old lady was nearly deaf and might not be able to hear the knocking. Or she was sitting out on her front porch in the rocking chair, enjoying a cool breeze blowing up from the river and watching for the steamboat that carried the news.

Becky strolled around the house. Upon seeing no one seated outside, she rapped on the front door. At the sound of rumbling wheels on the brick pavement, Becky whirled around.

A block away, a six-man patrol had started up the hill, followed by caged transport.

Who were they after? Could it be they were looking for Tom?

Becky gave another rapid series of knocks. "Mrs. Bent!"

The patrol came steadily onward.

Who was to say it was Tom they were after? It could be anyone. The military police had filled the jail with civilians.

Just in case, she ought not to wait around and risk being questioned.

Becky hurried to the sidewalk.

The clatter of hooves got louder.

"Good afternoon, Miss Thatcher."

Out of the side of her eye, she spotted the provost marshal on his black horse.

Drat.

He rode out in front of the patrol and turned into her path. "Might I have a word with you?"

The nervous flutter in her stomach rose to her chest, but she faced the commander of the military police with her head held high. "You wish to speak to *me*? Aren't you in a hurry?"

Sid leaned forward. The crisp brim of a gold-braided hat shadowed a long, serious face, but she didn't need to see his features to know this wasn't a social call. "You are the one who appears to be in a hurry, Miss Thatcher."

He implied her rushing made her a suspicious character.

She kept her hands out of her pockets so he wouldn't ask her to empty them. Explaining where she'd gotten a note from a prisoner in St. Louis would be very awkward for both her and Alfred. "Is being in a hurry a crime?"

"Depends on what you're running from or where you might be going." Sid's saddle creaked as he dismounted. He strode over to her with an air bordering on arrogance, a trait he and Tom shared, though both would be offended by any comparison.

Tom's half-brother had changed a great deal since those long-ago days when he'd crept around after her and Tom, thinking they wouldn't notice him. Tom had called Sid a *little sneak*. He wasn't little anymore. But he was still a sneak.

Becky pasted on a smile. "I am sorry I don't have time for a proper visit. My father is expecting breakfast, which is why I was returning home at a brisk walk."

"Awful hot day for a brisk walk." Sid removed his hat, revealing damp, black hair. Another trait he shared with his brother. Except Tom's hair curled where Sid's was straight, and Tom's dark eyes had flecks of gold and green. Sid's were brown as dirt.

He kept his fathomless gaze locked on hers. "You shouldn't be out alone. It's dangerous."

Sid also had an annoying habit of pretending concern to advance his own purposes, whereas Tom's concern... Well, in the past it had been genuine. Who knew what motivated him now?

Becky shrugged. "As you can see, I am perfectly fine."

Sid peered up the street. "Night before last, a stowaway jumped off a steamboat a short time before it docked. No one seems to know who he is or where he might be headed. Have you noticed anyone around who doesn't belong?"

Fear closed invisible fingers around Becky's throat. Tom's hair had been damp. So had his clothes, come to think of it. Sid had no proof Tom was at her house or he would've already barged in. If he failed to sniff out anything amiss, he would move on.

"No, I haven't seen any strangers," she managed without choking. "Good luck finding the stowaway."

She turned to leave.

"Just a moment."

Becky halted, holding her breath. "Yes?"

"Before you go, perhaps you could help me with something else." Sid reached inside a leather pouch attached to his gun belt and withdrew a folded paper. "Have you seen this before?"

A pamphlet? Did it have something to do with Tom?

"No."

"Look closer." He handed it to her.

The cover had an illustration of the skull and crossbones overlaid with other odd symbols she didn't recognize. She flipped it open and scanned the inside—a fiery treatise urging the secession of northern and western states into a second confederacy.

Dear God. Not even Jeff would become involved in such madness. If Tom were mixed up in it, she and her father could hang out simply for sheltering him.

She returned the pamphlet. "No one in his right mind would promote this nonsense."

"What about the judge?"

When she found her voice, she tried to laugh. "You're joking, of course. It is riddled with misspellings and grammatical errors. He would be offended by the attribution."

"We found dozens of those at the newspaper office," Sid replied without smiling.

Was he was attempting to frame her father with this piece of treasonous tripe?

"You know full well the judge isn't a Copperhead or a Democrat. He's a loyal Unionist, a Republican like you. He wouldn't have anything to do with this trash."

"Would he have anything to do with his rebel nephew?"

"Jeff is gone." She found it easier to lie when indignant.

Sid's expression reminded her of the one her father wore the instant before he said *checkmate*. "If that's the case, why won't your father sign the oath of loyalty?"

"The judge has given his word that he is loyal. That should be enough."

"Not for the army. Good day, Miss Thatcher." The provost marshal mounted his horse, waved his men forward, and the prisoner transport rumbled away.

Becky's relief lasted but a moment before panic struck. Sid wasn't off to torment some other poor soul. He was headed to her house to arrest the judge.

CHAPTER THREE

Bells from the old cathedral rang the noon hour. Quickening his pace, Tom turned a corner, his boot heels rapping on the bricked sidewalk as he strode alongside the high wall of a fortress. That's what it looked like, at any rate. In a previous life, the massive structure had been a medical college. Now, it served as a federal prison.

A sentry in front of the barred doors snapped pencil-sharp with a salute, and after peering for a moment at Tom's papers, directed him inside.

Golden light spilled through an opening in the ceiling onto the stone floor of the octagonal courtyard, adjoined by two wings. From the right echoed a measured tread before an officer appeared. His hat brim—tipped at a jaunty angle—shadowed the upper half of his face. A groomed mustache framed lips twisted into a smug, self-satisfied smile.

Tom snapped his eyes open and stared in confusion at a white, bead-board ceiling. It took his pounding heart another moment to realize he'd been dreaming. He curled his fingers into soft sheets. Sure enough, he lay in bed.

Whose bed? The scent reminded him of...

Becky.

He'd dreamed about her, too. Or was she real?

With deliberate slowness, he turned his aching head toward a window. The shifting daylight behind a pair of delicate lace curtains wasn't all that bright, still, it hurt his eyes. Reaching up, he encountered a bandage swaddling his head. The pounding headache wasn't a dream.

The woman resembled Becky, only more mature, and weary, and worried. During the night, or day, he wasn't sure, whenever he'd opened his eyes, she had been at his bedside.

Before that? He had no recollection. One minute he had been at Miss Mamie's, chatting up Pemberton to tease more information out of the Confederate general, and then he'd woken up at Becky's house, hundreds of miles away.

Tom pinched the bridge of his nose, struggling to find a memory, from a month ago, a week, yesterday. Becky told him he had fallen through her back door. What had he been doing before someone struck him from above?

Wait. That was new. He snatched at the fragment, little more than a bit of straw in a tornado.

Artillery? No. Rustling leaves...

Out behind Becky's house, an ancient oak tree spread its branches from the roof all the way back to the fence separating their property from a narrow alley. Had someone been crouched up there, hiding? Rarely did humans hang out in trees, so he had to assume whoever it was meant to ambush him.

Who would want to stop him from reaching her and why? Nothing came to mind, save a blinding headache.

Tom released a sigh. He wouldn't discover the answer while lying in bed. He had to get up, find Becky, and collect the other pieces needed to solve the puzzle. His life depended on it— possibly hers, too.

He sat up slowly, swallowing fast when his head grew light. Deep breathing eased the dizziness. With a grunt, he swung his legs over the side and braced his hands on the edge. After another moment, he tried standing.

The floor didn't tip nor did the room spin.

With careful steps, he progressed to the washstand. He peered into the mirror and unwrapped a bloodstained bandage from around his head. Someone had stitched up a half-inch cut above his left temple. He couldn't imagine Becky doing such a thing. Once, when he had shown off a hurt toe, she'd fallen over in a dead faint.

Tom washed up as best he could, using the pitcher of water and a sliver of soap. The towel had a fresh, summery scent that made his throat tighten and his eyes burn.

Of all things, he might get choked up about. But it wasn't the damn towel, was it? Rather, what it represented. Love. Dreams. A future he'd once imagined. Everything he'd lost.

Lost because of his own choices.

Tom tossed the towel across the washbasin and dispensed with self-pity. He had no time for that useless emotion. Something had compelled him to return and it damn sure wasn't to ask Becky for a pardon he didn't deserve.

Inside the wardrobe, he found a federal officer's uniform, along with a clean shirt and underclothes. A gunnysack contained a gun belt and ammunition. The judge had asked if those things belonged to him. He supposed so. Any self-respecting robber would've stolen the weapons. Whoever had hit him hadn't bothered, which made theft as a motive questionable.

Pondering the implications, he pulled on the shirt, buttoned the blue trousers with the yellow stripe down the side, and tried on the dress coat and the hat with the gold braid. Everything fit.

A dizzying array of images flashed through his mind. He grabbed the side of the wardrobe to retain his balance.

One of many uniforms, each worn for different purposes.

The gold bars, the rank of captain. A ruse. He didn't command a unit or even work with the same people twice.

Tom lifted a shaking hand and rubbed it over the beard. Upon occasion, he altered his appearance. Stealth wasn't something new. Neither was changing his identity. This much, he remembered. He'd been operating as a spy since before the war started, first in the gold fields and then closer to home. But never here. Never where he would have to betray people he'd grown up with. He wouldn't agree to that.

So why had he come to see Becky? Was she in trouble? Danger? He had to determine the answer to that question before he left her with only an old man to defend her.

From below, a door banged as if blown open—or someone had thrown it open. The tromping indicated more than one person.

"What's going on here?" a man called out.

Sounded like the judge, and he wasn't expecting visitors.

Tom buckled the gun belt and checked the revolver. Hadn't even gotten off a shot before he'd been hit. He'd better be more alert if he expected to live through the next encounter.

He exited the bedroom and went to the top of the stairs to take in the scene below.

The judge had made it as far as the doorway to his study. Half a dozen blue-coated soldiers filled the foyer with their weapons at the ready. Here to arrest someone or kill them, didn't take a genius to figure that out. Nor did it take it long to guess their target.

Tom considered his options. Escape through the open window in the bedroom. Too late for that. One of the invaders had noticed him. He'd have to bluff his way through whatever conundrum he faced. After all, he had a nice uniform. Why not use it?

He made the unhurried descent of an officer who outranked everyone else in the room. "What's the meaning of this, soldiers?"

The other men below turned their attention up the stairs. Thankfully, they didn't shoot him.

"Wait! You can't do this!" A female voice shrieked from outside an instant before a soldier backed through the door, attempting to restrain the woman from entering.

Her bonnet list to one side and her face shone beet-red. She swatted at the sergeant. "Keep your hands off me!"

Tom observed the interaction with a mixture of admiration and alarm. Was Becky defending him against arrest? Whilst he appreciated her concern, she was bound to get hurt if he didn't do something quickly.

He crossed the foyer, pushed past two privates, and grabbed her by the arm. "Back off, sergeant. This woman is confused and overwrought."

She raked him with a look of pure astonishment. "Why didn't you stay hidden, you idiot?" she whispered.

He liked that she was concerned. He didn't like that she thought him an idiot.

Becky pulled out of Tom's grasp and ran to her father, who swung her around behind him.

"Halt! You're under arrest!" The barked command came from another officer who had entered the house.

Tom met a dark gaze and recognition jolted him, followed by an inward groan.

Just his luck. The little sneak.

His half-brother's frown deepened before surprise flared in his eyes. "You!"

"Yes, its me." No point in denying it. Sid should've recognized who he was arresting. "What do you want?"

"For the record, you are speaking to the provost marshal." Sid straightened to his full height, which put him eye-level with Tom.

The runt had grown.

"I take it that means you're the one in charge of this band of bullies. Is there some reason you need so many of them to arrest one man?"

"That's none of your business. What are you doing here?" Sid demanded.

Tom's mind whirred as he sought a proper answer, one that wouldn't reveal much. He couldn't give away too much until he regained his cursed memories. In the meantime, he had to blunt Sid's natural nosiness.

"Not, *how are you*, or, *glad to see you're not dead*? No filial hug?" Tom held out his arms and then dropped them. "Ah, well. We can dispense with the pleasantries. I'm here to take over your position."

Sid didn't crack a smile. He still hadn't developed a sense of humor. "You have the proper papers for traveling, I assume. May I see them?"

Tom debated taking hold of Sid's extended hand and twisting his arm behind his back. As provost marshal, Sid held sweeping powers, including the right to demand travel documents and to jail people he didn't like. Best to play along for now.

"Don't have them at the moment. I was attacked on my way into town. The rascals knocked me out, stole my papers, and left me for dead." Tom removed his hat to show off the freshly stitched cut. "I made it as far as Becky's house before I collapsed."

All of this was true to the best of his knowledge.

Whether Sid believed him was another matter.

His brother's eyes narrowed with suspicion. "If you had come to see me, I could've helped."

If he'd been on his way to see Sid, he wouldn't have collapsed across Becky's doorstep. Besides, the fact that Sid conveniently showed up to arrest someone triggered suspicion. Somehow, it all had to be connected. If only he could remember...

"And bother you? I wouldn't dream of it. Becky was more than happy to nurse me back to health."

She made a noise that sounded like she'd swallowed her tongue and twin spots of color bloomed on her cheeks. All right, so she might not be happy about helping, but she had taken very good care of him and he wanted to give her credit.

Sid surveyed the two of them as if he were calculating the odds at a faro table. "Interesting. Miss Thatcher has been known to exhibit poor judgment when it comes to renegades and outlaws. Apparently, she's also too quick to take in strays."

Tom's anger flared at the unacceptable counter-attack. "That's flat-out rude and insulting. You owe this lady an apology."

"And you need to get your paperwork in order, captain, or risk being arrested for desertion," Sid shot back. "Give me the name of your commanding officer. I'll send word you've arrived."

Only one man directed his assignments. Despite a faulty memory, Tom suspected his chain of command hadn't changed all that much. Not that it mattered. Sid wouldn't believe him anyway. "You could try General Grant. Not sure how you'll find him. He's on the march somewhere."

Sid's lips thinned with irritation. "If we can't reach *the general*, I'll lock you up along with your friend the judge."

Becky moved in front of her father. "My father has done nothing wrong!"

Tom could not say the same for himself. He simply couldn't recall what he'd done wrong in the recent past.

Again, Judge Thatcher pulled her behind him. "Stay out of this, Rebecca."

Good fatherly advice.

"You are under arrest, your honor." Sid gestured for the soldiers standing next to him, who locked handcuffs on the unresisting judge.

It struck Tom that Sid hadn't come here to arrest or harass him. Apparently, the judge had done something to annoy the local authorities. Whatever it was, there was no need to humiliate the older man, and in front of his daughter, no less.

Tom clenched his fists, longing to plant one right into Sid's nose for being a first-class jerk. But if he interfered, it would give the military police a perfect excuse to lock him up. To be of any use to Becky, he had to let this drama play out until he could gather more information.

"Stop! You can't do this!" Becky started after the soldiers.

Tom caught hold of the back of her dress, reeled her in and held her firmly with his arm around her waist. "On what grounds are you arresting the judge?" he asked Sid.

"Treason."

"Your evidence?"

"He doesn't have any." Becky stomped on Tom's instep.

Ouch.

He held Becky fast while Sid withdrew a pamphlet from the pouch on his belt.

"Judge Thatcher and his friend, Mr. Sterns, have been printing and distributing seditious literature. We found dozens of these pamphlets stacked up over at the newspaper office where he's been working."

Using his free hand, Tom examined the evidence. Seditious, to be sure, but it didn't read like the kind of well-crafted piece that would be penned by a learned jurist. "You really think the judge authored this?"

"The evidence points to the fact that he conspired to publish it."

The judge stood stalwart despite his hands being cuffed and his arms held by soldiers on either side of him. "I don't deny helping my friend put the newspaper out, but we did not print that pamphlet. Someone else put them there."

"Who might that be?" Sid inquired.

The judge's chin went up. "I don't know."

"Escort Judge Thatcher to the prisoner transport," Sid instructed his men.

27

"You can't connect him to that drivel and you know it." Becky twisted and grabbed Tom's lapels. "*Do* something!"

It was clear to everyone except her that Sid wasn't leaving without his prisoner, and creating a ruckus would only result in being jailed. In order to discover the truth and help the judge, they had to remain free.

"Now is not the time," he replied to Becky in a low voice.

"Coward!" She flung the insult, pushed him away and ran outside, shouting at the soldiers.

This older Becky had grit, but she didn't take good advice.

Tom caught her before she reached the street. *Enough chasing.* He slung her over his shoulder to haul her back to the house.

She wriggled and kicked her feet. "Let me *go*. I'm going after them."

"No, you're not," Tom tightened his hold on her backside. Slippery fish were easier to manage. "You'll end up in jail."

"I don't care!" Becky twisted frantically as the prison transport pulled away. "If we don't stop them, they'll hang him before he even gets to jail!"

Tom turned without putting her down. She could be right. He'd seen firsthand how *justice* was meted out during wartime. "Provost Marshal!" he called out. "The army has strict procedures for the treatment of prisoners. Will you guarantee the judge's safety?"

Sid rode back and gazed down at Tom with an expression that couldn't be called *brotherly* on a good day. "Judge Thatcher will be held with the other prisoners until his trial. As for you, I'll expect to see you at my office tomorrow bright and early, with the appropriate traveling papers. And don't get it into your head to slip off. My men will be watching the house."

CHAPTER FOUR

om Sawyer—the low-down, lying, ungrateful reprobate—
carted her through the front door. Once they were inside,
he set her on her feet.

Becky kicked him in the shin. "*That* is for treating me like a
grain sack."

In a state of fury, she marched down the hall, removing her
bonnet before it fell off. Her father would need food, a change of
clothes, his pipe and tobacco, and a few books. She would gather
everything and go sit in jail with him. Anything to ensure his
safety. The last man arrested for treason had ended up hanging
from a tree near the river. No one admitted to knowing how he got
there.

"Becky, wait!" Tom limped after her. "We need to talk. I can
help you."

"Help me? You've done quite enough, thank you. By making
your presence known without having the proper papers or even an
explanation, you've cast doubt on me and my father."

She entered the kitchen to wrap up the leftovers from
breakfast.

Tom continued to stalk her. "Appears the doubt was already there. They came looking for the judge, not me."

Admittedly, it wasn't Tom's fault that her father was under suspicion. However, Tom's misguided heroics sent a snowball rolling downhill, amassing consequences he hadn't even considered. He hadn't changed one bit—except for growing bigger, and, sadly, better looking.

She shoved a chair into his path. "Go away and leave me alone."

"Can't do that. Didn't you hear Sid?"

"Yes. Do you always do what he says?"

Tom cleared her makeshift defense and straightened with a frown. "I'll deal with him tomorrow."

"How? By *taking his position*? He'll lock you up for that lie the minute you walk into his office, see if he doesn't."

"Aw, come on Becky. It was a joke and he knew it."

"He's no fool."

Tom shrugged. "That's debatable. But I trust he'll make inquiries before we meet tomorrow then I'll find out what he finds out. Before that, I need to know what's going on around here. Why is he so sure your father is a traitor?"

She wrapped bacon and cornbread in a napkin and tucked them into a basket on the table. Picked up a knife and considered throwing it, but then she'd have to clean the blood off the floor. Better to force Tom's hand and get to the truth, which might produce something she could use as leverage to gain her father's release.

"Why don't you start by telling me why you stowed away on a steamboat."

"What steamboat?" Tom set his hat on the table, visibly perplexed. He'd removed the bandage covering the injury she had carefully cleaned and stitched.

"Why did you remove the dressing?"

"I don't need it anymore."

His complete lack of concern pretty well summed up the problem. He would do as he pleased, as he had always done, and chaos would follow.

She refused to be caught up in it. "No, of course not. Just as I don't need you."

"Is that so? I don't see anybody else offering to help." He eyed the pan containing a single piece of cornbread. The longing in his expression reminded her of a dog begging for scraps. If he was starving, he needed more help than she did.

She pushed the pan in his direction.

He finished off the bread in two bites, licking the crumbs from his fingers. "Why did you ask me if I'd stowed away?"

"Sid told me they were looking for a man who jumped off the last steamboat that docked on the night you arrived. Your clothes and hair were damp."

He pursed his lips. "Hmm. Could've been me. Wonder who it was that hit me to prevent me from reaching you?"

A shiver lifted the hairs on her arm. "Why would you think it had anything to do with me?

"Whoever whacked me was hiding in that oak tree. That much I put together. I reckon he ambushed me when I got to the backyard."

She'd never seen members of the local militia crouched in trees. Jeff might have an interest in stopping intruders. But he wouldn't have allowed Tom to reach the house. Not unless he belatedly recognized him. She wasn't about to mention the possible presence of her fugitive cousin to a man she wasn't sure she could trust.

"You arrived in dirty civilian clothing. Maybe someone walking down the alley mistook you for a criminal—or a deserter."

Tom reached across the table and took the knife out of her

hand. He must've read her thoughts. Or maybe other women, like Miss Mamie, had thrown knives at him.

"Is that what you figure, that I'm yellow?" he asked softly.

She stared at the front of his coat at the row of brass buttons embossed with bold eagles. The youth she'd once loved had been recklessly brave. No one could call Tom a coward.

That was years ago. She didn't know this man or what he had done since leaving town and exiting her life. He hadn't seen fit to enlighten her. "Last I heard, you were in the gold fields. Now you show up with a uniform. What should I think?"

"You could think I earned this rank," he said in a soft voice. "Or that I might be here to protect you."

"Protect *me?*"

It was ludicrous. Cruel to even suggest. How could he say such a thing after virtually ignoring her for years?

He circled the table, coming closer.

She'd been so worried while he was lying there, vulnerable and hurt. Now that he was awake and moving around, his presence filled the room. So much so, she could hardly breathe.

She backed away to open more space between them. Her trembling response came from fear, certainly not because she was still attracted to him. "You're in trouble, I suspect."

"Let's see, oh…" He presented his wrists. "I'm not the one in shackles."

No, she would not stand for Tom's avoidance tactic, his attempt to make this *her* problem.

"Mercy, you sure are nosy for someone who hasn't communicated in years."

"That's an interesting idea." He took a step toward her. She froze when he reached out and lifted a strand of hair from her cheek. "Did *you* send for me?"

His absurd question shocked her out of her daze and she knocked his hand away, glowering. "And just how would I send for you? I had no idea where you were. Far as I knew, you were dead."

His eyes softened, and for a split second, sadness emerged. "Becky, I never meant to hurt you. I'm sorry."

The unexpected apology clamped her heart in a vise. How long she had waited to hear him say those words, and now...

What did he expect? That she'd collapse into his arms, let him kiss her and wipe away her tears, give him anything he wanted? She wasn't that naïve girl anymore. "If you need my forgiveness, fine, you've got it. But I won't listen to any more of your lies."

"I don't expect you to forgive me, and I haven't lied to you."

Their entire relationship had been built on a lie. He'd never loved her.

She pointed a shaking finger at him. "You told Sid I welcomed you into my home. That's a lie. You broke in and passed out."

"Broke in? Why would I...?" He threaded his fingers through his rumpled hair and ejected a sound of frustration. "Look here, it was an honest mistake. I'm having trouble remembering things, and I just thought...well, it seemed logical."

"Only to you."

"All right!" His voice went up a notch in volume. "Let's stop hashing over my misunderstandings. We've both got bigger problems at the moment. Tell me what's going on. I'll find out anyway, but I'd rather hear it from you."

'Sakes, he was like a dog with a bone, gnawing and gnawing until he reached the juicy center. She might as well tell him the truth, part of it anyway. He might decide the effort was too much trouble even for him.

"My father is being persecuted. They removed him from the bench after he dared to speak out against the army's heavy-handed tactics. Now they want to blame him for something he had nothing to do with."

"The judge lost his position?" Tom shook his head, clearly

amazed, and no wonder. Her father had been the single most influential man in the county, well-liked and respected by all— except the invading army.

"When did that happen?"

"Two years ago. And he's not been allowed to practice his profession since." She could fairly see the wheels turning in Tom's mind.

"Prohibited from practicing law? That's generally reserved for men considered disloyal."

Becky turned away and busied herself with fixing her hair. If Tom couldn't see her face, he wouldn't guess he'd struck the nail squarely. She had no intention of going into details about her family's dilemma concerning loyalties. It was none of his business anyhow. "I can assure you, the judge had nothing to do with those flyers. Someone is trying to make him look bad."

"Could it be the publisher?" Tom asked.

"Mr. Stearns has been publishing a Unionist paper for years. Why would he suddenly start spouting treason? I'll bet Sid made it up."

Tom pursed his lips as if giving her theory consideration. "I agree that Sid's a conniving snake, but he wouldn't flat-out lie. He's afraid he might go to hell."

"Don't be so sure. Your brother doesn't like us. Papa ruled against him in a property case."

"Your defense is that Sid holds a grudge?"

"Why not? That's what this war is about, settling grudges. Anyone with a uniform and a gun thinks he has the right to strike out at whoever offended him in the past." She picked up the basket and went to the back door.

When she opened it, a soldier stood outside on the stoop.

"Sorry, Miss. I got orders to make sure nobody leaves."

"But I need to take food to my father."

"I'll ask someone to take it down there." The soldier eagerly reached for the basket.

She jerked it away and slammed the door in his face. "Scavengers! I know what you're up to. My father won't get a crumb."

Tom took the basket from her and set it on the table. "*I'll* make sure he gets this."

"What will you do? Send a message to *General Grant*?" You won't get away with that lie either."

Tom dared to smile. "I expect Sid will contact his commander."

His commander. The colonel who oversaw the state's military police reported to the same general that Alfred served.

Worse. Tom had made things worse, and he didn't even realize it.

Becky sank onto the bench next to the table before her knees gave way. "Yes, Sid will tell his commanding officer, then Alfred will find out about you and about my father being arrested, and the wedding will be off."

So would her chance to secure a safe life for herself and her father.

Tom scooted next to her. "Alfred?"

She might as well give him another blunt truth.

"You know Alfred. He's *Captain* Temple now, stationed in St. Louis. He's asked me to marry him. I want to accept, but—" Her voice cracked as the dam restraining her emotions gave way and Tom's face became a blur.

She couldn't ascertain his reaction to her news. If it bothered him at all, it was only because he'd always hated losing to Alfred.

He lifted his arm, and for a moment it appeared he might draw her to him, but then he put his hand on his knee. Just as well. He had no business offering her comfort. She wouldn't accept it from him anyway. "You've got nothing to be ashamed of. If Alfred cares for you, he won't let anything stop him. He'll marry you regardless."

E.E. BURKE

Did he know how insulting that sounded to both her and Alfred?

Becky straightened her spine. "For one, I am not ashamed of anything, and Alfred would never abandon me."

Like you.

She hadn't said it, but Tom would have to be dense as a brick not to catch her meaning. Nevertheless, his expression told her nothing.

"If my father is charged with treason, it will be difficult for Alfred to associate with us without putting himself and his career at risk. I wouldn't ask him to do it."

"He ought not to care what it costs," Tom declared.

"Oh, I see, and *you* are one to judge the cost."

She half-expected him to defend himself or get angry, as he would have in the past. Instead, he lowered his head. After a moment, he rubbed at his temple as if to ease some ache or pain.

Becky drew her lower lip between her teeth. She'd become as irritable as a snapping turtle. Tom brought out the worst in her.

At one time, he had also brought out the best. She mustn't forget that.

It had been Tom who'd always encouraged her to dream. Of course, he'd also crushed those dreams. But making him suffer wouldn't change anything other than increasing her regrets.

She gently touched his shoulder. "Does your head hurt?"

"Feels like an anvil."

She suspected his heart hurt as well. He just wouldn't admit it. "It appears you've been serving in this awful war, so you would know plenty about sacrifice. I have no call to question your understanding of the cost, and I certainly occupy no higher ground."

"You don't have to apologize. Not to me."

But he had begged her pardon, and not offering him the same grace would turn her resentment into an unbearable weight.

Slowly, he straightened. He had relegated his pain to somewhere it wouldn't show on his face. He fished the pamphlet Sid had given him out of his coat pocket. "Have you ever heard of the Knights of the Golden Circle?"

The abrupt change of subject came as a surprise. "No. Who are they?"

"A secessionist organization that's been operating in secret for years. I first ran into them when I was out in the gold fields of California five years ago."

She took the pamphlet from his hands. If the organization was a secret, how did Tom know about it? At the moment, the answer wasn't as important as why he had brought this flyer to her attention. "Are they the ones who wrote this?"

"Those symbols on the front would lead me to believe so. Or it could be a diversion. Either way, it's only useful to Sid if he can connect it to the judge."

Her stomach knotted with fear. "My father wouldn't be part of anything like that."

Her cousin's associations, however, were unknown to her so she couldn't say one way or the other. Besides, she wasn't about to confide in Tom concerning Jeff's mishaps or her father's heartbreaking vow to watch over his nephew. Some secrets were better kept to oneself.

Tom continued to regard her with unsettling frankness. "We have to convince Sid that your father had nothing to do with that pamphlet."

Unease rippled through her. "We?"

"Let me have a look at it again." He held out his hand for the flyer, assuming, as always, that she would let him take over and solve her problem.

Accepting Tom's help, even in the smallest way, was akin to throwing a rock into a still pond. The impact of such a decision would spread and spread until it affected every part of her life, quite possibly ruining it. He had a special skill for that.

What chance did she have to free her father on her own? Sid wouldn't listen to her or her friends. If she dragged Alfred into this mess, she risked harming his career, or, God forbid, losing her opportunity to make a good marriage.

On the other hand, Tom might know something about the possible source of the treasonous literature. What harm could there be in letting him take a look at it and offer a suggestion? She didn't have to agree to anything else.

A half-hour later, Becky returned from the kitchen to her father's study where Tom sat at the desk with the pamphlet spread out in front of him. He had told her there might be a way to ascertain whether the evidence was planted. If he could prove that, he deserved to be fed.

"You haven't eaten much more than broth. You must be starving." She set down a plate with corncakes and molasses, and what remained of the fruit she hadn't packed for the judge. "There were a few peaches left on the tree. What the soldiers didn't hook."

"They don't care which side you're on if they're hungry." Tom turned his head, which put him at eye-level with her bosom.

Heat flushed into her face and she backed up. Given her unfortunate response to his nearness, she'd be wise to keep her distance. "I don't trust Sid to make sure my father isn't harmed."

"Sid will keep his word."

"How do you know? You haven't been around him for years."

"Some things don't change. Sid likes to follow the rules. In this case, his unfortunate tendency will be helpful." Tom stabbed a peach slice with the fork and popped it in his mouth.

"I pray you're right. What have you discovered?"

"Fresh peaches beat the dickens out of canned fruit."

"I meant about the pamphlet."

"Give me a moment." He gestured to the stack of newspapers on the corner of the desk. "Are those current?"

She picked up the top copy and handed it to him. "This one was printed last week."

"Let's have a look." He opened it, folded the pages back, and placed it next to the pamphlet. Bent over the paper with his nose almost touching it, he used his finger as a guide the way her father did whenever he misplaced his glasses. "Hmm. Same font."

"Is that important?"

"Perhaps. I need more light."

She opened the curtain and the afternoon sun brightened the room. "Is that better?"

"It is, thank you."

After a moment, he placed a finger on the newspaper. "Come over here and look at this. See how this *f* drops down?" He indicated a spot on the pamphlet. "It's a tad different from the same letter that shows up here. And the *q* as well."

Becky leaned over his shoulder to get a better look and smelled the soap he'd used along with a warm, manly scent that distracted her, momentarily. "Why, I *do* see a difference."

"They weren't printed using the same type sorts, so likely not on the same press."

It took a moment for the significance to sink in because she was still fighting the distraction of being so close to him, but when it did, her mouth dropped open.

She hadn't even considered there might be differences. Despite his injury, Tom's mind remained quick. "Brilliant," she murmured.

He leaned back, smiling, with his hands behind his head. "I like to think so."

Still cheeky and full of himself. She would have to ration the compliments. If his head got any bigger, it wouldn't fit through the door.

"Let's check the other papers before I give you a medal."

Becky pulled up a chair and they worked diligently through the stack of newspapers, comparing each to the pamphlet. She hugged the one to her chest, lightheaded with relief. *"None* of them match. They couldn't have been printed on the same press."

Tom rubbed his temple again as if his poor head still ached. "It appears that way. I have to check the type case to be certain."

Showing Sid the difference wasn't enough? Did they need *more* proof?

"Fine. I'll go look." She circled the desk.

Tom turned in the swivel chair, regarding her quizzically. "Even if you could get away from the soldiers outside, you can't just waltz into the newspaper office and start searching. If I know Sid, he has the place shut up tight."

"I can get in with this." She retrieved a key from the top drawer and held it up.

"Good thinking." Tom stood and cupped her shoulders with his hands. It was his compliment, not his touch, that sent a delightful current coursing through her. "Let me sneak over after dark and take care of it. You can wait here."

Sit around waiting and wondering. She'd done enough of that already. Besides, she would be a fool to put her complete faith in Tom. She'd seen where that had gotten her before.

Becky shrugged off his grip. "I'll go with you. I want to see the evidence with my own eyes."

He studied her with a thoughtful frown. "It's dangerous."

"Anything you're involved in usually is."

"How would you know that?"

She repeated his reasoning back to him. "Some things don't change."

His lips twitched. "True. My bravery in the face of danger, and how trustworthy I am."

"Don't you find that people are often deluded about their shortcomings?" Becky pocketed the key in her apron just in case he'd be tempted to sneak away without her. She went to the window. "There's a guard by the front gate."

"And the other one at the back door, as you know. Any ideas for how you plan to get around them? Tom asked from behind her.

She didn't have to look to know how close he stood. Her traitorous body vibrated like a divining rod.

Resist, and the Devil will flee. Or was *she* the one who was supposed to flee and the Devil would resist? Either way, she'd make dead certain Tom kept his hands to himself.

Becky moved to one side. "When it's dark, we can sneak out through my upstairs window and climb across the old oak tree to get to the fence."

"That's it. And use a disguise so we won't draw attention when we're walking through town. I'll come up with a strategy."

She turned to tell him his strategy for arriving hadn't worked out so well, but he'd gone over to her father's desk and was thumbing through the newspapers.

Years ago, she might've accepted Tom's leadership. But now? She didn't want to depend on him. If she did, he might trick her out of going.

The only civilians who didn't get stopped were the old midwives who went about their business around town. She smiled to herself when she imagined how silly Tom would look wearing one of the old housekeeper's dresses they had stored in the attic.

Silly? No, it was perfect.

"I know what we can do."

"What's that?" Tom glanced at her with a slight smile, which she took to mean he didn't expect much.

"The soldiers will take notice of a man and a woman together. But they won't be suspicious of two old women. I'll put on my granny's clothes, you can wear one of Lucy's old dresses and a big sunbonnet. We'll go out together as midwives. They won't give us a second glance."

Tom frowned. "Midwives? I don't think so."

"Why not? You were the one who said we need a disguise."

"And I'll come up with one."

"Such as?"

"We go out as soldiers and attract even less notice."

"How you talk!" she exclaimed. "You don't have an extra uniform. Besides, no one will believe I'm a man."

He'd been at eye-level with her bosom so he knew better.

"But they'll believe *I'm* a woman?" Tom stood up, to prove his point perhaps.

"Old Lucy was almost as tall you are, and one of her dresses will be big enough to conceal your, um, shoulders and..." She waved her hand in his direction to indicate the rest of him.

"My hands and feet?" He stepped away from the desk to show her. "Your housekeeper didn't wear boots this big."

"Hm. Those might give you away up close, but in the dark, who can tell?"

She goaded him with a comparison to his childhood idol. "Your friend Huck put on a dress and pretended to be a girl once, and he's taller and uglier than you are."

Tom harumphed. "No one would believe it."

"Precisely. Nobody would expect you to wear a dress. Admit it, my idea is a good one."

CHAPTER FIVE

S hortly after dark, Tom followed Becky out a second-story window and crawled along the branches of the old oak tree to the alley in the back. At this time, he learned two things: Becky was astoundingly nimble, and it was next to impossible to climb trees while wearing a dress.

A short time later, they were shuffling along the sidewalk in the direction of the newspaper office. He hunched over to look crippled and to keep his ankles from showing beneath the voluminous skirts. The sunbonnet concealed his face, but he had to turn his head to see anything except what was right in front of him.

Becky adjusted a basket on her arm, which she'd filled with supplies a midwife might use in case they were stopped and questioned. Getting into the role, she bowed her back and hung her head to give the impression of a tired old lady.

From behind them came the echo of hooves striking the cobbled street before a mounted patrol rode past. One of the soldiers stared at them for so long it put Tom in a sweat.

He fought the urge to thrust his hand inside the deep pocket of the apron where he'd put his revolver. "You assured me no one would spare us a glance," he whispered to Becky.

"Keep your head down. They'll be gone in a moment." She continued at her hobbling pace, which was excruciatingly slow. They were supposed to be old, not dead.

"Let's pick up the pace before they change their minds," he muttered.

From the moment they'd climbed onto the tree branch, he had regretted his agreement to bring her along. This wasn't a childish prank or a game of pretend, it was a dangerous mission. Though she'd made it clear she would go with or without him, and short of tying her up, he couldn't prevent her. At least this way, he could keep an eye on her.

With any luck, he would find what he sought and convince his brother to release the judge. In the process, he might come across something that would trigger his memories.

He had gone to Becky's house for a reason, which could have something to do with those pamphlets or whatever underlying motive Sid had for arresting the judge.

By the time they reached the corner where the newspaper office was located, Tom struggled for air. Becky had insisted the outfit would be more convincing if he wore a corset. She meant to torture him for his past sins.

Moonlight silvered the tops of the army tents pitched around the old schoolhouse. Dozens of campfires flickered in the darkness. From across the square, fiddle music accompanied a rich baritone crooning a heartfelt rendition of *Ellie Rhee*. The entertainment had drawn a crowd and no one appeared interested in the two old ladies.

The disguise appeared to be working.

Becky turned into the alley alongside the brick building where he'd once worked as a printer's assistant. He knew his way around a press better than she did, but she seemed happier when he let her think she was in charge. She stopped at the side door, which had been padlocked, inserted the key, and a moment later it opened.

Tom cast a furtive glance around to ensure no one had seen them before following her inside the unlit building. From the darkness came a scrape. Then a match flared.

She lit one of the tapers they'd brought along and held it up. Light spilled over newspapers stacked up against a wall. Next to them, neat as pins, were more pamphlets.

"How thoughtful that someone put them there so Sid would trip over them," Tom remarked.

"Or Sid put them there."

Tom considered Becky's accusation. "Why would Sid go to such lengths? What does he have against your father, other than a difference over property rights?"

Becky glanced away. Too quickly. She would never have succeeded as a gambler.

Tom untied the sunbonnet and tossed the blamed thing on a nearby desk. He raked his fingers over his itchy head. "I'd like to hear the theory you haven't shared yet."

She used the taper to light a desk lamp and held it up. "Let's find what we're after."

Fine, he could wait a little longer, but he would discover her secret one way or another. It might have something to do with why he'd returned.

The brighter light illuminated a steam-powered press across the room, and next to it, a framed case with narrow drawers.

"Over there," he pointed out. "That's where they keep the metal sorts."

Becky positioned the lamp on top of the type case. "I'll start with the top drawer. You take the bottom."

"Gee, thanks." He squished the pillow forming his makeshift bosom as he knelt.

They collected cast metal sorts and spread them out near the light. He compared the *q, f,* and *t* with the printed letters on the pamphlet.

"Can you tell if they're the same?" Becky peered around his shoulder, teasing him with her summery scent.

Her soft breast pressed against his arm and every nerve in his body sprang to life. He couldn't be held responsible for imagining what was beneath granny's dress.

Tom straightened to escape the sweet torment. "Nope, nary a match."

"This is the proof we need. Oh, Tom. Thank you!" Becky grasped his shoulders and lifted on her toes, aiming for his cheek.

Instinctively, he turned his head and their lips brushed in a brief kiss. Simmering desire roared into a full-blown bonfire. But she jerked away before he could get his arms around her and draw her into the flames with him.

"I-I'm sorry, I didn't mean to," she stammered.

"I'm sorry you didn't mean to as well."

She spun away and scooped up the metal pieces of type, dropping one in her haste. Tom knelt to pick it up. He wouldn't apologize for his intentions. She might not have *meant* to kiss him, but her actions showed she felt the same stirrings he did.

He could test his theory by kissing her again.

Even if he could succeed at wooing her away from Alfred, he wasn't free to make plans until he'd recovered his memory. Then, after he told her the truth, she would undoubtedly reject him, and with good reason. He was less deserving of her now than when he'd been an aimless orphan.

As a naive youth, he had promised her the world on a silver platter—then failed to deliver even the smallest part.

This time, he wouldn't disappoint her. He would convince Sid to release the judge so she could take her father to St. Louis where Alfred would use his influence to protect her.

Tom straightened and held out his hand for the remaining sorts, concealing his frustrated yearning behind a devil-may-care expression. "We need to put those away. I'll talk to Sid in the morning."

She frowned with distrust. "Shouldn't we go to him now with this evidence?"

Greeting Sid while dressed as a midwife? No, that wasn't a good idea. Not only that, he needed time to think through how best to present his findings without incriminating Becky. If she had anything to do with the mission he'd been sent on, she was in danger, which made it doubly imperative to get her out of harm's way at the earliest opportunity.

"It's too late tonight. Let's go before we get caught in these infernal outfits."

While Becky returned the lamp to its proper place, he grabbed the massive sunbonnet he'd left on a desk and they exited into the alley.

As they reached the corner, a shout rang out.

"Ladies!"

The hail came from the direction of the tents.

A soldier ran across the street, coming in their direction. "You, ladies! Stop there!"

Tom bit back a curse. Given his current run of rotten luck, he should've expected a wrinkle in their plan.

Correction, *Becky's* plan.

He might be able to pull off this disguise at a distance, but up close he could make no guarantees. At least he'd shaved off the beard. That would be a dead giveaway.

Becky grabbed his arm "What do we do now? We can't outrun him."

Not dressed like this.

"Shooting him will attract too much attention. There are other ways to silence him." Tom removed the scissors from Becky's basket.

~

The lanky soldier stopped in front of them, planting his hands on his knees, huffing and puffing. "Whew. Evenin', ladies. Glad I spotted you." He twisted his head to look up at them. "Can you come right away? My gal needs help birthing a baby."

Becky held in a gust of relief. Thank God, he hadn't come over here to arrest them. She prayed the moonlight wasn't so bright that it would give her and Tom away.

"I'm sorry, sonny," she warbled in her best granny voice. "We are plum tuckered out and on our way home. Widow Hayes delivers babies. She lives—"

"Yeah, I already tried her. She's out." The soldier removed his hat and wiped his forehead with the back of his sleeve. His youthful face twisted with anxious hope.

"Have you tried Mrs. Rogers?" Becky suggested.

The soldier cradled his rifle and made an exasperated sound. "There's no time to find someone else. If you want, let your friend go on while you come with me. I promised Nora I'd bring help."

"No need to be in such a hurry, young man. I'll go with ye." Tom's cackle fit a witch better than a kindly old woman. His right hand, holding the scissors, twitched.

Did Tom intend to stab the young man? Enough blood had been spilled in this war to turn the Mississippi red. They could pretend a little longer until she found a way out of this predicament.

Becky licked dry lips. "Never mind. We can both come along. Show us the way." She purposely handed Tom her basket to keep his hands occupied and started after the soldier.

She didn't have to see her companion's face to know he wasn't happy with her decision. It would work out better this way. Once they arrived at their destination, she would send the young man off on an errand, and she and Tom could slip away. No one would hurt.

The anxious soldier led them at a brisk clip down the hill toward the river. The further along they went, the more nervous she became. Each street closer to the docks appeared wilder than the one before. Soon, they would be in the worst area of town.

He turned onto the last street. "This way."

Becky hesitated—surely his wife didn't live down there—but she moved before Tom could catch up, then stayed between him and the young solider to prevent any unpleasantness.

They passed numerous seedy saloons and low places ladies didn't talk about, much less visit. Raucous laughter came from inside a dance hall. Outside, scantily dressed women boldly draped their bare arms around the necks of soldiers.

One of the young women was an old friend from school who had lost her husband and child a few years earlier. Without protection or resources, the poor girl had been left with few choices.

Becky swallowed a lump in her throat. If her father went to prison and she didn't marry, she could end up in worse straights than being an old spinster.

Their guide made a hard left down a muddy alley. "Nora's upstairs. We can go in through the back."

Becky climbed a twisting stairway attached to the outside of one of the buildings. They entered from a second-story door into a dimly lit hallway that reeked of chemicals, cloying perfume, and unwashed bodies.

A woman's screams startled her. She jerked to a halt so fast that Tom bumped into her. He laid his hands over her shoulders. The simple touch had a calming effect.

The soldier stopped in front of one of the rooms where the

screaming continued. He took off his hat and waved it at the sheen on his face. "Nora's in there. She's having a hard time."

Another shriek erupted.

Hard time? It sounded as if she were dying.

Becky entertained some serious second thoughts. She had tended injuries, patched up gunshot wounds, and mixed tonics for everything from warts to the ague, but she had never actually delivered a baby. She had only watched and helped when the elderly housekeeper took her along. Her mother had put an end to it before she'd gotten first-hand experience.

Tom curled his fingers around Becky's arms and squeezed gently. "Go on," he whispered in her ear. "I'll find a way to distract the bluecoat and come back for you."

What choice did she have? Becky couldn't bring herself to abandon that poor woman without at least trying to help her.

"Don't hurt him," she whispered to Tom.

Tom turned to the sweating soldier. "Got any whiskey?" he cackled.

The young fellow appeared relieved to have a task. "I'll get some."

"I'll go with you to be sure it's the right kind." Tom followed the soldier down the hall.

Becky gathered her courage and entered the girl's room. The pungent odors grew stronger and she had to resist the urge to hold her nose.

Light from an oil lamp on the nightstand shone onto the figure of a young woman. Her nightgown, bunched beneath her arms, exposed a distended belly resembling a beached and bloated fish.

A thin girl in a cotton shift sat beside the laboring woman. She gazed at Becky with wide, deep-set eyes that registered surprise. "Are ye the midwife?"

Becky was tempted to shake her head and run. Instead, she removed her bonnet and placed her basket at the end of the bed.

The scissors, bandages, and various herbal tonics she'd brought along were supposed to be for show. At least she had them. The rest she would have to recall from past observations. "Will you fetch hot water? And some clean towels to wrap the baby?"

"Yes, ma'am."

As the girl ran off, Becky sent up a silent prayer, asking for deliverance for the woman, the baby, and herself.

"Hello, Nora. I'm here to help you." She leaned over and gently stroked the woman's sweat-drenched hair away from her drawn features. Up close, it became apparent that Nora was little more than a girl herself. "How long have you been laboring?"

"Seems like forever," Nora gasped. "Maybe since yesterday."

Becky straightened, fighting panic. What if something prevented the baby from coming out? She wouldn't know what to do.

Cain't solve a problem if'n you don't know what it is.

Becky's mind grew clearer as the midwife's words came back to her. "I need to check the baby's position."

Nora gave a weary nod.

Becky placed her hands on the woman's bulging abdomen. Was that the baby's bottom? If so, the child was positioned correctly, so Nature ought to take its course. "Is this your first child?"

"Yes, ma'am. Hope it's my last."

It was an understandable sentiment.

"First babies like to take their time." Or so Becky had heard. She had no personal experience, but she'd seen Old Lucy pace the floor for hours with one woman whose labor had slowed. "Have you gotten up recently?"

"No, it hurts to move."

"I'm sure it does. But if you get up and walk, that'll help the baby drop down to where it needs to be and give Nature some help."

The girl squeezed her eyes shut and tears leaked out. "Oh ma'am, I don't know if I can."

"Let me help you." Becky helped the woman to a sitting position, then took her hands and pulled her to her feet.

The two women inched across the room between the washstand and a chair.

Nora sagged against Becky, who had to use every ounce of strength to keep the laboring woman on her feet. She wouldn't be able to manage if Nora collapsed.

A soft knock sounded at the door.

Was it the other girl with the requested items? Hopefully, she would be strong enough to help.

"Come in," Becky called out.

The person who entered wasn't the one she expected.

Tom peered at her from beneath the massive sunbonnet. "How are you coming along, dearie?" he asked in that awful witch-like voice. "Ready to go?"

"Not yet." Becky adjusted her grip on the panting woman's thick waist. "Nora needs to walk to hurry things along. She needs my help. You go on without me, I'll catch up later."

Rather than leave, Tom shut the door. "Honey, you're no bigger than a chick. Let this old hen help her out."

She'd given him a way out. Any man with half a grain of sense would've taken to his heels. Childbirth was women's business. Tom was taking this role a little too seriously. But he was correct in assuming she needed assistance.

"Nora, this is my friend. She's, um, strong, and can help."

"Thank you both," Nora murmured.

Tom slipped an arm around their patient and supported her weight. He nodded at Becky. "You make preparations. I've got her."

Becky moved the chair, the washstand, and a slop bucket, and kicked a rug out of the way to make more room.

The other girl returned long enough to hand over the hot

water, towels, and a threadbare shawl before vanishing. She would not be much use.

Becky laid out the other items she needed: scissors, a needle, and silk thread. Her mind swam with details. When she had tagged along, it had been out of boredom. She hadn't expected to take over as a midwife one day. Thank heavens she had paid attention.

Nora gasped in pain and grabbed Tom's arm. When her knees buckled, he supported her full weight. "You'll be fine, lambkins," he warbled.

Lambkins? Becky shook her head. Where had he come up with these endearments?

She joined Tom to help the laboring woman.

Time ticked slowly by. As each moment passed, she feared they would be discovered. She prayed Tom hadn't harmed that young soldier who mistook them for midwives, but it wasn't the right time to ask him about it.

Nora cried out. Water splashed the floor between her legs.

"Your water broke," Becky pointed out, in case Nora wasn't clear on the process. She recalled being horrified the first time she'd seen it. "The birth should go faster now. Let's get you ready."

Becky smoothed the sheets and patted the bed.

Tom helped Nora lie down and then moved back against the wall nearest the door. It would give him an easy escape route if he wished to skedaddle. But he didn't leave. He stood watch as Becky coaxed the mother through the delivery.

Sometime later, Becky held up a wet, squalling baby boy. Joy eclipsed worry and fear, and for a single perfect moment, all was right with the world.

After she cleaned up the baby, wrapped him in the shawl, and handed him to his mother, the door banged open.

"Nora?" The young soldier staggered inside, clutching a whiskey bottle. His glazed eyes fastened on the new mother and her baby and a look of wonder transformed his expression. He didn't notice anything or anyone else, including the still, silent figure standing against the wall.

Thank God, Tom hadn't killed him. Yet.

Becky jumped to her feet to avert disaster. "Sir, we aren't ready for you."

The soldier approached the tired woman on the bed. "Are you all right, darlin'? I heard you hollering."

"We're fine, Archie." Nora nuzzled her newborn. "Thanks to you."

"Shucks, it wasn't me. These old ladies..." The young man finally looked straight at Becky and his eyes widened.

She reached for her bonnet, too late.

"Why, you...you aren't an old lady," he declared. "You're the *judge's* daughter."

CHAPTER SIX

Tom had a choice: rely on his stellar reputation for spinning believable tales or crack the idiot kid over the head so they could escape. Of the two options, Becky's anxious face conveyed the one she would prefer.

"We can't fool you, can we sonny?" Tom said in his best old lady voice.

The young soldier jerked around with a look of surprise. Apparently, he hadn't noticed the tall, ugly crone hovering near the door. If he didn't start paying better attention to his surroundings, he'd get his head blown off.

"Miss Thatcher is my apprentice," Tom continued in a falsetto. "She wears a disguise so folks won't be put off by how young she is. You won't spoil it by telling her secret, will you?"

"N-no, ma'am." The soldier squinted at Tom.

Good thing he'd kept on *his* bonnet. Earlier, the kid hadn't peered at him very closely. He'd been way too distracted by all the hollering.

"All right, then." Becky blurted, drawing the soldier's attention.

She threw her instruments into the basket. "We'll run along now. Time for you two to get to know your new son."

Tom snagged Becky's arm and they left in a hurry, going out the way they'd come in so as not to attract more attention than necessary, and to spare Becky a longer excursion through the whorehouse. She'd gotten enough exposure to squalor for one night.

"That fool was supposed to stay put until I sent for him," Tom grumbled. "I purloined a whole bottle of whiskey. He should've been too drunk to care."

Becky deftly stepped over the refuse in the street. "He loves her."

"Or she promised to pay him well to fetch help. Bartering is a common enough practice."

"You shouldn't be so cynical."

"That's a joke. If I was being cynical, I'd say she duped him into thinking that baby is his."

"Poor girl. She deserves better than that life she chose for herself."

Tom couldn't see past the bonnet to ascertain Becky's expression, but he could hear the sadness in her voice. "You won't find many who'd agree with you."

"What they think shouldn't matter."

"No, it shouldn't."

That it did matter what people thought underscored Becky's tenuous situation. With her father in jail and her cousin wanted as a criminal, her good reputation was all she had left. Without it, she couldn't hope to marry a man who prized his lofty position in society.

If Alfred knew what she'd been up to he might renege on his offer. That wouldn't break Tom's heart, but it might break Becky's, which meant this would have to remain their little secret. Oh, and Archie's. If he could keep his mouth shut.

On the way home, they encountered no one else in need of a midwife.

As they neared the Thatcher property, Becky veered off the sidewalk and crept alongside the fence to the backyard.

Tom peered over the gate.

A guard sat on the stoop. His head bobbed as he dozed off.

"Let's get inside before he wakes."

"Secure your skirts," Becky demonstrated by pulling the length between her legs and tucking it into the waistband of her apron.

Everything was so much easier in trousers.

Tom lifted her to a low branch, handed her the basket, and climbed up.

A sturdy limb that stretched over a section of the roof gave them access to the second-story window they had left open. She crawled through first then hauled him into her bedroom, something he never would've imagined as a boy.

"We did it!" She twirled in a circle, tossed her bonnet aside, and fell back onto on the bed. "I can't believe we delivered a baby."

"*You* delivered a baby. I stood by and watched."

She sat up. "That's not so. You helped."

"But you did the hard work, and remained calm throughout the ordeal." He wouldn't have predicted it.

When he'd fallen in love with her as a smitten lad of twelve, she'd been a spoiled, sheltered girl, the only child of an aging couple who had envisioned marrying her into royalty, or at least someone with more polish, influence and wealth than an orphaned troublemaker. She had upon occasion shown him glimpses of her adventurous, curious nature when she wasn't working so hard to mold herself into someone else.

"Where did you learn how to deliver babies? From your mother?"

"Oh, heavens no! Mama would've gone into fits if someone

asked her to assist. I snuck out to go with our housekeeper, Old Lucy. She knew loads about doctoring and delivering babies."

"Did she also teach you how to break into newspaper offices?"

"*You* taught me those things." Becky bounced off the bed, lifted her arms, and stepped into a waltz without a partner, humming slightly off-key.

Tom smiled. God, he had missed her sunny smile and infectious laugh. Even her awful humming.

She deftly avoided the edge of the bed with a pirouette. "Now we have the evidence we need to get my father out of jail."

"Yep. Time to celebrate." Tom yanked off the bonnet. He untied the apron and flung it aside, then went for the buttons down the front of the dress. "I'll dance with you, soon as I get out of this confounded contraption."

Becky swayed to the music in her head. "Why Tom, you look right smart in Lucy's best gown. Your figure is a good bit trimmer, though."

"I'll say. Old Lucy was built like a bale of hemp."

Moonlight spilled through the open window, illuminating Becky's smile. Amazing how a little danger could put her at ease and erase the signs of strain around her eyes and mouth.

He'd relished the thrill as well, except for the disguise. He tossed the ugly gown aside and removed the makeshift bosom—a pillow knotted with ribbon on each end and hung over his neck—for which he credited her ingenuity. "You enjoyed dressing me up and sneaking over there."

She made a soft sound of disbelief. "Whatever gave you that idea? I was scared to death."

"Scared, eh? You hid it well."

He fumbled with the hooks. "Whoever invented corsets ought to be hanged with one. Help me here before I suffocate."

"What a baby you are. Women wear corsets all the time."

Tom braced his hands on her shoulders and sucked in his

stomach so she could more easily undo the treacherous device. "Good thing they haven't figured out how to use them as a weapon."

"How do you know they haven't?"

He released his breath with a laugh. "I do like this saucy side of you."

"Don't get used to it."

"Why not? Don't you think it's an improvement?" He considered kissing the top of her bent head, then thought better of it. She wouldn't finish setting him loose. "When I first saw you, I thought you were made of angel clay. Far too good for the unholy likes of me."

"Hm," she murmured. "From what I could see, you worked very hard at being unholy, and took perverse pleasure in giving your aunt the fantods, poor thing."

"Sad to say, there might be some truth to it. She regularly held up Sid as the example of perfection, which spurred me to greater depravations. But I repented of my sins every night, I truly did. It's just that my good intentions were vanquished by the bright light of day."

"How convenient that your conscience only bothered you at night." Laughter sparkled in her blue eyes as she looked up.

"It doesn't work that way for everybody?" He gave in to temptation and stroked her silky-smooth cheek with the side of his thumb.

Surprise flickered across her face, her lips parted, beckoning, but before he could put thought into action, she refocused her attention on the last hook, which took longer than all the rest. "I can't blame the sun for letting you talk me into trouble."

He sighed at his lost opportunity. "Who do you blame for your poor choices? Me?" he asked, partly joking.

"No. I know who to blame."

Her implication was clear enough. She blamed her infatuation with him for whatever misfortune had befallen her. He couldn't deny being a bad influence, but...

He tipped her chin so she'd look at him. "You go no reason to be ashamed of anything. I know your folks were always proud of you. So am I. Even if you do have a wild streak," he added with a grin.

Tears welled in her eyes, which acted like acid on his conscience. He should've simply offered a compliment and not teased her. Before he could formulate a proper apology, she pulled away. "Don't get me confused with that silly girl I used to be."

She snatched his shirt from the bed and held it out to him with her back turned.

Tom frowned as he pulled it on over his head. "I'm not the confused one. What you did tonight wasn't *silly*. You were clever and brave. I'd take you along as a partner anytime."

She paused to light a lamp beside the bed before she untied her apron and flung it aside, apparently aiming for the bed but missing. "I didn't go with you because I wanted an adventure. I have to get Papa freed and take him away from here. Then you have to leave."

Becky kept a wary eye on Tom when she bent to pick up her apron. She shook it out before she hung it from a hook on the wall next to where she'd put her bonnet.

She had let down her guard for a few stolen moments of joy and the old feelings had ignited a glorious happiness. When he'd tilted her chin to look into her eyes, her pulse had quickened and her lips had tingled with remembered passion. Dangerous emotions when she would soon be wed to another man.

Tread carefully. Her mother would warn. Too much was at

stake to risk a stolen kiss, no matter how much she might think she wanted it.

Hearts were fickle. Tom's more than anyone's. At some point, he would leave again and she'd be left to pick up the pieces.

She glanced out the window to make sure no one was watching before she pulled the curtains.

"Why does the judge have to leave town? Has he done something wrong?" Tom propped his fists on his hips, frowning in a way that implied he had mulled over what she said and formed the wrong conclusions.

"He's done nothing except to be too honorable."

"Generally, a man isn't arrested for being too honorable."

How could she explain without going through the whole sordid tale? It wasn't something that would put the family or her father in a good light. "He made a promise he can't break, and that got him into trouble."

Tom's eyes narrowed. "What kind of promise?"

She gathered the clothing Tom had left strewn on the floor and stuffed it into the wardrobe, partly to avoid answering his question.

"I can't help you if I don't know the truth. No matter how distasteful."

Tom wouldn't let up. When he eventually talked to Sid, he would unearth the story, although it wouldn't be the truth. She couldn't understand why he cared so much about her father's fate or hers, for that matter. Still, if anyone could manage Sid it would be Tom, and he appeared to be willing. She had to take the chance.

"Let me tell you what's *distasteful*, and it has nothing to do with my father's behavior. Three years ago, federal soldiers looted our town. They killed my Uncle George when he tried to stop them. Jeff went wild with grief. He joined a band of rebel guerrillas and vowed to drive out his father's murderers and—"

Her throat closed from a rush of emotion and she had to pause long enough to collect herself. Tom had been Jeff's friend. "Jeff has changed. He isn't the same person, but the judge promised..."

Tom threaded his fingers through his hair and released a heavy sigh. "What promise did your father make to Jeff?"

"Not Jeff. Papa vowed to my uncle before he died to watch out for his son."

His only brother was gone, and his only nephew might as well be dead.

"My father never supported Jeff's choices. He begged him to stop, to handle his grief differently. When it did no good, he banished Jeff from the house and told him not to come back. But he couldn't swear an oath to deny his nephew food or medicine and break a deathbed vow."

Tom paced to the window and back. "Your father is giving Jeff aid."

She dared not give Tom a confession that might seal her father's fate. "No one has seen Jeff for over a year. His men were hunted down, killed, or driven out. For all we know, he's dead or gone."

"Except he isn't, is he? And the judge knows where he is." Tom continued his slow pace. Always moving. In this way, he hadn't changed.

Becky would not lie, but she couldn't confirm his suspicions either. "You know my father, Tom. He's as loyal as you are."

Tom hadn't been loyal to her, but that didn't mean he couldn't be loyal to something he considered more worthy of allegiance.

"Sid needs proof of the judge's alleged treason," Tom reasoned. "Thus, the pamphlet. Maybe he did plant it."

Despair swamped her earlier buoyancy. "If so, he won't care that we have evidence to show it wasn't printed out of the newspaper office. He'll just cover it up."

Her worst fears had been realized and there was nothing she could do. Not even Alfred would be able to save her father.

She covered her face with her hands.

A moment later, Tom drew her into his arms. "Don't cry, sweetheart."

How tempting to lean into the fairytale, that Tom had returned for her sake and would be her hero. Whether he'd truly lost his memory or not, he was hiding secrets. She couldn't count on him now any more than she'd been able to count on him before.

"Let me go. I am not your sweetheart."

"You were at one time." He pressed a tender kiss to her cheek before releasing her, which relieved Becky of having to push him away.

To put her hands somewhere other than on Tom, she arranged the perfume bottles on her dressing table.

Tom came up behind her. "What if Sid isn't after your father? He wants to capture Jeff. Arresting the judge would be one way to draw out the culprit. Where do they meet?"

"Where does who meet?" Becky closed a hinged frame containing a cabinet card Tom had sent to her shortly after he left. She hadn't been able to force herself to put it away, despite foreswearing any remaining affection for him long ago. How silly to have left it on display. She slipped it into a drawer.

"Where do Jeff and your father meet?" he asked from over her shoulder.

If Tom meant to capture Jeff, she would not help him. Her cousin had vowed not to be taken alive and she would not aid the two men in killing one another. "We never see Jeff anymore. He and my father only met a few times. I can't say where."

"Or won't say. If he's meeting Jeff, exchanging anything, that makes him a traitor."

A chill swept over her. Had she confided too much, *trusted* too much?

She gripped Tom's shirt and pleaded. "Tell me, if someone you loved was starving, would you refuse them food? If they were cold, would you withhold a blanket? My father could have lied about it and signed the oath then violated his word, but he didn't because he is an honorable man. He isn't lying when he says he's done nothing to aid the rebel cause. You've got to believe me."

Tom grasped her arms with a gentleness that seemed at odds with his stern expression. "I believe you will do anything to save him."

"That's not the same as believing me." She twisted out of his grasp. "Someone else put those brochures at the newspaper office. You said so. They're trying to make it look like the judge is involved in something he isn't."

"But Jeff could be."

She had thought of that too, except it didn't make sense. "Jeff wouldn't deliberately implicate my father in treasonous activities."

"War brings out the worst in men."

"I suppose you'd know," she shot back.

Tom folded his arms over his chest. Perhaps the barb had pierced his armor. "How much does Alfred know about what's going on?"

She had purposely avoided talking about Jeff in her letters, and Alfred hadn't asked. "He works for the general who oversees the District of Missouri so I suspect he's privy to a great deal of sensitive information. He doesn't share it with me. He only said I should come to St. Louis where I'll be safe."

Tom nodded. "Then he knows enough to give you good advice."

The answer stunned her. Tom siding with Alfred? Even more surprising, encouraging her to go to him? She didn't know whether to feel relieved or angry. Regardless, her answer was the same. "I won't leave without my father. I have to find a way to clear his name. Will you help me now that you know the truth?"

Tom paced the length of the room, touching the spot above his temple as if the injury continued to plague him. She experienced a twinge of guilt for asking him to help her when he needed to be in bed recuperating.

It encouraged her that he didn't give her an immediate answer. If he did, it would be a glib one. He was thinking about it, considering the consequences. Quite a change from his younger self, who had never hesitated to jump into anything that smacked of danger.

"It isn't going to be easy."

"But you'll do it?"

He nodded.

Despite his obvious misgivings, Tom had chosen to help her.

She had to make a choice, as well, even though she didn't have an option. She couldn't do this on her own. Until her father could be freed, she had to rely on Tom.

God help him if he betrayed them.

CHAPTER SEVEN

The next morning, two of Sid's guards escorted Tom to a brick warehouse near the docks. Sid didn't trust him to walk a few blocks on his own without vanishing. He didn't trust Sid as far as he could throw him, so they were even in that regard.

To complicate matters, Becky insisted on coming along, and couldn't be talked out of it. He had agreed not to oppose her if she promised to stay with her father and keep out of trouble.

One of the soldiers stationed in front of the freight house ushered them up the steps into the two-story building, which had been previously used to store goods delivered to the docks. The only boats on the river these days were Union steamers, and the warehouse now served as military police headquarters.

They parted ways at the stairs leading down to a makeshift jail in the basement before Tom headed up to the second floor. He returned a salute from two guards posted at the door to the former dock manager's office. "I'm here to meet with the provost marshal. He's expecting me."

After entering, Tom shut the door to discourage eavesdropping.

Sid glanced up from his seat behind the desk and frowned. "I was beginning to wonder whether you'd show up."

Tom feigned surprise. "Me? Ignore your orders?"

"You wouldn't obey an order from me if I held a gun to your head."

"I would if it was loaded." Tom sat in one of two armchairs arranged in front of Sid's desk and adopted the role of the devil-may-care black sheep. The role fit comfortably, plus Sid would expect it and therefore lower his guard enough to let something slip that might help the judge.

Neat stacks of paperwork confirmed his brother's persnickety habits, and the jar of candy indicated a sweet tooth remained intact. What changes had time wrought?

Sid leaned back in his chair and folded his arms. Completely comfortable, in charge, at least that was the impression he wanted to give. He'd honed his ass-kissing skills enough to advance in the army's rigid caste system. Not just anyone got assigned as a provost marshal, and he must've set a record for being the youngest, at a mere twenty-one years. He had always looked, and acted, like an old man.

"You are a surprise," he said.

"A pleasant one, I hope." Tom removed his hat and shook his hair out of his eyes before he casually propped an ankle on one knee.

As far back as he could remember, he and his younger half-brother had been in fierce competition to gain the upper hand. He might be persuaded to be more charitable should Sid choose to extend an olive branch.

"I half expected to hear you were dead." The terse remark answered whether Sid might be interested in a brotherly relationship. He hadn't mellowed with age.

"If that's what you were hoping, you might get your wish yet."

E.E. BURKE

Sid's frown deepened, but it was impossible to tell whether he was annoyed or simply disappointed.

Tom unclenched his teeth. He, for one, wasn't disappointed that their relationship remained unchanged. Sid would do his level best to make life miserable. Why not play along to see if he could be goaded into revealing something useful?

Without a doubt, the provost marshal had made inquiries. Tom needed to know what, if anything, had come of it before he challenged the judge's arrest. But it wouldn't do to appear anxious.

"May I?" Tom asked, indicating the peppermints.

"Sure." Sid tipped the jar. "Since you asked so nicely."

"Why wouldn't I? I'm not the one who steals candy and blames an innocent soul for breaking the dish." Tom popped a piece of candy into his mouth. Their aunt had believed most any accusation Sid made, whether it was true or not, and Sid had sworn up and down he hadn't broken it, and he *never lied*.

Sid's mouth flattened into a thin line. Couldn't be embarrassment or guilt. Maybe he suffered from a peptic stomach. That would also explain the presence of peppermints. "Let's get down to business." He pulled over a piece of paper and dipped his ink pen. "Why are you here?"

Taking notes? How official.

Sucking on candy spared Tom from answering right away. He pretended a casual interest in the office while noting details.

The framed illustrations of the river's course had been here when the building was used as a freight warehouse and might come in handy at some point. Another item of interest was a large map of the region with pins placed on it. Those pins meant something and he would eventually find out what.

Behind the desk, a Stars and Stripes had been tacked to the wall above a framed picture of President Lincoln. It sparked an idea for how to sidestep Sid's direct question.

Tom gestured with his hat to the portrait. "Ever meet him?"

"No, I haven't," Sid replied crisply.

"Nice fellow. *He* has a sense of humor."

"We're not here to talk about the President."

"No, suppose not." Tom settled more comfortably into the chair. He'd led up to the next question by implying he had a connection to important people in high places. Sid would suspect he was joking, yet couldn't be sure. "Did you get an answer from General Grant?"

A muscle by Sid's eye twitched. "I didn't contact General Grant."

Even if Sid had reached out, he wouldn't have received a reply. The man responsible for directing Tom's movements maintained strict secrecy. Even Ulysses Grant didn't know where Pinkerton's agents were at any given time. The chain of command likely hadn't changed. Tom just couldn't recall his assignment. Whoever Sid had messaged might provide a clue.

"Who did you contact?"

"Before I say, tell me who sent you."

So that's how Sid intended to play it, *tit-for-tat*.

Tom dared not confide about his memory loss until he knew more about what Sid was up to and why. "Too bad I'm not free to share that information."

Sid returned a baleful stare. "I can lock you up until you do."

Tom examined his nails in a show of utter boredom and called the bluff. "You can risk it, yes."

"Why are you staying with Miss Thatcher rather than at home?"

Did he mean Aunt Polly's old house? Sid had inherited it, so it might be *his* home.

Tom shrugged. "Becky's prettier than you are?"

Sid came out of the chair, bracing his hands on the table, hunched forward in the perfect imitation of a snapping turtle. "Stop playing games! I have no time for your craftiness."

Tom didn't move a muscle. "I am not playing a game and I have no time for your ill temper. If you can't hold a civil conversation, I'll be forced to make a negative report. Without your input."

Panic flared in Sid's eyes for a second before he retreated into his shell. "Report? About what?"

Well, well. What did the provost marshal fear would be found out? It opened up an opportunity to rattle Sid and see what might fall out.

"The report about you. For being ineffective, inept, and a general nuisance..." Tom touched the first three fingers then spread all ten. "It's a long list."

A dull stain spread up Sid's neck, reddening his swarthy skin, something they'd both inherited from their father. Only Sid had gotten the old man's sour disposition. "The colonel didn't mention sending anyone down here to make a report."

Interesting. Sid wasn't so sure.

Tom leaned back, marveling that Sid might have something to hide, something worse than a broken candy tray. "What are you afraid of? That I'll find out you aren't the perfect soldier?"

"*Damn* you." Sid's fervent condemnation hit Tom with the force of a punch.

Over all the years they'd wrangled and fought and tried to outwit each other, Sid never resorted to calling down curses. Unlike Tom, Sid took them seriously.

"That's already taken care of." Tom maintained a light tone to hide the unexpected sting. He shouldn't be surprised that Sid would resort to the same low opinion held by their father. "Didn't Pa declare I was only fit for the devil?"

Sid jerked away and paced to an open window that faced the river. He crossed his hands behind his back, flexing his fingers in a gesture that put a knot in Tom's gut.

Pa had stood like that, right before he administered a beating.

Something he did with frequency to take out his anger on the child whose birth had cost him his beloved first wife.

Tom took little comfort from the fact that his half-brother had enjoyed a brief reign before their parents succumbed to typhoid. He also couldn't whip up any pleasure in baiting the younger man. Sid could be an ass, but he hadn't started this particular fight.

"I'm surprised you haven't made inquiries up the line."

"You'd like that, wouldn't you?" Sid ground out. "Bad enough Colonel Sanderson thinks I'm too soft—"

The telling remark slipped before Sid could cut it off and gave Tom another glimpse into his brother's inner demons. It also disturbed ghosts he would prefer to remain buried.

Sid had been four years old when the two of them were orphaned and bundled off to live with a widowed aunt. For nearly a month, the small boy with the big frightened eyes had ventured to his seven-year-old brother's bedside at night to seek comfort where none was to be found. Tom had since come to regret his jealousy and what it had brought out in him. But like many things he regretted, it was in the past and couldn't be changed.

Besides, Sid wasn't a frightened child anymore. He wasn't weak or helpless. He sure as hell wasn't *soft*. But he was still motivated by fear and ambition. Both could be applied to gain leverage and get the judge released.

"If you tell me who planted those pamphlets, I'll consider changing the report and recommending you for a promotion."

"We got word Thatcher printed them out of the newspaper office. Found boxes, ready to distribute." Sid clung to his story. The part about finding the boxes might be true, but he didn't want to work hard enough to figure out the other part that didn't make sense.

"A smart man like the judge put those things out where anybody could find them to make it easier for you to hang him? That's what you believe?"

Sid remained silent and stared out the window.

Frustrated and angry, Tom shot to his feet. "Dang it, Sid, you *know* the judge. You can't think he's guilty of treason."

"If he wasn't, I wouldn't have him locked up."

Time to roll out the big guns.

"So, I don't suppose you're interested in evidence proving your arrest is an obvious set-up. I'll save it for your commander."

Sid spun around with the swiftness of a hawk. "What evidence?"

"Take a look." Tom reached inside his coat pocket and laid the newspaper clipping on the desk next to the pamphlet. "These weren't printed on the same press. I've circled where the letters are different."

Sid leaned over to examine the two papers. "Hmm. Different type. Doesn't prove anything."

"Sure, it does. Check the type drawer. The sorts used for the flyer aren't in it."

"Did you break in and remove them?"

Assuming the worst, as usual.

Tom shook his head and sat down. "Go take a look. You'll find nothing removed. Though I can't promise that *you'll* be here after I file my report."

He waited, growing nervous at the extended silence. If threats and hard evidence didn't work, what was left?

"I haven't contacted anyone about you being here," Sid said in low voice.

Sid hadn't tattled on him? If someone had offered a wager, he would've lost that bet. He still wasn't sure he believed it. "Seems strange you wouldn't send a message through your chain of command."

"I would if I thought I'd receive a truthful answer."

Another revelation that flummoxed him. "Why would they lie to you?"

Sid sat down with a weary sigh. "They don't trust me? I don't know. I used to think they gave me this job because I'm honest and committed to keeping the peace. Now, I wonder if they put me here because they see me as dispensable. No other provost marshal has lasted more than a year."

He didn't have to say what had happened to the others. It was chillingly apparent.

"Who can you trust?" Tom asked.

"No one." Sid leaned on his arms. His stern expression had softened, making him appear younger, and more vulnerable. "Everybody claims to be loyal then they plot behind your back. Every week we lose soldiers to snipers. Our informants are hunted down and hanged from the nearest tree. This town *reeks* of treason, but we can't find the source."

This shed light on why his commander might not be pleased. It also suggested a reason for a spy to be dispatched, to ferret out a traitor's nest that local authorities hadn't been able to find and destroy.

Tom rubbed his temple and tried to remember. Anything that might help him solve the puzzle. Too many pieces were still missing, and his headache had returned. "Tough spot you're in," he said with honest sympathy.

"You have no idea," Sid muttered.

The provost marshal's antipathy toward Becky's father might make sense if he believed the judge would betray him.

"I'd stake my life on the judge's integrity," Tom stated.

"Of course, you would. He treated you like a son."

"A son? He talked Aunt Polly into packing me off so I'd stay away from Becky." Tom released a humorless laugh. "Is that what's bothering you? The judge didn't tell her to send you away to school?"

"I wouldn't have dropped out," Sid said under his breath. "Not that it matters."

Well, it did matter. It mattered so much he'd carried around a chip on his shoulder.

"Keeping the judge locked up won't make him like you any better," Tom pointed out.

"You think convincing me to let him go will make Becky like you any better?"

That was low, even for Sid.

Tom heaved a weary sigh. He didn't have the energy to fire back an insult. "Let him go, Sid. He and Becky will leave then we can concentrate on finding Jeff. He's the one you want."

Sid straightened, narrowing his eyes. "Leave? Where are they going?"

Tom debated about how much to reveal. Information, like currency, had to be spent carefully. Knowledge about Becky's imminent betrothal amounted to a few coins, at best, and the whole town would know soon enough. "St. Louis. She has a marriage offer from Alfred Temple. He's stationed there, working for some general at a desk job."

Sid regarded Tom with a slight smile. "Did she tell you that Captain Temple is the adjutant to General Rosecrans? A very important *desk job.*"

"If you say so." Tom tucked away another bit of information. Now Becky's concern about Alfred's reaction made more sense. Although why Alfred would pursue her in the first place didn't, given her father's tenuous situation. The only possible reason made Tom's stomach knot. Alfred loved Becky enough to risk everything. Her former beau, fool that he was, had risked her love to seek something more. Only, there wasn't anything more.

"You don't care that he's marrying your girl?"

Tom stared at his hands rather than looking Sid in the eye. "What makes you think I care? She's not my girl. We're just old friends."

"If you say so. She's relieved, I'm sure, that you have no intention of messing up her plans."

It had entered Tom's mind, much as he hated to admit it even to himself. But why would Sid care about Becky's plans? He considered her a tool to get information. Either way, she would soon be beyond their reach and out of danger. "She thinks she'll be better off in St. Louis with Alfred. I reckon she knows her mind."

"Yes, I imagine she does." Sid straightened up and cleared his throat. "Miss Thatcher is free to leave. Her father remains here until I have a chance to check out the newspaper office and confer with the authorities. We can't afford to make a misstep. I'm sure your commander would agree. Why don't you send him a message?"

Tom lifted his head and a flush hit his face. He should've known better than to let down his guard. "The charges are phony."

Sid held Tom's gaze. "Judge Thatcher refused to sign the oath of loyalty. Did Becky tell you that?"

"As a matter of fact, she did. He didn't break any law. Taking that oath is an act of free will, not evidence of guilt."

"Unless your nephew happens to be a rebel guerilla."

Tom stood and planted his hands on the desk. "You admit it! The judge is a pawn in some game you're playing to catch Jeff."

"It's no game. Jeff is in the middle of whatever treacherous plan is being hatched, and the judge is his uncle."

"So? I'm your brother. Does that make me complicit in your lies?"

Sid came up on his hands until they were nose to nose. "That's rich. You accusing *me* of lying. I wager you've never met my commander."

Tom scored his empty mind. He had no idea, but he wasn't about to back down. He picked up the pamphlet to wave it in Sid's face. "Why are you so bent on seeing the judge hang for something he didn't do?"

Sid snatched the flyer, his eyes flashing with anger and another emotion more difficult to decipher. "Why are *you* so determined to defend him? Which side are you on, Tom? Now that might be worth checking out."

CHAPTER EIGHT

The basement of the freight house had been turned into a holding pen for the military police. Prisoners, a startling number of them boys, stretched out on the dirty straw. The lucky ones had blankets. One of the guards dragged a bench inside the cell for Becky to sit on while she visited with her father.

The judge sagged as if his spare frame weighed a ton. He brushed straw off the sleeve of his rumpled suit. His eyes looked rheumy and weighted with bags. He coughed into his elbow. If he was forced to remain behind bars, the rancid air and filth would sicken him.

Alarmed, but not wanting to distress him, Becky adopted false cheer and handed him a napkin along with a piece of cornbread. "I'm sure you must be starved."

"Strangely enough, I'm not hungry. But I know someone who is." Her father bent to hand his portion to a gaunt youth sprawled at his feet.

"God bless ya, judge." The boy's hoarse voice wavered and his hand trembled as he reached for the gift. It was a sight that would've wrenched even the hardest heart, and Becky's was no exception.

She couldn't scold her father for having compassion. Soon, he would be home where she could feed him and take care of him. "I'll speak with Tom about making sure these prisoners are fed. He's with Sid now, presenting evidence that will clear up this misunderstanding about those pamphlets. You'll be out of here in no time."

"What evidence?" Her father's studied gaze gave her the impression he could see through her bravado.

"It's brilliant. Tom found a way to show Sid the pamphlets weren't printed at the newspaper office."

"Did he now?" Her father's slow smile brought a flicker of life back into his eyes that for a moment made him appear like his old self. "He's always been clever."

"Yes, very clever." She chewed her lower lip. Too clever, sometimes. "Do you doubt he's trustworthy?"

"Is anyone trustworthy these days?" the judge mused. "Whatever Tom presents to the provost marshal may not be enough. Sid can still hold me for not signing that document while they take their time investigating."

"But the truth—"

"The truth isn't always easy to find."

She steeled herself against a spurt of panic. "Tom has a gift of persuasion. He will prevail with Sid. And as soon as you're released, we'll board the next steamboat bound for St. Louis."

The judge rummaged through her basket and retrieved the jar of peaches. These he also gave away to another hollow-eyed boy, who shared it with his comrades. "Don't expect I'll be going with you."

She gaped at him in astonishment. "Why would you choose to remain behind? There is nothing you can do. Your every move will be watched."

He shifted back onto the bench and folded his hands. "It's not a matter of choice. They want to set a trap and I'm the bait. That's why you must leave, child. I don't want you mixed up in this."

"I'm already mixed up in it, so you can save your breath telling me to leave without you. If Sid refuses to listen to Tom, he can appeal to a higher authority."

"Has Tom regained his memories?"

"Not that he's said."

Her father sandwiched her hand between palms that were soothingly warm and smooth. "The best thing Tom can do is to escort you away from here," he said in a low voice. "In time, I may be released. But you cannot stay. It's too dangerous. Pray Jeff will realize it's over."

His words sent a wave of unease over her. "What do you mean? What's over?"

"The only thing that matters to me anymore is your safety. Relieve my heart and see to it."

A dreadful premonition prickled her skin. What had her cousin involved her father in that was too awful to talk about? The honorable judge wouldn't have participated in treason, not knowingly.

By now Jeff had to be aware of her father's imprisonment. What, if anything, did he have to do with those pamphlets? He might be knee-deep in a conspiracy and had dragged the judge down with him, once again.

She gripped her father's arm. "Tom knows about your vow. He wants to talk to Jeff."

"I'm sure he does, but I can't help him."

Her father refused to acknowledge what Jeff had become. He could only see his nephew as the brilliant, sensitive, compassionate young man he had once been.

"What have you done? What has Jeff drawn you into?"

"Don't cry, dearest."

"I'm not crying."

Not yet.

Her father wrapped his arm around her and hugged her against him. "Things aren't as bad as they seem. Tell Tom that, and tell him I'll confess everything at the right time."

Now the tears came.

"Should you confess to treason you'll hang, regardless of how you explain it? I won't let you do it." She wrapped her arms around him and squeezed. "Not for Jeff, not for me, not for anybody."

Her father rubbed her shoulder. "Becky, trust me in this."

Given what he had just revealed, she could trust no one. She had already involved Tom too much. Appealing to Alfred was out of the question. She had to seek out Jeff and plead with him to give himself up rather than allow her father to be his sacrificial lamb.

Becky stuffed the napkin into the basket. "All right, I'll be leaving."

Her father released a heavy sigh. "Good. You've given me peace in knowing you'll be safe."

Safe was the last thing she would be if she were caught.

She leaned over to kiss her father's papery cheek. "If Tom comes downstairs looking for me, tell him I've gone home to pack my bags and will return soon."

That should give her enough time to find Jeff and knock some sense into him.

She motioned for the guard.

Her father stood as they removed the bench. "Are you sure you don't want to wait for Tom?"

"Very sure. This way will be better."

The soldier who offered to accompany Becky home was the same young man she had helped while posing as a midwife. He grinned and offered her his arm. "Private Archie Hendrix. Remember me?"

How could she forget what had turned out to be one of the most memorable evenings of her life? Hopefully, the private would not ask about her *friend*.

"Yes, nice to see you again." She worked up a half-hearted smile.

Somehow, she had to find a way to lose her escort so she could go look for Jeff. She didn't have much time left before Tom would come looking for her.

"How are Nora and the baby?"

"They're doin' well. I asked her to get married."

"Good for you. Congratulations."

He frowned rather than appearing pleased. "She didn't accept right off. Said she'd think about it. I don't know why she wouldn't want me to lay claim to my son."

They walked past the wild street where Archie had taken her the previous night.

Becky could guess why Nora might've refused the gallant young man. "Perhaps the child isn't yours?"

Archie jerked up his chin. "He's mine, and that's that."

Whether it was true or not, the fact that he was willing to take on responsibility spoke well of him. It also gave Becky an idea. "Perhaps Nora has another reason. Why don't you go talk to her? I can make it home on my own."

Archie slowed his steps, but then he sped up, pulling her along. "No, I got to get you home, and not let you out of my sight."

So, it wouldn't be as easy as that.

Halfway home, she passed a tumbledown fence meandering across the front of the Lawrence property. The two-story house, with its crooked shutters and peeling yellow paint, appeared deserted. At one time, a family with three boys and a girl lived

81

there. Now, only one person remained, and Amy had become a recluse.

Movement on the front porch caught Becky's eye. Someone, a man, crouched behind the railing. Overgrown bushes concealed him before she could get a good look, but there for an instant—

"Miss Thatcher?"

"What?" Becky jerked her attention to her escort. Had Archie seen the man on the porch? She'd seen him only an instant, but she would swear it was Jeff. If she went over there and found him, she would force a confrontation that would endanger her escort.

She tried to speak normally despite her hammering heart. "I'm sorry, I just thought of a faster route to my house. Let's cross here."

Becky tugged the soldier's arm to turn him away. As they reached the opposite side of the street, she glanced over her shoulder.

The man on the porch had vanished.

Becky couldn't imagine why her cousin would be sneaking around Amy's house, of all places. Unless Jeff suspected the resentful woman of stirring up trouble for the judge.

"I can make it home from here, Private Hendrix. I'm sure there's more important business for you to attend to."

"Not as important as escorting you home. Got to follow orders."

Had he been *following orders* when he'd dragged them off to a brothel? Archie had a weakness, and her name was Nora.

"Aren't those pretty?" Becky gestured to the climbing roses intertwined along the fence in front of her home. "I've been mulling over your dilemma. You don't want Nora to think you're only marrying her for the child. You need to woo her. Why not take her some flowers and tell her how much you care for her?"

It was good advice, trickery or not.

Archie scrunched his face into a confused expression. "Where would I get flowers?"

He couldn't have seen Jeff. He paid no attention to his surroundings.

She motioned to the blooming bush. "We have a profusion of roses. My father planted them for my mother years ago, and she considered them a sign of his true love. You can snip some off for Nora and show her how special she is to you."

Archie's pinched expression gave way to a look of amazement. "That's a grand idea, Miss Thatcher. Should've thought of it myself."

"Glad to be of assistance."

Archie held open the front gate. "Thank you, ma'am. I'll give her the flowers tonight."

"Why not now? There's no reason for you to stay here and wait on me. I have some packing to do, and you know how long that takes a woman."

"I suppose I could..." Archie pulled a knife from a sheath on his belt. "I'll do it. I'll go get them flowers and take them to her, and be back before you finish packing."

While Archie got busy cutting flowers, Becky started up the steps. She would slip out the rear door and double back through the alley.

She made it as far as the kitchen.

Widow Bent sat at the table with her head on her arms. She jerked awake with a snort and straightened her glasses. "About time you got home," she grumbled.

Frustration at encountering another obstacle made Becky cross. "You'll excuse me, I'm rather busy."

The old lady used her cane to get to her feet. "Is the judge in jail?"

Word traveled fast.

"It's nothing for you to worry about. Just a misunderstanding about some ugly pamphlets left at the newspaper office."

Mrs. Bent blinked with confusion behind thick lenses that

made her eyes look owlish. "Why on earth do they care if your father is keeping ugly blankets?"

Her hearing was as bad as her sight.

"No, I didn't say blankets. *Pamphlets*. Like a booklet or a treatise."

"Trees? What trees?"

"Never mind."

"Where's my letter?" the old lady demanded.

Being quarrelsome was not how one received favors, but if that would get rid of her...

Becky crossed to retrieve her apron from where she hung it by the stove. "I brought it over the other day. You weren't at home. Since then my life has become a bit more... difficult."

The old lady clutched her shawl. "Yes, yes, I understand. Do you have it handy?"

"Right here." Becky reached into an empty pocket. Frowning, she checked the other pocket. "That's odd, it isn't where I left it."

Good grief, she didn't have time to worry about a misplaced letter. She had to get away and locate Jeff before Tom came looking for her.

"Do you mind if I bring it by tomorrow?"

The old lady grunted with annoyance. "Yes, I do mind."

Becky retained a sweet smile while simmering inside. "After supper perhaps? I'm sure it's around somewhere."

The widow pulled her lips into a thin line. "Careless girl. You must find Anne's letter, and bring it to me no later than tomorrow morning."

Becky held her tongue rather than respond to the old woman's surprising venom. She could find and deliver the blasted letter tonight. With any luck, she wouldn't be around tomorrow morning. She would be on a boat headed north to St. Louis with her father at her side.

CHAPTER NINE

Meanwhile, back at the freight house, Tom tromped down to the basement to find Becky and deliver the bad news —that her father would, for the time being, remain in jail.

Managing Sid should have been an easy enough task. Tom blamed faulty memories for his poor performance. At best, he'd gleaned a bit of information about Jeff Thatcher. If his assignment was to root out traitors, any fool could figure out that Becky's cousin would be first on the list.

The guard sat on a bench outside the holding cell. Becky was nowhere to be seen.

"Where's Miss Thatcher? She was supposed to wait for me," Tom asked.

The guard shrugged, unconcerned.

The judge approached the bars. "She insisted on going home to pack and one of the soldiers offered to escort her. Don't be too upset with her. She's anxious to leave."

Anxious to leave with her father, that's what he meant.

Tom's stomach sank. Becky had put her faith in him, and

again, he would disappoint her. "The two of you won't be leaving together, I'm sorry to say," he informed the judge.

"I expected as much. Thank you for trying, son."

The affectionate address twisted the knife in Tom's conscience. He shouldn't have let Sid's suspicions poison his faith in the man who had been like a father to him. The judge's active involvement in his life had opened doors that would've remained shut otherwise. He'd loaned Tom books from his private library, encouraged a boy's curiosity and endless questions, and had done his best to improve a young man's mind and his prospects, going so far as to recommend him to a school, which he'd dropped out of.

"It's poor thanks for all you did for me," Tom conceded. "But I'm not giving up."

The judge motioned Tom closer and lowered his voice. "See to Becky. Take her away from this place."

Curious. He hadn't mentioned anything about delivering her to Alfred. It might go without saying. Regardless, she would resist leaving without her father. They wouldn't convince Sid to release him with a handful of metal sorts. They needed a viable suspect.

"Tell me who you think put those brochures in the newspaper office?" Tom asked.

"If I knew, I'd tell you."

"What about your nephew?"

The judge met Tom's gaze without flinching. "As misguided as he's been in the past, he wouldn't intentionally put my neck on the chopping block."

The jurist who had presided over the county court hadn't been blind to reality. Yet, it had to be painful to consider that his own flesh and blood could betray him.

"You're saying Jeff is no longer misguided?"

"I can't speak for his state of mind."

"But you know enough to surmise his present intentions. Where can I find him? I'd be happy to convey a message. If you could convince him to turn himself in, Sid may agree to let you go."

A flush stained the judge's hollow cheeks. His eyes flashed with anger. "You're asking me to hand over my nephew in exchange for my freedom?"

Tom would turn Jeff over without losing sleep. Becky's cousin bore the responsibility for his family's troubles, and he was the only one who could resolve them.

"As distasteful as it sounds, that may be your only option."

The older man's shoulders sagged although his mouth remained stubborn. "If you were in my place, what would you do?"

"I wouldn't hesitate to do whatever it took to keep Becky safe."

Her father gripped the bars with a plea in his eyes. "Then do it. Convince her to leave. Take her somewhere she'll be secure. Don't let her throw her life away because of me."

The judge wouldn't betray his nephew. Becky wouldn't leave her father behind. It came down to one option. Track down Jeff and bring him in.

In a sense, Becky's disobedience might serve them well. She would be busy packing, which would give him time to do some reconnaissance.

Tom eluded Sid's guards by leaving through an open window on the first floor. He headed away from the river, across the rail yard toward the woods. He had an idea of a few places where his old friend might be hiding.

Based on Sid's report, the men under Jeff's command had scattered and fled or been tracked down and killed. Capturing their commander had proved more difficult than Sid anticipated, which explained why he was certain the judge was supplying Jeff with information.

Becky insisted her father wasn't guilty of anything.

Who was right?

Awareness prickled the hair on the back of Tom's neck. He dipped his chin and pulled at the brim of his hat, leaning forward as if to fight the wind, and slid a furtive glance around his shoulder.

Well, well. He and Sid were still playing chess. Sid had anticipated his move and sent a tracker after him.

Further along up the hill, Tom slipped in between two houses to make it appear he was taking a shortcut through the alley behind Becky's place. He hid beneath a porch until the man tailing him passed, then he ran, hopped a fence, and doubled back in the direction of the river before disappearing into the trees.

Summer had woven the forest into a tapestry of overgrown bushes and vines. During school days when the sunshine had called and Tom couldn't keep his mind on his studies, he coerced his friends into playing hooky. He'd take Jim Harper and Jeff Thatcher to a secret spot in the woods where they would meet up with Huck. It was easy to miss, and Tom had never told anyone else about its location. Jeff would remember the place. He might've used the concealed cave as a convenient place to hide.

Back then, the four boys had formed armies and agreed to meet the next day on a field to fight it out. Jeff had not shown up. Later, he admitted he didn't enjoy war games, even pretend battles. He had been the least adventurous of the friend group and had avoided fights whenever possible. Unlike Tom, who had relished the chance to thrash a rival.

Becky said her cousin had changed. Based on Sid's reports, he had changed into someone unrecognizable as the peace-loving, scholarly boy Tom had known.

As he got closer to his destination, Tom sniffed the air. *Smoke,* and the scent of cooked meat. Someone was camping out.

Tendrils of gray smoke rose from behind a natural barrier of sumac bushes and overgrown vines. The snorts and rustling coming from the other side indicated multiple horses, which meant more than one man was over there. Jeff and his rebel friends?

Tom knelt and slowly parted the branches. He spotted three men hunkered around a low-burning fire. Didn't recognize any of them. Even if Jeff wasn't here, these might be some of his henchmen.

The scrawniest one used a stick to roast a rabbit while his companions rested on their heels, fairly licking their chops. Armed to the teeth with rifles, pistols and knives, they weren't here for a cookout. None were in uniform, although each had a bit of red cloth pinned to the shoulder of his jacket. An identifier, no doubt, so they wouldn't accidentally shoot each other.

Tom leaned in, straining to hear their conversation.

"After this job, we got to pull heel," the skinny cook whined in a nasal tone. "There's more Federals in these woods than fleas on a dog."

"Stop your bellyachin'. We've given them another target." The speaker, who had his back to Tom, wore his hair in a long black braid secured with a leather tie, Indian style.

"What's our next move?" This remark came from a heavy man with hooded eyes and a florid complexion.

"Deliver the goods," the man with the braid answered.

"When?"

"When we get word." He withdrew a long hunting knife from a sheath on his belt. "If we don't hear something soon, I'll have a chat with the messenger."

The men's dark chuckles sent a chill over Tom's skin.

They were plotting something. Who was the messenger and what were they delivering?

Tom leaned in so he could see better.

Next to the black-haired man lay a felt hat with a wide brim and a wig with long, white hair. Something awful familiar about that disguise.

"What about the Thatcher gal?" one of them asked.

Tom jerked to attention at Becky's name.

"Don't worry about her," the leader replied. "She'll be taken care of, right after we get rid of—"

A loud eruption sounded. Flatulence.

"Whew, you got a problem?" The cook waved his hand, sending the awful smell in Tom's direction.

"Not for long." The third one stood up.

As he moved toward the bush, Tom sank back into the shadows with his revolver at the ready. The leaves rustled an instant before the heavyset man stepped around the end, unbuttoning his trousers. Surprised, he went for his gun.

Tom shot the weapon out of his hand.

The wounded man screamed and stumbled backward, crashing into the bushes.

Startled cries came from his partners, followed by gunshots.

Tom darted behind a tree for cover. Jangling sounds, men mounting up, in the next instant, a horse cleared the bush, landing within a few feet of where Tom hid.

The rider whirled his mount about and fired. A chunk of bark flew past Tom's cheek.

He eased around the trunk, took aim at the departing rider, and squeezed the trigger. The cook toppled off his horse. Two down, and the third man riding away in a different direction.

Tom swung around to take a shot. The crack of a gun resounded and pain seared his side. He twisted, astounded. The first man he'd wounded, using his left hand to fire.

Another gunshot rang out.

The attacker jerked and fell back.

Tom's heart hammered in his chest. Where the hell had that shot come from? He pressed his hand against his burning side and crouched in the leafy foliage as he scanned the trees and bushes around him for the sharpshooter.

The surrounding woods had gone silent. Not even the birds stirred.

Was the mystery gunman a disgruntled companion of the others or one of Sid's men?

Only a fool would stick around to find out.

Keeping an eye on his surroundings, Tom crept over to the dead man's horse. He made soothing sounds as he took up the dangling reins. Something warm and sticky oozed from his side through his fingers.

Blood.

If he went back to military headquarters, his brother would find a doctor and send more men out to search, and that would send the one who escaped into hiding. He applied pressure to the wound and mounted with a grunt of pain. No time to seek help. He had to get to Becky before that black-haired bastard got to her first.

CHAPTER TEN

Becky returned to the Lawrence property posthaste. Her pace slowed as she mounted the front steps to the porch. Unpleasant as it would be, she had to face Amy. Jeff would have no earthly reason to sneak around spying on the unfortunate young woman—unless he suspected she had something to do with the judge's predicament.

Becky raised her fist, her heart thudding with dread, and knocked.

After a moment, she ventured to a window overlooking the porch and rubbed her handkerchief over one of the dirty panes. Grime had built up on the inside as well, but she could make out parlor furniture covered with sheets. Had the lone occupant left town without anyone knowing?

Becky knocked again, this time, harder.

The door opened a crack, revealing a golden-hued eye in the sliver of a pale face. "What do *you* want?"

She hadn't expected a welcome. "Amy, I know you think my cousin murdered your brother, but that's not why I'm here. We need to talk—"

"We have nothing to talk about. Go away."

"I've brought you something." Becky held out a jar of jam, her last one, as a peace offering. "It's blackberry, your favorite."

Amy reached out and grabbed the jar before retreating.

Quick as a wink, Becky stuck her foot inside the door to prevent it from being slammed in her face. "The jam is a gift. But if you take it, you have to talk to me."

Amy struggled to close the door. *"You have not pleased me with your sacrifices. You have burdened me with your sins."*

The Lawrence clan had always been fond of quoting scripture, mostly paraphrased to fit their particular views at the time.

Becky pushed back. *"Blessed are the merciful,"* she grunted. *"For they shall receive mercy."*

"You don't need my mercy."

"We all need mercy, Amy. Every last one of us."

The door flew open and Becky stumbled inside, nearly falling on her face. At the last moment, she caught herself.

Amy had already retreated into the house without a word of welcome. She'd lost most of her manners or didn't care to waste them on a woman she despised.

Becky didn't bother removing her bonnet, knowing she wouldn't be there for long. She followed Amy down the dark hallway. The house had a musty smell as if it hadn't been dusted in a while, and another, more unpleasant odor. Perhaps reclusive people didn't bathe regularly.

The reluctant hostess led her into a sitting room. In here, no sheets covered comfortable-looking chairs and a well-used sofa. Books were stacked on tables and several lay open.

Amy plopped into a cushioned chair. Her chestnut hair hung over one shoulder in an untidy braid and loose curls framed a heart-shaped face marred by a frown. "Short of wrestling you out the door, it doesn't appear I will be rid of you until I hear you out."

"May I?" Becky gestured to the armchair nearby. She'd rather be across the room than within spitting range, but she'd get nowhere if she didn't at least attempt politeness.

Amy flicked her wrist in a dismissive gesture. "Suit yourself."

Becky settled into the chair. On the arm, someone's dirty fingers had left a smudge. A blanket lay discarded on the floor and crumbs were scattered beneath the table.

Amy hadn't planned on welcoming guests. Not only was the house unkempt, but her dress also showed worn places, several of which had been patched, and the lace trim on the frayed neckline didn't match what was on the sleeves.

Something twisted in Becky's chest. Nothing so shallow as pity. Rather, a deep sense of empathy. They were, both of them, victims of this wretched war. But Amy wouldn't see it that way. She would just as soon the interloper spoke her mind and was gone as quickly as possible.

Becky fiddled with the folds of her skirt. Where did she start? What did she say to someone who hated her to the marrow of her bones? She should start with an apology for what she could've done differently. "I am deeply sorry that I have not been a better friend."

"You were never my friend," Amy said with a baleful stare.

"We might've been."

Except for Tom, which went without saying. The two of them had vied for his affection in the schoolyard. Would Amy set her cap for Tom now that he was back?

Becky quashed a spurt of jealousy. She had a beau in St. Louis and would soon be married. Whatever might happen between Tom and Amy was none of her concern. "Even if we aren't friends, we both have enemies enough. We need not add each other to the list."

Rather than accept the olive branch, Amy was affronted. "What are you talking about? I haven't done anything to you. Your cousin, on the other hand, did us a great injustice."

Her brother, Asa, a fervent abolitionist, had led a band of loyal-ists who weren't connected with either army. They'd called them-selves *Freedom Fighters* and had aided runaway slaves. The group disbanded after its leader was ambushed and killed. Jeff and his men were blamed.

From that moment on, Becky had no choice but to disavow her cousin and refuse to help him. Her father had grieved as intensely as if his nephew were already dead, but then he'd snuck out to give him food. Or was there more to the story?

"Jeff didn't kill your brother."

"If that's what he says, I don't believe him. He would've been with his men."

"He wasn't with them. I know because he was with us at the time."

Twin spots of color stained the hollows of Amy's cheeks, and hatred from an unquenchable fire flickered in her eyes. "Then I'd say you're a liar, too. Regardless, it doesn't change the fact that he was their captain. He had control over their activities. Your cousin has my brother's blood on his hands no matter where he was that day."

Her cousin had made many mistakes, but he hadn't sanctioned that despicable murder. Those who carried it out had acted alone, without orders. But the facts didn't matter. Amy would never forgive or forget, not in a million years. She hated every Thatcher so much she might've recruited others who shared her thirst for revenge. That could explain why Jeff had been sneaking around, seeking information about who had betrayed his uncle.

"Is that why you told Sid my father is a traitor?" Becky asked.

"What?" Amy's shocked expression couldn't have been faked. It was too fast, too real.

Even if she wasn't the culprit, she might know more than she was letting on.

"Someone put treasonous pamphlets in the newspaper office

and tipped off Sid. He arrested my father and the publisher for printing them."

Amy's surprise faded and her eyes took on a speculative look. "Maybe they did."

"I have proof they didn't."

Amy harrumphed. "Then why are you bothering me? I don't know anything about it."

A muted bump came from somewhere inside the house.

Becky jerked around, startled. "What was that?"

"What was what?" Amy replied, wide-eyed.

The thump sounded again.

"You must hear it."

"I believe you're the one hearing things. Maybe ghosts. My brother, haunting you?"

Becky shot to her feet, trembling with fear. "Stop feigning ignorance. Someone is in this house, and it's not a ghost. Is it one of your brother's friends?"

"There's no one here but me and you." Amy's flushed cheeks declared otherwise.

"You know, I turn that exact shade of red whenever I lie." Becky started across the room toward the hallway. If bogeymen lurked in the shadows, confronting them was preferable to being caught unawares.

Amy scampered after her. "That's why you came here, isn't it, to accuse me? I should've expected you would make up something like that. You always did hate me because of Tom."

Becky whirled around, anger blistering away her usual cautiousness. "This has *nothing* to do with Tom. I want to know why Jeff is so interested in what you're doing over here.

"Jeff?" Confusion clouded the anger on Amy's face. "Why would he be...?" She darted a fearful glance down the hall.

Whoever she was hiding, she didn't want Jeff to discover them either.

"What are you plotting?" Becky demanded.

"Nothing." Amy shoved Becky down the hall and out the door. "Get out this instant and don't come back. If I see you or Jeff anywhere near my house, I'll shoot both of you!"

CHAPTER ELEVEN

A soft click startled Tom out of a somnolent state. The sound had come from the front of the house. If it was Becky, she was awfully quiet. Could be the rascal who'd gotten away, trying to sneak inside.

Tom struggled to move his sluggish limbs and get up, must've drifted off after tending to his injury. When he lifted his foot over the bench, a knife-like pain sliced through him. Biting off a groan, he groped for his gun and removed it from the holster on the kitchen table, then cautiously crept toward the entrance into the hall.

Sweat from his scalp stung his eyes. He wiped it away and leaned against the wall next to the doorway to steady himself, and prayed his hand wouldn't shake if he had to take a shot. In the stillness, the sound of rapid breathing raised the hairs on the back of his neck.

"Tom?" Becky peeked inside.

Releasing a sigh of relief, he lowered his gun and sagged against the wall, sliding lower and lower.

"Tom!" She caught him beneath his arms with surprising

strength and helped him to his feet. "Sweet mercy, is that blood on your shirt? Are you all right? Is the judge all right? Where is he?"

"Yes, to the first three questions," Tom muttered. "But Sid won't release him."

Her eyes dimmed with disappointment before she turned away to go to the cupboard. She started rummaging around. "I have salve somewhere and bandages."

Tom dragged his weary body to the table. He returned his gun to its holster before sinking onto the bench. "Trust me when I say jail is the safest place for the judge at the moment. Until I figure out who those men are."

"What men? The ones who hurt you?" She set her supplies on the table.

His head swam and her form turned dark and fuzzy. He licked his lips with a thick tongue and attempted to string together a coherent response. "I came back to protect you, but you weren't here. Where've you been?"

"Lift your arms and let me take your shirt off."

Tom pressed his lips together to keep from moaning as he allowed her to pull the shirt over his head. She dropped the bloody garment on the floor and then bent to remove the dish-cloth he'd used to staunch the bleeding. He struggled to remain still while she poked and prodded. "The judge said—ow—you were packing."

"You're a fortunate man. The bullet only tore away a piece of your flesh. Hm. You may need stitches if the wound doesn't stop bleeding."

It wasn't hard to figure out where she'd gone, given her evasiveness. "Did you find Jeff?"

"No." She smeared a pungent salve over the wound.

Tom hissed between his teeth. Stung like hell. She'd done that on purpose. "I have to talk to him."

"I have no idea where he is."

99

E.E. BURKE

If she wasn't outright lying, she was still dodging. "Tell me where he meets your father."

"Don't be ridiculous. You have no business going anywhere." She pressed a dressing against his wound then wrapped soft lengths from an old sheet around him to hold it in place. "The salve will ease the pain and help you heal faster."

Her knowledge of midwifery had surprised him. Tending a gunshot injury made him suspicious.

"You've been treating wounded men real regular, have you?"

"Only an ornery one who doesn't know when to quit." She held out her hand. "Let me help you upstairs. You'll feel better after you get some rest."

"I'll feel better if you stop evading my questions." Rather than accepting her assistance, Tom grasped a bottle of whiskey he'd found and took a swig to cut the pain and clear his head.

She remained planted in front of him, perhaps waiting to catch him if he fell on his face. "We can continue our discussion upstairs while you're in bed."

"Promise to join me?"

Her expression remained stoic.

"Meant no disrespect. Just thought you'd worry less if you knew I wasn't close to death."

She was right about one thing. Remaining upright would soon become a problem.

He snagged his gun belt before they left the kitchen, and tried not to lean too heavily on her as she helped him up the stairs and into the bedroom. He'd rest for a spell while remaining alert, in case the man who'd gotten away decided to show up.

The mattress sagged as he sat down. He put his gun within reach. "Why were you so quiet when you came in? Who did you expect?"

"I didn't expect you to be hiding."

"Wasn't hiding. I was being cautious."

100

Becky eyed the revolver on the bed. "It appears you are expecting someone."

"Someone you don't want to meet." Tom provided a brief account of how he'd stumbled onto the trio of irregulars and their cryptic conversation, including the threat against her.

The color drained from her face and she sank onto the mattress next to him. "God help us... Who do you think they mean to get rid of?"

Tom didn't want to scare her any more than he already had. "Not you. Could be your father. They want him in jail."

"*Get rid of* sounds more permanent. It might not be me or my father they were talking about. It could be you."

"I don't know enough to be sure who they meant." Tom scrubbed his fingers through his hair in frustration. As a spy, he'd made more than a few enemies, and his insistence on keeping her close might put her in more danger.

The next Union steamer was scheduled to arrive the following afternoon. He'd make sure she was on it, even if he had to hogtie her.

In the meantime, he would find the one person most likely to know the answers to his questions. "Tell me where to find Jeff."

Becky put her face in her hands. "I don't know where to find him, and that's the truth," she said with anguish melting her voice. "He-he wouldn't send those animals after me."

"He might not know about that part of the plan. The man who got away might be acting on his own. He talked about getting a message from someone."

"What does that mean?"

"Didn't get the details before the party broke up."

She stood abruptly and crossed to the window to draw the curtains.

Fighting fatigue, Tom propped his hands on the edge of the bed. If anything happened to her, he'd never forgive himself. At the same time, she wasn't helping. She'd been up to something and it had nothing to do with packing. "Where were you? I can't help you if you won't confide in me."

She spun with anger flashing in her eyes. "Why should I confide in you? You don't trust me, either. You've kept things from me that pertain to why you're here."

He combed his fingers through his hair again. "What I've told you is the truth."

But it wasn't the whole truth.

Tom leaned to one side to relieve the pain. He had made little progress today in learning his mission, other than guesswork based on Sid's reports, and the hints he'd picked up from the unknown men in the woods. But he couldn't confide in her until he was sure she would not act to her detriment. "Becky..." he heaved a weary sigh. "I'm trying to protect you. If you don't believe anything else, believe that."

She turned away from the window, regarding him with an inscrutable expression that didn't tell him whether she believed him or not. "Do you remember Amy Lawrence's older brother?"

Tom searched the memories he could retrieve, none of them recent. "Bright red hair. Hot temper. Yeah, I remember. He blackened my eye when I was ten for flirting with his sister."

Becky didn't find the remark funny. She was rarely amused by anything having to do with his one-time sweetheart.

"Go on," Tom encouraged. "I'm done making jokes."

"You weren't around, so you may not know that Asa Lawrence stirred up men in arms against southern sympathizers after fighting broke out. They burned homes and farms all over Marion County. Needless to say, they made more than a few enemies. Last year, Captain Lawrence was ambushed and killed in a despicable fashion."

"Let me guess. Jeff was involved?"

Becky shook her head. "Several men in his company were, but

Jeff had no part in it. The truth doesn't matter because the authorities are eager to hang him."

Tom wouldn't argue about Jeff's guilt. He'd fought with the guerrilla forces, which was enough to get him hanged, regardless. "How does all this pertain to the men who shot me?"

Becky returned to the side of the bed and faced Tom with her hands on her hips. "The militia under Asa's command supposedly disbanded. Now, I'm not so sure. You might've encountered some of them today."

Tom digested what she'd told him. "The men I encountered didn't sound like vengeful loyalists. They were plotting something, some sort of delivery. Stolen goods perhaps. The one who got away has long black hair he wears in a braid."

"No one I know fits that description."

Why she'd suddenly decide to cast suspicion on Asa Lawrence's friends made sense. It took the focus off her family. Tom wasn't convinced. "Something tells me Jeff is the key to fitting everything together. I intend to find him."

Her lips tightened with irritation. "Unless you are determined to die, at least try to rest a little while."

She had a point. He couldn't even lean over to remove his boots without toppling over like an old man. He attempted to push off his right boot with his left.

"Here, let me help." She knelt and tugged.

The boot came off. His big toe poked out of a tear in his sock.

She rolled off the threadbare stocking and examined it with a grimace. "You might as well go barefoot as expect these to keep your feet dry. I can repair them while you sleep."

Her life and future hung in the balance and she was concerned about his feet getting wet. That she would care about something so insignificant revealed the depth of her compassion. Her offer was an act of mercy he didn't deserve.

Tom's eyes burned. He pinched the bridge of his nose with his thumb and forefinger and squeezed his lids shut. The time for indulging in tears of regret had long passed.

"Is it the wound in your side?" she asked softly.

He shook his head. "The frightful condition of my socks."

"You aren't fooling me, Tom. I know you're in pain."

She meant physical discomfort, not the ache in his heart.

He had failed this brave, compassionate woman instead of becoming worthy of her. By the time he'd grasped the enormity of his decision to pursue a life of deception, it had been too late to retrace his steps. If his intention in coming here was to set things right, he had only made it worse, as was his peculiar talent.

His limbs felt heavy as anchors as he shucked off his trousers and crawled into bed. He had to get some rest or he would be in no condition to help anyone, but he couldn't let her leave and risk losing her to an enemy. He patted the covers. "Here, lay beside me where I can watch over you."

She got to her feet and eyed him doubtfully. "If I do, you won't rest."

"I'll rest better if you're sleeping next to me. That's God's-honest-truth."

"You need food to build your strength up. I'll go make something."

"I'm not hungry. If you don't lie down, I'll get up and follow you to the kitchen."

That did it. She moved to sit beside him. "Hush now, don't you dare move. You'll start bleeding again."

"It's up to you whether I move or remain still."

She signaled her aggravation with a hefty sigh but then bent down to remove her shoes and stretched out beside him, facing the door. Her body fairly vibrated with tension.

"Promise you won't leave." His eyelids drooped.

"Go to sleep."

She hadn't promised, which could mean she intended to sneak

out after he drifted off.

Another thing about her that had changed—she'd become unpredictable. That in itself wasn't a bad thing, except for when some cutthroat was out there who'd threatened her.

Shifting onto his uninjured side, Tom slipped his arm around her waist and spooned his body to hers. If she moved a muscle, he would wake up.

"Comfortable?" he whispered.

"I can't say I'm comfortable, no."

He was so tired he couldn't fully enjoy being *uncomfortable* either.

"I'll bet these hairpins aren't helping." He plucked off the hair net and the pins securing it and used his fingers to comb through her silken tresses. He could honestly say his only intention was to help her relax, even if he took a great deal of enjoyment in the process. "Better?"

She batted his hand away. "My hair isn't the problem."

"No, not a problem at all." He nuzzled her hair.

She still smelled of lilacs. Like the first time he had dared come close enough to press his lips to hers when they'd been sitting together in a deserted schoolroom.

Tom inhaled and sighed. How many nights had he dreamt of holding her again? And there were days he'd wanted her so badly it was a physical ache. If she turned to him and he positioned them just so, he could make love to her.

He dragged his thoughts away from Temptation to the reason he had insisted she lay next to him. The man who escaped would either run and hide or sneak back to finish the job. Tom bet his money on the latter. He would be ready when they met again.

Draping his arm over Becky, he placed his gun within easy reach.

"Is that supposed to comfort me?" she asked in a wry tone.

"Do you mean my arm—or the gun?"

CHAPTER TWELVE

T wo dark-eyed scamps and a fair-haired little girl crouched behind furniture in the judge's study, giggling. Her children. No...she didn't have any children. Yes, she did. Tom's children...

A rooster's crow interrupted, dissolving the images and high-pitched laughter. With a sigh, Becky snuggled closer to the warm body next to her and turned her face into his sleep-warmed flesh. Still enmeshed in the remnants of a lovely dream, she flung her arm across his broad chest and curled her fingers into crisp hair. It felt so real.

Her eyelids flickered open. She stared at a furred chest as real as the flush heating her skin. She had only intended to lie down until Tom fell asleep but must've succumbed to fatigue. At some point during the night, he had rolled onto his back and she had turned over and scooted closer, using his arm and shoulder as a pillow. Safe and secure. At home in his arms.

She sighed wistfully. Those feelings, like the dream, were nothing but illusions. No more than a longing for a past she couldn't recapture.

Moving carefully, she slipped out of bed. Physical distance enabled her to maintain emotional distance.

Tom stretched out his arm although his eyes remained closed. She waited until his breathing became rhythmic again. He had to be beyond exhausted. The bandage wrapped around his middle had darkened from bloodstains.

Guilt niggled her conscience.

They had fallen back into old habits. Tom, true to his nature, had taken on the mantle of protector, and she'd gone along, desiring a hero. If she'd been stronger and refused his offer of help, he wouldn't have become an unwitting target for those who hated her family. Old habits were dangerous for both of them.

She would go to the military headquarters and speak to the provost marshal about releasing her father in exchange for information about where she'd seen Jeff. Let Sid pry Amy's secrets out of her. If Sid refused to cooperate, she would send word to Alfred. Given his position, he had to know something of her situation, and, despite everything, had asked for her hand. She must trust that he would believe her father wasn't a traitor.

Becky gathered her hairpins and shoes from the floor.

"What's your hurry?" came a sleepy voice from behind her.

She hesitated with her hand on the doorknob. "I'm sorry I woke you." If she didn't offer a valid excuse for leaving the room, Tom might try to get up, and then he'd start bleeding again. "The army doesn't feed civilian prisoners. I have to fix Papa something to eat. You don't have to get up yet. I'll be in the kitchen."

It wasn't a lie. She would be there until she left.

"Wait, I'll come with you." Tom levered upward with a grunt and swung his legs over the edge of the bed. With a determined set of his jaw, he got to his feet, clothed only in knee-length drawers barely held up by a drawstring.

Even wounded, he had a magnificent body.

She snipped the thrill before it could grow into outright lust and put her hand out to ward off temptation. "No! Don't get up. You're bleeding."

He glanced with unconcern at the bandage. "It's dried blood, nothing to worry about. I'll go with you and talk to Sid. He can send soldiers to search the woods for that rascal who got away while I look for Jeff."

Had Tom lost his mind? The fool would get himself killed.

She snatched his trousers, shirt, and coat off the floor before he could retrieve them. "I'll clean these up and bring them to you. Go back to bed."

"I don't care if they're stained."

She slammed the door in his face.

He jerked it open, his mouth tight with anger or pain. "What the devil is wrong with you?"

"What's wrong with *me*? You were shot, Tom. You need to be in bed."

"Where are you going?"

He hadn't guessed she was leaving. Best not to explain because he would insist on accompanying her. If she happened across Jeff, she would plead with him to turn himself in. If not, he had made his decision and she must make hers.

"I've already told you. I'm taking my father's breakfast."

Tom snagged her arm before she could turn away. "Give me my trousers and wait for me."

"No, I won't help you be foolish." She twisted out of his grasp and hurried off, clutching the clothes to her chest.

Halfway down the stairs, Tom caught up with her.

When she cast a panicked glance over her shoulder, she missed the next step and would've tumbled the rest of the way if he hadn't caught her around the waist and grabbed the railing to stop their momentum. She clung to him, balancing on her toes to avoid dragging him down with her.

Fear burst into outrage. "Have you lost your mind? You'll kill both of us!"

He shifted her to a more secure spot on the riser then dropped a kiss on the top of her head. "No worse than letting you kill yourself because you're so hardheaded."

With a resigned sigh, she rested her forehead on his shoulder. Just her luck, the one vow he kept would be his pledge to follow her around. "I don't want you risking your life on account of me."

He hugged her close. "It's nothing, just a scratch. I'll be right as rain as soon as I work out the stiffness. I've suffered worse."

He'd been shot before?

A shudder passed through her. "Take care that you don't tempt Fate once too often."

"Fate and I reached an agreement long ago."

His cocksure attitude infuriated her. He didn't have a care for himself so why should she?

"Stop playing the hero and go to bed." She pushed at his hard chest to get him moving back up the stairs.

He remained solidly planted, gazing down at her with mild amusement.

The props she'd used to prevent a total collapse gave way under the strain. Tears flooded her eyes. God help her. How could she keep him safe if she couldn't even convince him to rest when he was injured?

He used his thumbs to wipe her cheeks. "Aw, sweetheart, don't cry over me."

Giving in would only make him more determined to follow her. "What makes you think it's you I'm crying over? And I am not your sweetheart."

~

Tom retrieved his clothes from Becky and finished dressing in the kitchen so he could keep his eye on her while she fixed breakfast. He strapped on his belt and gun, keeping it low near his hips so as not to aggravate the wound in his side. With his coat buttoned, it would cover up the bloodstains on his shirt.

Her decision to leave him behind might be rooted in concern, but it also indicated a lack of trust. A few hours of snuggling weren't going to erase years of doubt.

The kitchen smelled heavenly. His stomach responded with loud rumbling.

She opened the oven door and set the pan of biscuits, golden and steaming, on top. "I'll let you have one if you promise to stay here and rest."

Her insistence on treating him like an invalid was wearing thin, as was her assumption he would be easy to fool. "I'll rest if you promise not to leave."

Telltale stains colored her cheeks. She didn't look at him but reached up to a shelf to collect a jar of molasses. "I don't take orders from you."

"It's not an order. It's a...strong request." He couldn't blame her for not trusting his competence. He hadn't gotten her father out of jail or caught the man who threatened her. On the other hand, she was the only link to Jeff, who, thus far, had the only logical connection to whatever plot was being hatched.

After he collected more facts, he would figure it out. In the meantime, he couldn't let her go off on her own unprotected. "While you take your father his breakfast, I'll talk to Sid. One of his guards was tailing me. He might've seen something or know the identity of the man in the woods who shot one of those scoundrels and saved my life."

"A fourth man?"

"Whoever it was didn't want to be seen, which makes me think he might know something about the others." Tom shifted his position on the bench, trying to get comfortable. The wound would be tender for a few days.

She approached with a frown and he braced for another round of arguing about the state of his health. Instead, she brushed back his hair and pressed her palm against his forehead, then slid her hand to his cheek. The loving touch inspired a sense of awe and joy akin to seeing the sunshine after many dreary days.

"You feel a tad warm," she murmured.

Feeling *warm* happened with unsettling regularity whenever she was around, though it would be unwise to mention this. Instead, he reached up to capture her hand so he could kiss it.

She escaped before he got his lips near her fingers or any other part of her.

Tom clapped a lid on his longing. Becky was off limits, and he would do well to remember that. She had her sights set on Alfred, and he had to keep his focus on figuring out his mission.

Unaware of the battle he waged, she took a basket from a hook on the rafter and set it on the worktable. "If you stay here, I promise to go straight to visit my father and not make any stops along the way."

He had a better idea. "How about this? I'll let you go visit your father in peace if you tell me how to find Jeff."

"You don't need to find Jeff. You need to fill your stomach." She smeared butter over the hot biscuits to emphasize her point or to torment him.

"I'll be happy to eat whatever you give me, and then I'll go find Jeff."

She carefully removed the biscuits from the pan and set them inside the basket. Did she think starving him would stop him? "If Jeff knew who was behind this, he would've done something by now."

"Maybe he can't, not without help."

"He won't accept your help."

111

"He will if he wants to keep you safe."

"If you rested as well as you argued, you wouldn't need to favor that side."

Tom used the table to push himself up and forced his back to straighten. Not for anything would he demonstrate that she was right. He went to where she stood at the work table, fussing with a napkin. Not only was he starving, but he was also quickly losing patience with her pigheadedness where Jeff was concerned. "Your cousin betrayed his country. He's endangered you and your father. Stop protecting him!"

She spun around with anguish twisting her features. "It's not *him* I'm protecting, you numskull. It's *you!*"

Her outburst put him back on his heels.

She was concerned for *his* safety, that's what all this dodging was about?

Tenderness swamped his heart. Unable to help himself, he reached out to draw her into his arms. "Becky, honey..."

"Take your hands off me!" She nearly tripped, moving so fast to get away from him. Something told him it wasn't because she despised him as much as she was afraid of him, afraid of what she was feeling.

He understood perfectly. The emotions she dredged up worried him more than his memory loss, and he was losing his battle to suppress them. At the same time, he couldn't act on them either. "I'll be careful," he promised her.

"Careful?" She laughed without humor. "Do you even know the meaning of the word? I don't want you to go after Jeff. I don't need your help."

She was lying. At least, she was lying about one of those things. She did need him, and he wasn't letting her push him away in a misguided effort to save him. His life wasn't the one that mattered.

Silently, she served up a plate with two biscuits slathered in butter and dropped it on the table. "Here. Have something to eat."

"Looks good. Thank you." Tom waited for her to serve herself a plate.

Instead, she loaded molasses and a jar of fruit into the basket before tucking a napkin over the top.

"Aren't you eating?" he asked.

"I'll eat at the jail with my father."

Tom picked up his plate of food. "Then I'll go with you."

She threaded the basket over her arm and started for the back door like she hadn't heard a word he said. He shoved a biscuit into his mouth. If he ate fast, he could finish before she got her bonnet tied.

No more tears on his behalf, this time she glared at him. "You are as stubborn as a cross-eyed mule. I won't cry at your funeral after you get yourself killed."

"Don't plan on getting myself killed." He mopped up the butter with the last biscuit and downed it in two bites. By then, she had on her shawl.

Setting the empty plate aside, he took the basket from her. "Here, let me carry that for you."

She took it back. "I said I don't need your help."

She didn't understand the gravity of the situation or the fact that he was the only person available to ensure her safety. Except she didn't care about her safety, so he would remind her of what she did care about.

"You do need my help. To get your father cleared."

CHAPTER THIRTEEN

Becky gave serious consideration to taking Tom's gun and shooting him in the foot to prevent him from following her and putting himself in harm's way.

Each scuff of his boot soles behind her in his valiant effort to keep apace made her cringe. He declared himself fit while continuing to favor his injured side.

Stubborn man.

He had already been shot once for sticking his nose where it didn't belong. His insistence on being her protector could get him killed the next time.

As she reached the center of town, soldiers patrolling the streets whistled and called out. She couldn't control the cold rush of fear, but she didn't have to give in to it or pay attention to their crude remarks.

Tom sped up next to her and took her arm. His possessive gesture should've annoyed her. Instead, it warmed her as surely as a crackling fire chased away the winter's chill. "They won't bother you if you have an escort."

"Sid's men don't answer to you. If they chose to bother me, you couldn't stop them."

He captured her fingers and tucked them into the crook of his elbow, effectively slowing her down. "You should have more faith in my powers of persuasion."

She had no problem believing in *those* powers, having been the object of them on numerous occasions, one of them as recent as the previous night. "Your charisma won't stop a bullet."

Outside the general store, the shopkeeper's wife, sweeping the sidewalk, edged closer with the broom and gawked at Tom.

He smiled and waved. "Morning, Mrs. Graves."

Becky gritted her teeth. Every biddy in town would know she'd been out with him before the day was done. Had she not succumbed to her weakness for him and fallen asleep in his arms, she could've slipped away before he'd awakened.

She withdrew her arm and adjusted the basket so that it was between them.

"Is that getting heavy?" he asked solicitously.

"No." Her heart, on the other hand, weighed a ton. She didn't want to push Tom away. Her traitorous body hummed with pleasure each time he touched her, and she had failed miserably at maintaining a wall of defense against his assault on her emotions.

Her gaze strayed to the strong line of his jaw. He'd shaved off the dense beard but hadn't applied the razor recently to remove a regrowth of dark whiskers. The roughness of his appearance didn't detract a bit. If anything, it made him dangerously appealing.

He caught her staring at him. "Is something wrong?"

She blurted the first thing she could think of. "You look like a pirate."

He responded with a wry smile that dimpled one cheek. "That's what's bothering you?"

E.E. BURKE

"No." She didn't add that she had loved the rogue long before he'd fashioned a respectable veneer. "I've always had a soft spot for Blackbeard."

"Had I known, I would've grown a beard for you and chopped off a few heads."

"How romantic. Rather than a love letter, a severed head."

Having his escort did make her feel safer, though she wasn't about to say so, and encourage him to continue following her around. With his penchant for heroics, she was surprised he'd stayed alive this long.

He leaned in. "Tell me, milady, what is your fondest desire?"

The whispered question teased her embattled senses, provoking a shiver and an illicit thought.

Heavens, no. Acknowledging her lust for him would be pure folly.

She gave a wave toward a cluster of bluecoats. "How about making all these soldiers disappear?"

Tom's smile turned rueful. "Wouldn't you rather set sail on my ship?"

"You don't have a ship."

"Steamboat then."

"You don't have one of those either."

"Piddling details."

Such a charmer. Despite pretending otherwise, she had missed his flirtatious banter, his persistent attentiveness, and even his bragging and swaggering. If she could have anything she wanted, she would wish for more time with Tom. More days to explore their renewed friendship. More hours to see where it might lead.

A dangerous wish to make. Continuing their association would ruin a future she'd carefully cultivated with Alfred. She would lose a chance to secure her father's safety and her security, throw it all away for the glittering lure of passion and adventure.

Fool's gold.

Tom startled her out of her musings when he shifted her to the inside to make room for a soldier using a crutch to compensate for his missing foot.

A loud crack rang out.

The lame soldier toppled into the street.

"Get down!" Tom yelled and shoved her.

Becky flung out her hands to break her fall and the basket went flying, its contents spilling out over the brick pavement. No sooner had she hit on the ground than Tom threw himself on top of her, his weight forcing the air from her lungs. She could only manage a squeak when she tried to tell him to get off and run.

More shots. Those came from Tom. Wedged beneath him, she couldn't see a thing. Who had started shooting? Why had they targeted a crippled soldier? Or had the bullet been meant for Tom?

Shouts came from around them, followed by the drum of boot heels.

Tom got up and pulled her to her feet. He clamped his hands around her waist and tossed her into a nearby hay wagon. "Keep your head down, and *don't move.*"

"Where are you going?" She thrashed about to untangle her legs from her skirts. Gripped the side of the wagon to cautiously peek over the edge. "Wait!"

Tom had crossed the deserted street and was entering an open doorway to the abandoned rope factory. *Alone.* None of the other soldiers were venturing over there. Everyone who'd been on the sidewalk and in the street had sought cover. Even the injured soldier had dragged himself behind a water trough, where a man wearing the uniform of the military police crouched.

"Captain Sawyer went into that building!" She pointed the way. "Go help him!"

No one paid her any mind.

Becky counted the seconds in an agony of uncertainty. A minute passed...two...an eternity. In the August heat, the itchy hay and the interminable waiting grew unbearable. Finally, she could take no more.

She clambered out of the wagon. Armed or not, she wasn't going to sit here and do nothing while Tom risked his life to protect her.

Tom held his revolver cocked and crept through the abandoned building. The shots had come from this direction, he was certain.

A musty odor hung in the air, charred ceiling beams lay scattered like matchsticks over ruined equipment, and a thick layer of dust coated everything. He knelt beside marks in the fine powder. Someone had recently walked through here.

On a long-abandoned workbench, someone had done a crude finger drawing in the dust. A skull-and-crossbones with the word DEATH written beneath it. Similar to the political symbols on the pamphlet. No, not quite the same...

Tom straightened with disbelief. The last time he'd seen an image like that, it was carved on an old box he and Huck had dug up. Injun Joe's treasure. Huck had warned him then that the old scoundrel might one day come back from the dead to haunt them.

Cold invaded the space. A sensation of fingernails rasping over his skin made him shiver. Motes disturbed by the chase drifted in the air.

He squelched an irrational fear. No murderer's specter was going to rise out of the grave and come after him. Someone was trying to spook him.

Ahead, a glimmer of light cut through the unlit interior.

He ducked beneath a collapsed beam and followed the bootprints to the back of the cavernous factory where an exit door stood open. The would-be assassin had left by this door.

Or he wanted his pursuer to believe that.

Tom stilled, waiting for telltale sounds, such as a hammer being cocked. After a moment, he approached the exit with caution and peered outside. Wheel ruts and numerous footprints crisscrossed the narrow alley, along with trash and waste.

Whoever it was, he'd vanished as swiftly as a ghost.

A soft scrape came from somewhere inside the building.

Tom jerked around with his revolver, barely restraining a wild shot. No, that's what the devil wanted him to do, then he'd reveal himself. As it was, he was too exposed.

He slipped into the shadows behind a blackened support with his finger curled around the trigger and waited for the hunter to come after him.

"Captain Sawyer? Hello? Are you in here?"

No voice he recognized.

Tom remained silent.

"Captain Sawyer, sir, call out if you're there. We don't want to shoot you by mistake."

We? Was there more than one?

Tom peered around the post. In the dust-speckled light, he counted four figures moving cautiously through the debris.

"Do you see anybody, Sam?" whispered one.

"Nope, but that gal outside said she'd seen him come in here. She would've gone off on her own if I hadn't agreed to check on him."

Gal outside? Did they mean Becky?

Damn it, he'd told her to stay put.

"I'm in here," Tom called from the shadows. "Where's that gal who sent you after me?"

Seconds later, Tom exited the warehouse ahead of the

bemused soldiers and stormed across the street to where Becky knelt beside the wounded man. In the time he'd been gone, she had rounded up a posse, dressed the crippled soldier's injury, and exposed herself to danger.

"What are you doing out in the open?" he bellowed.

"Tom!" She jumped up and ran over to hug him. "Thank goodness you're all right. I was so worried."

Worried? She appeared oblivious. Strands of her hair hung loose around her face and dirt marred the pretty blue dress she'd donned for her visit. She could've been killed.

"I gave you strict orders for a good reason. What if that killer had come out the front and seen you?"

Her expression flattened. "Why did *you* go into that warehouse alone? You're injured and not at your best. You should've taken precautions."

His energy had been running so high, pain from the gunshot wound hadn't entered his mind. Now it hurt like the dickens. He fought the urge to put his hand over his side. "Don't worry about me, I'm fine."

"You're impossible, that's what you are," she muttered, before turning her attention to the wounded man. "Be careful not to jostle him too much," she advised the soldiers, as they lifted their fallen comrade into the wagon and went off in the direction of the doctor's office.

Tom surveyed the gathering crowd. It was too much to hope for that he'd catch a glimpse of that black-haired scoundrel, Injun Joe's lookalike. Wearing his hair in that long, black braid and using the same disguise, it had to be intentional.

"Did you see who was shooting?" Becky asked.

"No, but I'm near certain it's the same man who got away."

"If you didn't see him, how can you be sure?"

"He left me a message."

"What kind of message?"

The kind meant to scare the tar out of him.

"I'll tell you later. Let's not stand around here and give him easy targets."

Tom took her arm. She didn't resist, which was a good thing, because if she had, he would've tossed her over his shoulder.

He marched her down to the freight house. By the time they arrived, he had to press his hand against the throbbing pain in his side. "You should've stayed where I put you."

She shook off his hand. "Stop chewing on me. I wasn't going to sit around twiddling my thumbs while you ran off and got yourself killed."

"Did you even consider he might be after you?"

She shook her head, but he didn't miss the alarm that flared in her eyes. "It's you he's after. Didn't you just say as much? That he'd left you a message?"

True, which meant he posed a hazard to her. At the same time, he couldn't let her wander around by herself.

As they climbed the stairs, Tom considered his next move. He had to secure Becky's safety while he searched for the perpetrator of all this mischief. It was too much to hope that she'd leave her father behind and get on a steamboat to St. Louis. Even if she would, going alone wouldn't be safe.

Inside the office, Sid stood in front of the large framed map on the wall. He was surrounded by a tight knot of soldiers. "Sergeant, take your men down here along the river. Lieutenant, lean on our informants to find out what you can."

Word traveled fast if the provost marshal was already mounting a search for the gunman.

"While you're at it, post guards to protect Becky," Tom added.

Sid jerked around with surprise and then annoyance flooded his features. "You don't give the orders here."

Tom bit back a sarcastic reply. If he let it rip, Sid would swell up like a toad and they wouldn't get anywhere. He patiently explained his reasoning. "I do when Becky's life is threatened."

"Tom has uncovered the real perpetrators behind those pamphlets," she chimed in. "One of them shot him. He'll give you the details and you can release my father."

Sid turned his frown on Becky. "No, I will not, Miss Thatcher."

Her chin went up. "You'd rather I send word to Captain Temple and ask him to investigate?"

Sid swelled up. "Send word to whomever you like. Your father isn't going anywhere."

Becky narrowed her eyes. "I will. Just as soon as I take the judge his breakfast. What I managed to salvage after being brutally assaulted by a madman."

Tom waited until Becky had finished raking Sid over the coals and turned to him. He had caused her to drop her basket of goodies when he pushed her to the ground. "Forgive me?" he pleaded, plucking a piece of hay from her bonnet.

The tension around her mouth eased and she placed her hand on his chest. "You are mad, but you're not who I meant. Your quick action saved my life. You don't require a pardon for that."

Even so, he'd done other things that did require forgiveness.

He ran his thumb over a dirty spot on her chin for an excuse to touch her. "Why don't you go see the judge? Give me and Sid a chance to talk."

Sid cleared his throat. "Miss Thatcher, you are to return home as soon as possible and remain there. If my men catch you out, they'll arrest you."

Thank God. Sid had listened, for once. Now, if he could be convinced to send her father with her to St. Louis. Should the authorities choose to keep him locked up, they could do it there just as well.

Tom jerked his thumb at the provost marshal. "You heard him,

Becky. After you give the judge his breakfast, go with the guards. They'll escort you home to pack. I'll join you soon."

Sid's wry expression turned almost, but not quite, amused. "You're not going anywhere, Tom. I'm detaining you. For questioning."

CHAPTER FOURTEEN

Tom waited until Becky left the room before he turned on Sid. "Why the hell are you detaining *me*? If you want to arrest somebody, go after the bastard that just tried to *kill* me!"

Sid stared pointedly at the place where Tom had his hand clapped over his aching side. "Do you need a doctor?"

Was he sincerely concerned or just worried that blood might drip onto his clean floor?

Tom let his arm fall to his side. "No. It's an old wound. Happened yesterday."

"Suit yourself." Sid gestured to a chair. "You might want to sit down before you fall down."

As much as Tom wished to remain stalwart, he couldn't straighten up without it hurting like hell. He'd overdone it, though he would never admit as much to Becky and confirm she'd been right again. Who knows what she might do with that knowledge?

He sank into one of the two leather chairs. "All right. Tell me why you're detaining me. And I assume it isn't so you can send for a doctor."

Sid moved to the front of his desk and propped his hip on the corner. He crossed his arms over his chest, exuding authority. "How did you come to be injured?"

Tom removed his hat and mopped his damp forehead with the back of his sleeve while he considered how much to tell the provost marshal. He could share enough information to gain a little in return. "Had a run-in yesterday with three irregulars who were camped out in the woods."

Sid studied Tom with those inscrutable black eyes he'd gotten from his mother. "Yes. We found the bodies of the two men you killed."

Interesting. Sid's spy in the woods had lied.

"I only killed one. Someone did me a favor and took down the second one. I assume it was the man you sent after me."

Sid frowned. "One of *my* men? They wouldn't dare. Those fellows you engaged work for Colonel Sanderson's agent. You killed men fighting on *our* side."

"Our side?" Tom sank against the leather back with a harsh laugh. "You've got to be kidding. Those men weren't soldiers. They're thugs."

"Hired thugs," Sid conceded.

"Mercenaries. I might've guessed," Tom muttered.

Both armies used soldiers for hire, despite the risks involved when dealing with men who were motivated by money.

"Something's not right." Tom shifted to cradle his injured side.

"Are you in pain?"

"Yes, but that's not the problem."

"What is?"

"Well, first off, the man you sent after me killed one of them."

Sid's frown deepened. "He came back here and said he lost sight of you. I got a report from someone else who came across the bodies. I've had men out searching for clues."

Tom shook his head. Sid didn't know a damn thing more than

he did—or his brother was a better actor than John Wilkes Booth. "Why am I detained?"

Sid released a humorless laugh. "I figured you must've had something to do with those killings. As it turns out, I was right, by your admission."

Tom considered his next words carefully. He needed his brother to believe him because he needed Sid's help to ensure Becky and her father made it safely to St. Louis.

He shifted forward, speaking lower so his words couldn't be overheard by the guards standing outside the door. "*If* those mercenaries were, at one time, working for our side, then I wager someone on the other side has paid them more. They talked about giving *the federals* another target—the judge, I presume. And they were planning some sort of delivery. It could be anything. Weapons. Stolen goods."

Sid's stunned expression gave Tom a moment of encouragement. "You should've come straight here to report what happened."

"And leave Becky unprotected?"

His brother slid off the desk and strode over to the big map on the wall.

Tom struggled to his feet. "You spend more time looking at maps and fretting over protocol than doing your job."

"I could *do* my job if they didn't keep sending in men like you."

"Those men aren't anything like me." Tom dragged his aching body over to where Sid stood. He had to keep moving or his muscles would get stiff. What would it take to fix the same problem with his brother's neck?

"The one who got away has a long black braid, but he could be wearing a disguise. A white wig. He tried to kill me yesterday. Tried again this morning when he took a shot at me from the old rope factory. He left a message in the dust, a skull-and-crossbones with the word *Death*. Same as what was on Injun's Joe's box of gold."

Sid reacted with incredulity. "How do you come up with these crazy tales? That image is a political symbol, used by a secret Confederate organization. It was on the front of those brochures."

Tom simmered. His tales weren't crazy, they were inspired, or in this case, true. "That's what I thought, at first, but it didn't look the same. I'd seen it before. On Injun Joe's treasure box."

At this, Sid huffed a laugh. "You ought to consult a doctor about that knock on the head if you're seeing ghosts."

"I am not *seeing* ghosts. That black-haired devil wants me to *believe* he's a ghost.

"You said he had white hair."

"Damn it, would you *listen*? I said he had a wig. The man who escaped has swarthy skin and black hair, the same as yours, only he wears it longer and in a braid."

"He looks like me and that makes him Injun Joe?"

Tom was ready to throttle his brother for treating him like an ignoramus. "Hell, I don't know who he is. But he knows about Injun Joe and the treasure, and he's using it to taunt me or distract me from finding the real culprit."

"Hundreds of people know about Injun Joe. It was in all the newspapers. You were quite the hero. Apparently, this copycat isn't a fan."

"For Pete's sake, Sid, this is serious."

Sid returned to his desk and put his hand on a stack of files. "Tell me about it. I have a pile of reports a mile deep that are all *serious*. Why is this Injun Joe lookalike after you?"

It wasn't the right time to get into a discussion about why he might be targeted.

"Based on what they said, I'm thinking those men are responsible for planting that secessionist literature to get the judge arrested."

"Can you prove that?"

"I will after I find the one who got away. Do you know where he is?"

Sid folded his arms over his chest. "Those men you ran into don't answer to me. I've been told to stay out of their business."

"Then tell me where to find him. I'll go after him so you don't get into trouble with the colonel. You can assign a couple of men to stay with Becky and keep her safe."

"I don't have extra men to assign. We're stretched thin as it is."

For some reason, Sid was choosing to be an ass instead of taking appropriate action.

"You know I can't be with her twenty-four hours a day."

One corner of Sid's mouth lifted in a smile that didn't reach his eyes. "Why not? You've been with her about that much since you got back."

Tom's neck grew hot beneath his collar. "That has nothing to do with what you're thinking. I'm trying to protect her, which is getting hard to do while being shot at."

"Yes, I'm curious as to why that is." Sid returned to his desk and took up his spot on the corner. "I sent a telegram notifying the district office of the judge's arrest, and the instructions are to send him to St. Louis for trial. He leaves on the next boat."

Damn it, Sid had good evidence the judge wasn't guilty.

"You want to impress your boss. That's what this is about, isn't it? You'd send an innocent man to the gallows to prove you aren't *soft*."

A dark stain appeared beneath Sid's high cheekbones. "Looks to me like you're the one who's letting personal feelings influence his judgment. What mission are you on, Tom? Your own personal crusade?"

Tom leaned into Sid's space. "At least I'm not compromising my principles to get back at somebody I don't like."

His brother didn't back down. If anything, he drew himself up straighter. His eyes gleamed with a kind of hatred reserved for siblings. Or mortal enemies.

"Your *principles?*" You come here and lie to me. Try to use me for your purposes and think you can get away with it because you know how to make people dance to your tune. But I know the truth. I know what a selfish, conceited son-of-a-bitch you are."

It took every ounce of willpower not to slam a fist into Sid's smug face. "Don't accuse me of being selfish when you'd throw away a man's life to salve your wounded pride."

Sid reached inside his coat. For a split second, Tom thought he might produce a firearm and shoot him on the spot. Instead, Sid withdrew a folded telegram and held it out. "Your orders, Captain Sawyer. In case you've forgotten."

BRING IN THE EVIDENCE YOU WERE SENT TO COLLECT AGAINST JUDGE THATCHER. HIS TRIAL WILL COMMENCE IMMEDIATELY UPON YOUR RETURN. GEN. ROSECRANS

Tom reread the missive, praying his memory would suddenly return and the words on the page would mean something different. Instead, a terrifying certainty pressed down on him. The authorities needed someone Judge Thatcher would trust, someone who knew how to build a case to ensure a swift and certain execution. Who better to send than a spy who could extract information from the judge's vulnerable daughter?

Tom dropped into one of the chairs in front of Sid's desk and gripped the arms. Could it be he had sunk so low? How was it possible to become that evil and not even recollect it?

His brother stepped in front of him. "Did you withhold this information because you want me to look incompetent?"

"I didn't remember...my orders." Tom stared at the damning telegram in a daze. "Someone did whack me on the head on my way here. When I came to, I was in Becky's house and had no idea why."

Sid heaved a disgusted sigh. "Your ridiculous ghost story is better than that."

He would've doubted himself if he didn't know better. He raked a trembling hand through his hair. "I did suspect I was on a mission. But until now, I didn't know for certain I was supposed to—"

"Bring in your lover's father?" Sid supplied.

"She's not my..." Tom's voice cracked. He was close to losing his composure, and with it, his chance to influence Sid on Becky's behalf. "Do you have any water? My mouth is bone dry."

Sid strode to a cabinet and rustled around. He returned with a short glass half full.

"Much obliged." Tom tossed back the clear contents.

Hell laid tracks down his throat.

He convulsed in a fit of coughing.

Sid pounded on his back.

Tom braced his hands on his knees and blinked back tears. Whatever Sid had given him was ten times more potent than whiskey. "You did that on purpose," he rasped.

"Well, yes. I admit I did." Sid took the chair next to Tom and set the bottle on the desk. "You looked like you could use something stronger than water," he explained calmly.

Hell, yes. God, he wanted to crawl into that bottle and ferment. Except, getting drunk would only ease the misery temporarily. Then he'd be in no condition to keep Becky safe—even if that meant keeping her safe from him.

He slid his eyes sideways to see Sid's reaction to his misery.

His brother crossed his right leg over his knee, looking perfectly relaxed.

"Are you enjoying this?" Tom asked, already knowing the answer.

"I thought I might, but, no..." His brother's expression turned reflective. "That's something I'd rather not dwell on. I might discover I have a heart."

Tom sat up, rubbing his chest where the whiskey still seared the hollowed-out space. "Mine's gone missing."

Sid nodded slowly. "You might check and see if that woman downstairs has it."

Tom's eyes burned. He squinted like he was peering at something outside the window. Sid would ridicule him for all eternity if he started bawling. Sid had it wrong on one account. Becky didn't just own his heart. She held his dreams. He had spent half his life trying to become deserving of her admiration and affection. The kind of man that boys emulated and adults held in high esteem. Instead...

The stone lodged in Tom's throat plummeted to his stomach. "She's going to hate me."

"Hate's probably too kind," Sid murmured.

Tom could imagine. Becky would call down heaven's fury. Then God would send his soul back to hell in a puff of smoke. "I can't follow those orders."

"Refuse and you'll be looking down the barrels of the same guns aimed at the judge. Worse, your honor will be besmirched."

"Honor?" Tom released a dark laugh. "Is that what you call betrayal?" He scanned the tersely worded message. "They want evidence. I'll give them evidence. What I found at the newspaper office."

"That won't be enough to clear the judge."

Furious, Tom waded the telegram in his fist. "Then I'll find that black-haired bastard and beat the truth out of him. Tell me who he is!"

Sid eyed him with curiosity. "You aren't making that up, are you?"

"Why would I?"

"None of Sanderson's agents look like the man you described."

"I haven't lost my mind."

"That remains to be seen."

"Don't tempt me to wipe the floor with your face. You said those other two were employed by Sanderson. I didn't dream them up."

"No...that's troubling." Sid drummed his fingers on the arm of the chair. After a moment, he uncrossed his leg and leaned forward. "If our agents were compromised, we need to find the man who's still alive and figure out what he's up to."

"More than theft, I wager."

"Indeed." Sid stared off into the distance and continued the annoying finger-tapping.

"What are you not telling me?"

Sid stopped tapping. "Should I trust you? You didn't trust me."

"I can't trust anybody, Sid. That's the hell of it." Tom gripped the leather chair arms and fought a tidal wave of despair. Spies lived in isolation surrounded by enemies. For the safety of those he loved, he had eschewed friendships and severed ties. Despite his self-imposed rule, he had come home.

Had he returned intending to betray the only woman he had ever loved? If so, he was a bigger bastard than even he guessed.

Sid cleared his throat. "We've been anticipating another rebel invasion. Sterling Price has his troops poised at the border, and they appear to be waiting for some kind of sign or opportunity. Did you get any intelligence from General Rosecrans before he sent you down here?"

Tom swept his mind. Nothing more substantial than the wisps of an abandoned spider web. He braced his elbows on his knees and cradled his cracked skull. "I don't know. All I can remember are bits and pieces. Not enough to fill in what's missing. The last thing I recall with clarity is being in Vicksburg."

"Were you leading troops there? Fighting with Grant?"

Tom shook his head. Things might go better for Becky and her father if treated his half-brother like a friend instead of an adversary. But Sid hadn't asked for friendship. He wanted honesty and respect.

"I was living inside the city, working deep undercover." Tom sat back to watch his brother's response. As usual, it wasn't telling. "Does that surprise you, that I was a double agent?"

"Not really."

Sid's opinion shouldn't matter, but for some reason it did.

"Most folks consider spies no better than Judas."

"You aren't betraying the Son of God. You're helping defeat an enemy who'd do the same to you in a heartbeat." Sid's matter-of-fact response was the last thing Tom expected to hear.

"Are you defending me?"

"I'm only pointing out the difference."

That wasn't all he'd done. With a few words, he had extended grace. Why would he do that? Any brotherly bonds that might've formed in childhood, Tom had relentlessly destroyed. Now, when Sid had the upper hand, he chose not to deliver the final blow.

Tom blinked back an embarrassing wash of tears. His brother had offered an olive branch. Sid might pull it back again, as he'd done in the past. The real test would be whether he gave up his greatest weapon—information.

"I've told you what I've been doing. Tell me why you're after the judge. You know as well as I, he's a Unionist. He didn't sign the oath because it requires him to turn in his kin. Dozens of men are in the same boat, but they just lied and signed it anyway. The judge is too honorable to do that."

Sid straightened in his chair. "He's protecting his nephew, and there's no one more likely to be involved in this conspiracy than Jeff Thatcher. He rode with the meanest bunch of bushwhackers north of Arkansas."

Put in Sid's position, Tom would assume the same. "All right, I can agree that Jeff knows *something*. But if the rebels are planning an invasion, it's going to take more than a recruiting brochure to pull it off."

"What, do you suppose?"

"Consider this. That black-haired agent—whoever he is—intended those pamphlets as a distraction to draw attention away from what is actually going on. We need to find out. Not waste time packing the judge off to a military court."

Tom waited to see how Sid would respond, which would tell him where they stood with each other.

Sid's frown didn't inspire confidence. "You'd disobey a direct command?"

"Send a message for me. Tell them you can't find me. Say we're still gathering evidence. Do whatever you have to, but keep the judge here until I figure this out.

"You want me to be dishonest?"

"Just present the facts differently. Delay."

"You mean lie."

"Why do you have to view choices as black or white?" Tom reframed the plea. "Help me save an innocent man's life."

Sid remained silent, staring at his desk. After a moment, he dragged his hand over his face in a weary gesture. When he stood, he moved like an old man. "Nobody in this war is innocent. Not Thatcher. Certainly not his nephew."

Tom came to his feet slowly. He hoped his brother was more than a puppet on strings held by bureaucrats. "Don't you want justice to be served?"

Sid sat behind his desk and opened up a file. "You want justice? Become a judge. Soldiers follow orders." Without looking up, he took a writing pen and dipped it into the ink well. "I suggest you get busy. The next boat arrives tomorrow and you're expected to be on it with your prisoner."

CHAPTER FIFTEEN

In the basement downstairs, the stench from unwashed bodies and an overflowing slop bucket made Becky's eyes water. This time the guard didn't allow her inside the cell, and he inspected the beat-up basket before he passed what food she'd salvaged through the bars to her father. She wasn't even allowed to stay and visit.

Sid had ordered her to go home.

Fine.

She would pack and prepare to leave after Alfred arrived and sorted things out, which he would do as soon as he received her telegram. Her mistake had been listening to Tom in the first place rather than trusting the man who wanted to marry her.

The fact that Sid had detained his brother worked out well because it meant Tom would be kept busy answering questions and wouldn't be able to follow her around and get himself killed.

While she still didn't entirely trust Tom, he had convinced her of his good intentions. However, he had not asked for her love. Even if he did, the both of them knew, deep inside, she would only hold him back. He thrived on adventure. She needed security, which Alfred could provide.

On her way out the door, a bearded soldier approached her. One of Sid's men, by the look of his uniform.

"Ready to go, miss?"

When she tipped her head to look at him, the sunlight blinded her. Shadows darkened the upper part of his face beneath the hat brim. Whoever he was, he was too tall to be the young private. Disappointing. But she had been frightened enough by the earlier attack to appreciate an escort, as long as he wasn't Tom.

When the soldier presented his arm, she curled her fingers around the dark blue sleeve. "I'm sure you heard about the shooting today. Did they catch the man responsible?"

The soldier shook his head.

"He's still on the loose, then." She glanced around nervously as they made their way up the hill in the direction of her house.

The mysterious assassin who tried to shoot Tom was likely the same one who had made threatening remarks about her. He could be anywhere.

"Don't you worry, Becky, I'll keep you safe," her escort drawled.

Her skin prickled with awareness. The soldier's voice had changed to one she recognized. She jerked her attention to his face and gasped.

Jeff.

He had used something to darken his fair hair and light brown beard. Even his skin had a slightly darker shade. Considering the disguise, it was obvious he hadn't shown up to turn himself in. If she called out or identified him, the soldiers would shoot him on sight.

He kept his head lowered as they passed the general store. Thankfully, the shopkeeper's wife had gone inside. After the shoot-out, everyone had to be scared. The only other people in the street were soldiers, who hardly spared them a glance.

"Why are you dressed like that and sneaking around?" she whispered.

"Why is Tom here?" he asked.

What else did he know?

"How long have you been spying on us?" she countered.

"Wasn't spying on you. I was near the freight house when you showed up with him."

"Why were you...? The answer came to her. He intended to break her father out of jail. Singlehandedly. "Have you lost *all* your marbles?"

"Only some of them." Beneath the beard, his lips curled sardonically.

"This isn't funny. You could've been caught and killed right in front of me."

Despite all he'd done, all the mistakes and bad choices, she loved her cousin dearly. Growing up, they'd been as close as brother and sister. She could no more betray him than she could abandon her father. But how on earth could she save them both?

"Calm down" Jeff patted the hand she had curled around his forearm. "I was only getting a lay of the land. Haven't decided yet what I'll do."

This wasn't the first time he'd put on a disguise and moseyed through town, bold as brass. "You'll get us both shot," she muttered.

"We'll be fine, so long as you don't make a scene."

Walking back toward the house, each moment stretched out forever. She'd been far calmer when she and Tom had donned old lady disguises. Somehow, with Tom, a sense of adventure overshadowed her fear of danger.

A mounted patrol trotted past without incident.

When at last they came to the corner closest to her house, she balked. "Sid might've posted guards at the house."

"We'll go another way." Jeff pulled her off the sidewalk onto a path alongside a fence that bordered the property, ending at the carriage house.

He removed a loose board on the back of the building. She stepped through the open space and he followed her inside, setting the board back in place. Her dress brushed against the wheels of a carriage that hadn't been used since the army had confiscated their horses.

A soft nicker came from the bay Tom had ridden home.

He wasn't the only one keeping secrets.

"Tom ran into some men yesterday. One of them shot him. He thinks they're the ones who got the judge in trouble by planting seditious brochures at the newspaper office. What do you know about that?"

"Not much. You sure Tom didn't do it and lie about it?"

"Why would you think that? If Tom wanted Papa jailed, he wouldn't have helped me look for evidence to clear him."

"Unless Tom wants to win your trust," Jeff said in a grim tone. "Maybe I should've done him in when I had the chance."

She halted in front of an empty stable. The light was too dim to make out whether he was joking or serious. "What do you mean, when you had the chance? Were you the one who hit him on the head?"

"Someone hit him on the head?" Jeff's laugh held no humor. "Nah, I was in the woods yesterday when he got into that shoot-out."

"That was you?" She grabbed her cousin's sleeve, elated. "Tom didn't see you. He has no idea it was you who saved his life."

Jeff huffed. "I don't give a damn about his life."

She didn't believe that. Jeff hadn't lost every shred of human decency. "What do you know about those men?"

"All I know is they aren't from around here."

"Why were you following them?"

"I wasn't. Was minding my own business when they showed up

near my hideout. I reckoned Tom was looking for me, so I stayed hidden to make sure he wouldn't interfere."

"Interfere with what?"

"None of his business."

Jeff's cagey answers damped her hopes that he might not live up to his criminal reputation.

"What are you involved in? Is it so terrible you can't tell me?"

Jeff rested a heavy hand on her shoulder. "I'm not so low down as you think."

Her heart sank at his pitiful attempt to reassure her. "Then tell me why you're still hanging around. Tell me what you've got Papa involved in."

"If he hasn't seen fit to tell you, I won't either. But it ain't as bad as you think. Don't doubt what you know to be true about the judge. He hasn't changed."

"But *you* have." She hammered her fist against Jeff's broad chest in frustrated anger. "Don't try to break him out, Jeff. They'll just kill both of you. Papa wants you to flee. He says there's nothing more you can do."

Short of turning himself in. Why couldn't she bring herself to demand it? If he did, he'd be hanged before sunset. She couldn't live with the guilt of having encouraged him to give himself up, and it would devastate her father. But there was nothing she could do to change her cousin's inevitable future. Nothing.

Tears spilled down her cheeks. "It's over, Jeff. Can't you see that?"

"Yeah. I see." Sunlight speared through cracks between the boards, illuminating Jeff's profile, which hinted at something tragic.

"What do you mean to do?"

"It's time I stopped running from my mistakes. I got into this war for all the wrong reasons and it ruined everything...for Uncle James, for you, for other people I never meant to hurt." He heaved a long sigh. "I have some unfinished business to take care of, but I'll be back tomorrow at noon to arrange an exchange."

Dread squeezed her chest. "You mean to trade yourself?"

Would it work? She hated even thinking such a thing, and her father would never accept it. For that matter, Sid would use it as an excuse to hold both of them on charges of treason.

"Giving yourself up won't achieve anything other than your death. They won't release the judge just because they get the chance to hang you. Someone planted evidence against him. Tom thinks the brochure came from some secret society. The Golden Circle is what he called it. They're Copperhead Democrats, northern secessionists."

"I know who they are. How does Tom know so much about them? Is that why he's here?"

"He got hit on the head and can't recall why he's here."

Jeff bent his head and his features gave her the impression of being carved from stone. "You sure he isn't putting on? I remember him being a good actor when it suited him. He faked a toothache so well his Aunt Polly pulled it."

"I did doubt him, at first. Now...I think he's telling the truth, some of it anyway. But I don't want him involved anymore. Someone tried to kill him because he was with me."

"Could be another reason. I overheard talk about there being a price on his head."

"A price? For what?"

"For being a spy."

Tom let himself into the front door of the Thatcher house and stopped to catch his breath, after having run the whole way with his side on fire. "Becky! Are you here?"

No one could tell him the identity of the soldier who'd

escorted her home. The escaped mercenary might have inter-cepted her at the freight office in disguise.

Tom eased his gun from its holster and moved forward quietly on the balls of his feet. He shouldn't have trusted Sid or anyone else with Becky's safety, even though intuition told him whoever had shot at them this morning was after him, not her. That didn't mean the devil wouldn't use her as a lure or a shield.

He searched the front of the house then crept through the kitchen and pushed the back door open a crack to peer outside. No one in the yard. Not even guards. Sid said he couldn't spare them.

Along the side of the carriage house, the shutters were closed. One was broken. An old ladder leaned against the building as if someone had been about to make repairs and had walked away.

Becky emerged from the side where the doors opened, halt-ingly, as if in a daze. Thank God. She'd made it home all right. Though it was a mystery as to why she'd be out there.

She turned around and stared at something or someone. Had the man who made off with her dragged her in there and molested her?

Tom swore a vicious oath. By God, he'd kill the bastard.

Before he'd made it halfway across the yard, she spun to face him. Her startled fear transformed into an expression reminiscent of a cornered animal.

"You *despicable* snake. I don't know why I didn't see through you earlier, you...you *Judas*."

Terrorized women sometimes struck out at those who tried to help them.

Tom holstered his weapon and spoke calmly. "What's got you so worked up?"

She took a fighting position. "Don't give me that innocent act. I know why you're here, you rascally, no good bottom-feeder. You came home to spy on me and my father."

Though surprised, Tom held his face expressionless. *Hell's bells.* How had she figured it out? The throbbing pain in his side traveled to his head, making clear thinking difficult. Sid wouldn't have told her. Had one of the prisoners said something to her father? Or was the man who escorted her home privy to classified information?

"You don't deny it?" Her face reflected a gut-wrenching cascade of emotions: anger, puzzlement, and hurt. She was so transparent, so trusting.

What he'd done was unforgivable.

He opened his hands in a gesture of surrender. "No point in denying it, considering you aren't the only one who knows. Who told you? That fellow who escorted you home? Nobody could tell me his name."

"He didn't give me his name."

She'd left with a stranger? That didn't sound like Becky, unless...

That *soldier* had been her cousin!

Tom dashed to the door of the carriage house. "Where is that possum?"

"He's not inside," she replied in a dull voice.

Not believing her, Tom went inside and did a cursory search. He found a loose board on the back wall and swore softly. Jeff had been in here.

Tom returned outside before she could slip away again. "Was he the one who told you I was spying on you?"

Tears welling along her lower eyelids spilled onto her cheeks. She dashed them away with the back of her hand. "Who else knows? Everyone but me?"

More people than Tom would prefer. "How did Jeff find out?"

Becky's expression flattened. "Someone put a price on your head. That's why those mercenaries are out to kill you."

Dread prickled Tom's skin. He had to find the real traitors

before his enemies succeeded in eliminating him and took aim at her. "Time is running out, Becky. I have to find Jeff and talk to him if we're to have a chance at getting your father freed."

"You don't care about him. Or me."

"Yes, I do."

"Liar."

"I don't expect you to believe me, I'm just setting the record straight."

"Then let me set the record straight. I *despise* you."

He could live with her hatred. He wouldn't want to live if anything happened to her.

Moving slowly, so as not to startle her, he closed the distance between them and gently took hold of her arm. "You can cuss me all you want after we get inside. Let's not stand out here where anybody can see us. It's too dangerous."

For a moment, she remained rooted. Finally, she moved her feet and walked stiffly in the direction of the house. When they reached the steps, she hesitated a split second, then shot through the door and slammed it in his face.

Before she could lock it, he shoved it open and marched inside. "Now you listen to me! You'll get yourself killed if you keep running off."

She backed up to the table. "I'm not running. I'm shutting you out."

"You can do that after we talk."

"There's nothing to talk about. You lied to me."

"What I told you was the truth. I'll admit there are a few things I didn't share, but I'm sworn to secrecy so I couldn't tell you everything."

"You didn't tell me *anything*." She went to the pantry and started rummaging around, grabbing tins of food and stuffing them into a flour sack.

"Who's that for, Jeff? Dang it, Becky, you can't keep helping him. It'll make things worse for the judge."

She threw a sharp glance over her shoulder. "Stop pretending you care what happens to my father. I don't believe you, and I won't help you find my cousin."

Tom took the sack away and set it on the table. "That's too bad because I'm the only chance you've got."

"Arrogant, as well as a liar! You are not my only chance. Alfred is on his way here. He'll help me, and I'll never have to speak to you again."

If she believed Alfred would help, she didn't know the worst of it. He had to tell her or she'd refuse to cooperate and only end up hurting herself. And she thought she hated him now...

"Alfred won't help you. His commander is the one who sent me here to bring your father in, along with the evidence to convict him. Those were the orders I couldn't remember."

The blood drained from her face.

She sank onto the bench next to the trestle table with a dazed expression.

Tom didn't think he could despise himself more than he did at that moment. He sat down beside her with his hand pressed against the burning in his side. That pain was nothing compared to the ruckus going on in his heart. "I didn't want to tell you like that. But you've got to stop fighting me."

Her eyes widened into gleaming pools of pain. "You, of all people...you would betray me in the worst way."

He would rather pour acid on his soul. Granted he had misled her and hidden things from her, but he would die before he let anyone, including himself, destroy her hope.

"When have you ever known me to follow orders blindly? Just because I can't remember them doesn't change my intentions. I mean to clear your father."

"How do I know you're not making that up? You could be pretending like you've been doing ever since you've been back."

God knows, he'd spent the better part of the war pretending, and before that he'd pretended as well. For most all his life, he had played different roles. Roles that made him feel smarter, braver, or in some way superior. Because deep down he'd known he was a nobody. Except for when he was with Becky. She had seen the truest part of him and had loved him anyway.

She had no such delusions anymore.

He braced his hands on his knees as desperation beat down on him in a deluge.

The truth was all he had to offer. He had to expose the thing he'd protected so fiercely for so many years. "I have never pretended when it comes to how I feel about you. I love you."

For once, he couldn't read her reaction.

"If that's what you think then you've fooled yourself, Tom Sawyer."

He released a ragged breath. His love had never been pure enough or strong enough to hold a woman like her. He'd known that for a long time. But he still had something of worth to offer. "I swear on my honor, you can depend on me—"

"Don't!" She squeezed her eyes shut. "*Do not* swear another vow. I don't want to hear it." Her voice cracked, and her throat worked convulsively. When she opened her eyes, they were filled with loathing. "You promised me everything. You've given me nothing. All you've done is dishonor me and double-cross my family."

She hung her head and released a wretched, defeated sound.

Tom couldn't speak. Couldn't even breathe. Must be because of the hole in his chest from that verbal attack she'd just fired at him. He dragged himself to his feet, in the process managed to suck air into his lungs, then he paced the breadth of the kitchen. Raked his fingers through his hair and paced some more.

Becky would never forgive him. As much as he wished he could take away the hurt he'd inflicted, he couldn't. He also couldn't walk away. Not yet.

"The man who shot me, I'm certain he's working for the insurrectionists, and somehow all of this is tied together. We just don't know what the plan is. But I have to catch him before tomorrow."

She raised her head to look at him with an expression so filled with despair it made his gut clench. "What happens tomorrow?"

"That's when I have to take your father to St. Louis to stand trial."

CHAPTER SIXTEEN

Becky fought a pathetic urge to fall into Tom's arms and let him hold her and comfort her as he had the previous night. If she was honest with herself, she would admit she longed to believe in his love, despite everything. But love was illusory. And the man sitting next to her was a charlatan of the worst sort.

The warmth and slight pressure of his grasp on her cold fingers gave the impression of tenderness. Yet, every word he said, everything he'd done, had been carefully crafted to manipulate her into believing in him so he could accomplish a cursed mission. To ensure her father would be hanged as a traitor.

Her heart shrank into a painful knot. He would not get the opportunity to pry it open again.

She withdrew her hand and hunched her shoulders.

Tom scooted away a few centimeters. "Tell me how to find Jeff before we run out of time. He has to know something about what's being planned."

Which man could she trust? Not Tom, who had been forced to admit his betrayal.

Alfred must've known about his commander's orders. Why

hadn't he done anything to help? Perhaps his hands were tied or he couldn't risk it. If so, she couldn't depend on him to save her family.

Her secretive cousin, for all his flaws, would offer up his life to save her father. But, dear Lord, she couldn't bear to think about what they would do to Jeff when he turned himself in. Shooting him would be too easy. They'd send him to a horrible, humiliating death on the gallows. He'd been labeled a murderer and her father branded a traitor. Neither of them would escape punishment.

She would track Jeff down and together they would figure out how to free the judge. They could flee. West. Start over with new identities. Somewhere no one would find them.

First, she had to escape from Tom. Being a terrible liar, she would need to be truthful enough to sound convincing.

She wiped her eyes and heaved a resigned sigh. "Jeff told me before he left that he would be back to talk to you about giving himself up in exchange for my father's freedom."

Most of that was the truth, except for the part about trusting Tom.

"Why didn't he stay here if that's the case?"

"He said he had something to do first."

"He knows the army doesn't negotiate with guerrilla fighters."

Another reason for her to find Jeff and work out some way to spring her father. If both men were executed, she would have no one left to care for, except for Tom and she didn't want him anymore.

"Well, that's what he told me. I suppose you'll have to wait and see." Becky stood up and untied her bonnet to give the impression she intended to remain inside. "I trust that Alfred will be here on the next boat, regardless. I plan to accompany him to St. Louis to be at my father's side when he stands trial. Now, if you'll excuse me, I'm going upstairs to my room to freshen up and pack."

Tom followed her as she left the kitchen and started down the hall. He favored his side. Had the fool torn the wound open while he was running after her? She fought an urge to tend to him. She ought to put a bullet in his other side.

"Why are you following me?"

"I won't allow you to put yourself in danger," he said dully.

She gave an exasperated huff. "I'm only going up to my room, Tom. You need to sit down and be patient. If Jeff said he'd be here, he will. I prefer to wait in privacy and not have to look at you."

Becky mounted the steps.

When she reached the top, Tom still stood at the base of the stairs. Even his stoic expression couldn't conceal his pain and misery. Now, when it was too late, she could see through him as easily as if he were made of glass.

Did he believe what he said about loving her?

She squelched her too-tender heart. Having listened to that unreliable source for too long, she would now rely on reason and common sense. Tom had deceived her before and he would do so again if she allowed it. "I'll be back downstairs shortly."

After she'd shut the door to her room, she changed into a work dress and apron and reached under her bed for a pair of sturdy boots. She would need to move freely and not lose her footing.

Her hand encountered what felt like a piece of paper. She withdrew it.

The missing letter for Mrs. Bent. It must've slipped out of her pocket when she was changing and had gotten pushed under the bed.

She could deliver it on the way to the Lawrence place. She hadn't gotten a chance to talk to Jeff about why he was snooping around earlier. It might be part of his *unfinished business*. If he wasn't there, she had an idea where he might be holed up in the caves.

Taking care to be quiet, she opened the window and crawled out onto the roof.

Her mind went back to a night when she had slipped out to meet Tom in a last-ditch attempt to change his mind about leaving. Being young and in love, she hadn't known any better than to take him at his word that he loved her and would return to marry her.

Foolish girl.

She inched across the rooftop toward an overhanging tree limb that she could use to make her escape. It took what seemed like an eternity to crawl across the branches and reach a spot beyond the fence where she could drop into the alley. There, she wouldn't be as likely to encounter soldiers.

Overgrown bushes lined the boundaries of the properties without fences. She turned onto the path between a vacant home and Mrs. Bent's small house.

Some innate warning tickled the back of her neck. She checked over her shoulder but didn't see anyone. Still, Tom could be sneaky.

Becky hurried to the widow's back door. It wasn't locked. She slipped inside.

"Hello? Mrs. Bent?" She called out in a loud whisper. The old lady was near deaf and wouldn't hear a grenade if it went off, much less a soft call.

Becky came to the bedroom and pushed the door open. She removed the letter from her pocket.

Mrs. Bent sat slumped in a rocker by the window with a shawl draped over her shoulders. She often sat there for the light while she was knitting, but today her chin rested on her chest and her hands had fallen to her sides.

Poor thing. She must've become fatigued.

Becky started to back away, then hesitated. Something didn't look right. The knitting needles and half-finished sock had fallen to the floor. Several skeins of yarn lay scattered, almost as if someone had kicked them out of the basket.

Some primitive warning raced up the base of Becky's neck, as she approached the rocker and reached out, gently shaking the widow's fragile shoulder.

The old lady's head drooped at an impossible angle.

The letter fell from Becky's nerveless fingers.

Tom slipped around the bushes and down the path Becky had taken. He had suspected she would try to escape using the oak tree and run to Jeff. Up to this point, he'd had no trouble following. Then, she'd vanished.

He crept alongside the wall outside the house where Oscar Bent's widow lived. The place was in worse shape than the house where he'd grown up. Not wanting to be seen, he slowly peered around the corner at the sagging porch.

A bloodcurdling scream sent chills down his spine.

Tom had his gun out of its holster before his feet hit the porch. The front door stood open. That scream had come from inside, he was sure of it. He approached the bedroom with the hammer cocked and peeked inside.

Becky stood stock still in front of a rocker where the old lady sagged to one side. No one else appeared to be in the room with them.

As Tom stepped inside, Becky whirled around, fear stretching the skin on her face into a mask of horror.

"She's...dead."

Tom holstered his gun and moved quickly to check the old woman's pulse. "Her neck's been snapped."

"Dear God," Becky moaned. "Who would do something so *evil*?"

He'd long since stopped asking that question. "Someone

looking for money or valuables? Did you see anybody when you came in?"

Becky averted her gaze from the widow's body. "No. She was sitting there when I found her."

Tom glanced at the items strewn across the floor, things that would've fallen from the old lady's lap. "No more struggle than that, I'd say she knew the killer well enough not to worry until it was too late. Do you know of anyone who wished her ill?"

"No, no one. She was just a lonely old lady." Becky shuddered. "Oh, Tom. This is awful."

He drew her into his arms, needing to protect her, comfort her. She trembled like a leaf in a high wind. "Why did you come in here? Did you see something amiss?"

"No. I was afraid you might be following me. I came in here to hide."

Of course, she had. She was smart. Too smart.

Tom used his fingers to comb the tangles out of her hair. He longed to scoop her into his arms and whisk her to a place where crazed killers didn't murder old women and threaten innocent young ladies.

Reluctantly, he released her and bent down for a closer look. The widow's wrinkled face had the appearance of a pale rag doll. Her flesh had gone cold, but her body hadn't yet stiffened, which meant she'd been killed recently.

Possibly, the murderer was hiding nearby.

"Let's get you out of here." He drew Becky into the hall. After he got her to a place of safety, he would return and search the house.

Once outside, she turned to him, in a panic. "Wait! I forgot."

He caught her. "Forgot what?"

"I didn't...I..." Tears welled in her eyes. "Didn't say goodbye."

Her compassion stirred his own sympathies, which he had

learned to keep tightly concealed. "You can say goodbye later," he said softly. "Come on."

He waved down a federal patrol. "There's been a murder in there. I'm seeing this young lady to safety. Secure the house until I return."

"A murder?" The sergeant glanced at the house but didn't dismount. "We'll need to report it to the provost marshal."

"I'll take care of that," Tom promised.

Becky cast a worried look over her shoulder. "Then I should go home."

She would run again. She no longer trusted him, and there were things she wasn't telling him, not just about her cousin, but something that had to do with the widow.

Her lack of faith didn't change his commitment. If he had come home years ago as he'd promised, she wouldn't be in this situation.

"It's not safe for you to be alone," he reminded her.

This time, he wouldn't let her down. No matter what trouble she'd landed in, he would protect her. Even if he had to lock her up to do it.

CHAPTER SEVENTEEN

Becky stumbled along, caught in a whirlwind of fear and doubt. Another wave of anxiety pounded against her dazed disbelief. People close to her were being murdered, shot at, and arrested, and she had no idea why.

Tom followed her up the stairs in the freight house.

The provost marshal, behind his desk, stood as they entered. A moment later Tom sent the guards away and closed the door.

"What's this about?" Sid grumbled.

Tom ushered her to a chair, which she gratefully accepted. Her limbs hadn't stopped shaking. She still couldn't believe what she'd seen with her own eyes. It was too terrible.

"We're here to report a murder. Someone killed Oscar Bent's widow in her home. I've alerted one of your patrols. They're over there now."

Sid sat back down. He picked up a pen, drew the inkwell closer, and opened a notebook. "Tell me what happened."

"We found the widow slumped in a rocking chair in her bedroom," Tom answered. "Her neck was broken. Quickly and cleanly. No sign of forced entry. Very little appeared to be disturbed. Doesn't look like a robbery gone wrong. Someone intended to kill her."

Sid stopped writing and leaned his arms on the desk. "Widow Bent's daughter is in prison for aiding a rebel guerilla."

"The old lady might've known something that would incriminate another traitor," Tom suggested.

Fear put a knot in Becky's throat. She shifted her eyes away from the provost marshal's penetrating gaze only to meet Tom's questioning one.

Did he expect *her* to suggest the killer's motivation? She didn't have anything to do with the old woman's death. The messages she delivered were brief, concerning Anne's health and longing for home. Nothing out of the ordinary.

"Perhaps the widow argued with someone who objected to her political views?" Becky suggested.

"Breaking her neck seems a rather extreme way to settle an argument," Sid said dryly.

If she brought up the letters, it would implicate her and drag Alfred into the whole mess, which would only make matters worse for her father. Anne's sentimental notes could have nothing to do with her mother's murder.

"It was a professional killing, not the work of a disgruntled neighbor," Tom said firmly. He walked over to the large map on the wall and studied it.

"What are you thinking?" Sid asked.

Becky twisted in her seat to hear Tom's answer.

"I encountered those mercenaries here." He pointed to a spot with an illustration of trees indicating a forested stretch of land. "It's close to the rail yard. Not that far from the docks."

"A hideout?" Sid suggested.

"Perhaps. Or a temporary camp."

"What does that have to do with the widow's murder?"

Tom scratched his head. "Not sure. I overheard the men who

attacked me talking about waiting for someone to send word about a delivery. The man who got away implied he might do violence if they were double-crossed."

Becky struggled to follow Tom's reasoning. Weren't those men the same ones who had brought her name into their conversation? She had no more to do with that pack of killers than Mrs. Bent did. Or Anne.

The air in the room grew warm.

"What would a half-deaf old woman know that's worth killing her for?" Sid mused.

Tom rubbed his chin. "Sounds far-fetched, I know, and there's no common thread."

Except for her.

The incidents couldn't be related. It made no sense. On the other hand, spies were reported to have uncanny intuition.

"What about Jeff Thatcher?" Sid proposed.

Of course, they'd blame her cousin. He'd become the Devil incarnate. "Jeff would never murder an old woman."

"He killed a man in cold blood." Sid's merciless gaze didn't falter.

She turned to Tom to state her case. "Jeff did nothing of the sort. I swore on a Bible that he wasn't there."

Tom rested his hand on her shoulder. "That may be. We still need to talk to him."

"Hang him, you mean. Or put him in front of a firing squad. The same as what they want to do with my father...with *your* help."

Tom didn't flinch at her bitter assault. Had his eyes not darkened, it would appear he was incapable of feeling anything. "To help your father, we have to find the real culprit. That would happen faster if you tell me what you know."

"I don't know *anything*. I have no idea who killed Mrs. Bent or why. She couldn't possibly be involved with those killers. She was just a lonely old woman. I did what I could to ease her suffering, nothing more."

"And your father?" Sid asked. "Did he have any dealings with her?"

Now they were attacking the judge as if no one else in a town under martial law could be involved.

"Why are you so intent on dragging my father's name through the mud? He is an honorable man. Not a traitor."

Tom's tightened his hold on her shoulder. "We aren't arguing that."

She pushed his hand away, not wanting comfort, not wanting anything from him. "I've told you what I know. There's nothing more to tell."

Rely on Alfred.

Reason and common sense rose to defend her decision. Alfred would come through for her. He wouldn't abandon her, regardless of his commander's orders.

Sid leaned back in his chair, watching her with the keen interest of a vulture observing an animal in its death throes. "What do you propose to do?" he asked Tom.

"Find our missing mercenary and hunt down Jeff Thatcher."

"What about her?" Sid motioned at Becky with his chin.

Tom wouldn't look at her. "We'll keep her locked up here. For her protection."

Tom escorted a grimly silent Becky to an upstairs storeroom, where he reminded her of his promise to ensure her safety. He didn't repeat for the umpteenth time that he would endeavor to clear her father. She didn't believe him, and he couldn't yet tell her how he might accomplish it. But he would figure it out. He wouldn't fail her. Even if she considered him lower than the mud on her boots.

He stepped back into Sid's office as his brother buckled his gun belt. "Where are you going?"

"To have a look at the body, check out the house." He frowned at Tom. "In case you've forgotten, I'm in charge of the military police. I'll lead any investigation in my district. Not you."

Tom had a difficult time not taking charge. It just came naturally. However, he needed Sid's help so he could at least act like he wanted it. "Sure, it's your investigation, but we need to be working together, right? Like partners."

Sid leveled a flat stare. "Don't flatter me, Tom. I like that less than when you're ordering me around. Tell me what you need."

"Assign a few men to go with me. I'd feel better if you stayed here and kept Becky safe."

"And I'd feel better if you'd tell me what the hell is going on."

"I don't know what's going on any more than you do." He had proposed a wild theory about the widow possibly being involved with the conspirators because he had nothing else, and he wanted to see how Becky would react.

She'd gone pale as a sheet and then avoided meeting his eyes. What did she know that might have a bearing on the murder? If the secret involved her father or her cousin, she wouldn't willingly give it up.

"You have an idea," Sid prompted.

Tom wasn't ready to share his theory. He didn't want to give Sid a trail to follow that might inadvertently lead him to Becky. "Having an idea would imply that what I know makes enough sense to form a coherent theory. All I've got are hunches."

Sid retrieved his hat from a brass tree. "That's a start. Share what you suspect. I'll tell you what I know. That's how partners work."

Partners? They would kill each other if they had to work together for an extended period.

"That mercenary who got away, he's part of a bigger plot," Tom offered.

"You're not telling me anything new. What kind of plot?"

"We have yet to figure it out."

"But you think Jeff Thatcher is involved."

Becky sure didn't see it that way. Then again, could she be trusted for objectivity?

"He's the most obvious suspect. But it seems too neat. Almost as if someone is working the strings to make sure that he and the judge take the fall for whatever trouble is being hatched. Why would Jeff knowingly do something that would result in his uncle's arrest and hanging? The same man who's been helping him stay alive?"

Sid hesitated at the door. "What do you suppose Becky is hiding?"

"Becky?"

"She looked ready to spew her supper all over my desk when you implied those men were somehow connected to the widow. You told me they mentioned Becky. If you hadn't locked her up, I would've arrested her as a party of interest."

Tom wished he hadn't been so forthcoming with his hare-brained theory. "I have no proof whatsoever. I was just spinning out crazy ideas to see where they'd take us."

Sid's facial muscles tightened. "Thanks for the honesty, partner. Anything else I can do for you?"

Tom chose to ignore the dripping sarcasm. "Keep Becky safe while I go look for that killer."

"We've got guards posted outside and inside. She'll be safe. I'm going to the crime scene."

Sid opened the door. Then he took an abrupt step backward as a giant man filled the frame.

His glower radiated from behind a tangled mane of dark hair and a heavy beard. Four armed soldiers escorted the bound man into the room.

"I'm here to give myself up," he drawled.

Tom recognized the voice. "Jeff?"

"Sure as hell ain't Abe Lincoln. I'm here to make a deal. Didn't Becky tell you?"

Tom's awe turned to unease. Becky had been telling the truth about Jeff's surrender. What other truths had she told that he'd ignored? "What is this deal you want to make?"

"I give myself up and you let my family go."

"You've been captured, you great lummox," Sid declared.

One of the guards cleared his throat. "We didn't capture him, sir. He just walked up and turned himself in. He said Captain Sawyer would be expecting him."

Tom shrugged at Sid's questioning glance. "Becky might've mentioned it. I wasn't sure he'd show up."

"The army doesn't negotiate with bushwhackers," Sid informed the prisoner.

Jeff understood the rules as well as they did, and he'd taken the risk anyway, which confirmed his honor—or proved he was crazy.

"He doesn't look like a bushwhacker to me. Where are the frills on his shirt? The feather in his hat?" Tom humored the sullen prisoner and pretended not to notice the black look Sid gave him as he untied Jeff's bindings. His brother would eventually catch on to what he was doing.

Jeff rubbed his wrists where the rope had burned the skin. A bruise on the side of his face had the size and shape of a rifle butt. He was fortunate the soldiers hadn't shot him on sight.

Sid rested his hand on his revolver and he addressed the guards. "You men can return to your posts."

Good. His precious protocol wasn't going to get them anywhere.

After the guards left, Tom crossed to Sid's liquor cabinet and poured a small glass of the home brew then handed it to Jeff. "Have a drink."

Jeff's resentful gaze flickered over the glass. He kept his hands at his sides. "I don't need a drink."

"Well, I do." Tom was prepared for the burn this time. He was also prepared to do whatever was necessary to ensure Jeff's cooperation. Lie. Cheat. Torture wasn't entirely out of the question. "Before we discuss any deal, tell us where to find your friend, that black-haired mercenary."

"I don't have any friends. They're all dead." Jeff's blunt, useless reply sent a wave of anger rolling through Tom. Was Jeff's primary goal to waste their time?

"He's about Sid's height and coloring," Tom said evenly. "Might also wear a disguise, a white wig. Does that jog your memory?"

Jeff's sullen stare didn't waver. "I don't know who he is or where to find him."

Tom's patience stretched hair-thin. He set the shot glass on the table with a thunk. "Did you come here to make a deal or not? If you don't cooperate, your uncle will be hanged. And Becky? She's locked away because she'd rather protect you than herself."

Quick as a flash, Jeff snagged Tom by the front of his uniform and jerked him nearly off his feet. "You stinking double-crosser."

The click of a hammer being cocked sounded loud in the sudden silence. Sid pressed the muzzle of his revolver against the big man's temple. "Let him go."

Jeff relaxed his hold, but his sky-blue eyes remained beacons of hatred, similar in coloring and expression to the look in Becky's eyes right before Tom had shut and locked the door. "I hope you both burn in hell."

Tom straightened his coat without breaking eye contact. "You'll be there with me, old friend. You're the one who got Becky and your uncle into this mess."

Jeff's face darkened to an alarming shade of red. He'd reached the verge of exploding despite Sid's gun being pointed at his head.

Tom raised his hand so Sid would not get trigger-happy. He didn't want to see this interrogation end with Jeff's brains splattered all over the walls.

"What do you want me to do?" Jeff thundered. "Sign a confession? Whatever it is, I'll do it. Just let Becky and my uncle go. They haven't done anything wrong."

"Then tell us where to find the traitor who's after Becky. Stop protecting him."

"Why would I protect a bastard who's trying to hurt my family? I don't know what you're talking about."

He sure as hell knew *something*.

"Where is the delivery taking place?" Tom demanded.

"What?" Jeff's frown dissolved into a look of confusion.

Now they were getting somewhere.

"We know you're involved. Give us the details then we'll talk about a trade."

"How did you...?" Jeff's question trailed off. He darted a look at the door, scratched his beard, then frowned reflectively, possibly considering his options. He had few and they were running out.

After another moment, he heaved a weary sigh. "All right. I'll show you where we make the delivery. But you got to swear to let my family go."

The rush of relief swept the tension out of Tom's shoulders. "Becky will be safe. I'll do what I can for your uncle. That's all I can promise."

He offered his hand. After a brief hesitation, Jeff took it in a firm grip.

"I'll round up some men." Sid started for the door.

"No." Jeff squeezed Tom's hand tighter. "Just Tom."

The sharp demand brought Sid to a standstill. "You must think he's an idiot. Tom isn't going with you alone so you can lead him into an ambush."

Retaining his hold, Jeff challenged Tom with a look. "If I lead a pack of Federals into the woods, we'll be picked off before we make it ten feet. Decide what you want."

Tom tightened his fingers around Jeff's hand to let him know he wasn't the only one who could apply pressure. He would do this Jeff's way for now. But if he sensed a trap, he would kill him. "You're right. Taking a patrol will send the rats back into hiding. I'll go with you. Alone."

Jeff released the death grip.

Tom flexed his fingers to get the blood flowing again.

Sid didn't holster his gun. "It's a trap, Tom. Don't fall for it."

He wasn't hesitating because he feared death. He feared what might happen to Becky if he wasn't around to mount a defense on her behalf. But it was as clear as the blue in Jeff's eyes this was the only way he'd cooperate, and time was running out.

"We've got a deal. If Jeff expects us to honor it, he won't double-cross us." Tom wasn't nearly as certain as he sounded.

"I'll go with him." Sid's surprising offer rendered Tom speechless.

Why would he risk his life? It couldn't be brotherly love or loyalty between friends. They enjoyed neither. Unless...Sid had changed.

No, it was too troubling to think about. Besides, he was in a better position to take care of someone more valuable.

Tom clasped Sid's shoulder in an awkward show of affection, just in case he didn't come back. "I appreciate the offer, but I've made a deal."

Based on Sid's hesitation, Tom suspected he would send a man to track them, and silently shook his head. That was a risk he wouldn't take, not with so much at stake. "Send your men out to search for our suspect. Be sure to keep Becky safe."

CHAPTER EIGHTEEN

Tom set out with his prisoner for a destination somewhere south along the river. Jeff hadn't been forthcoming with specific, responding to questions with grunts or monosyllabic replies. Whether he would stay true to his word remained to be seen.

The wind picked up as they trekked past the wharf with Tom bringing up the rear. He cradled his repeating rifle, and also carried Jeff's fine hunting knife, two Army revolvers, and belts lined with bullets. If he had to dig in and defend himself, he would be ready.

By the time they exited the rail yard, gray clouds bunched overhead and he could smell the imminent rain. It appeared first as pencil-dark streaks over a towering bluff that jutted into the river like a giant fist.

The precipice had been one of his favorite childhood spots to while away the hours on days he played hooky from school. He would lay about with his friend Huck, the both of them puffing on corncob pipes, talking about adventures they would have when they grew up. He did most of the talking while Huck listened.

When the war came, Huck had lit out to avoid the conflict. Tom had chosen a different path. Even if he could turn the clock back, he wasn't positive he would make a different decision. Becky was sharp enough to realize this and not fall for him again. She didn't need his love anymore. However, she did need his skills to escape a dangerous situation and that much he could give her.

Jeff silently traipsed along the treeless shoreline. Soon, they were picking their way through sedgy grass and stiff river cane.

Tom adjusted one of the ammunition belts crisscrossing his chest. "Where are you taking us?"

Jeff threw the answer over his shoulder. "You'll see."

"Hold up." Tom snagged the back of Jeff's coat. "I'm not going any further until you tell me where we're headed. Is it a cave?"

Jeff glowered at him. "Are we gonna stand here all day jawin' or do you want to see where I deliver the contraband?"

The contraband? Could be weapons or ammunition.

Tom's suspicions were confirmed. "Are you the ring leader? Becky said you'd gone bad. She didn't reckon how bad."

Jeff moved quietly through the river cane. "Tain't bad, what I'm doing. She'd understand if she knew."

"Don't talk in riddles. Who's helping you?"

"You'll meet him soon enough."

Tom drew the rifle around and kept a sharp eye on the bushes along the shore. He could very well be walking into an ambush, just as Sid feared. Was Jeff lying when he'd said he didn't know the black-haired mercenary? That man might be his partner. If so, Jeff betrayed his family as well as his country.

"Did you promise him that he could molest Becky?"

Jeff halted and turned so fast that Tom had to walk backward. He pointed the rifle at the big man glowering down at him. "Becky doesn't have a damn thing to do with my crimes. I'll kill you or anybody else that hurts her."

The fury in Jeff's expression and tone confirmed he wasn't

aware that his partner had threatened his cousin. Mercenaries couldn't be trusted. Jeff ought to know better.

Tom kept his gun leveled on the unpredictable prisoner. "Whether you intended it or not, she's in danger."

Jeff's anger melted into an expression bordering on despair. He spread his arms in open appeal. "Look here, Tom. I don't care what happens to me. Just don't let anyone hurt her."

Damn, he was hard to read. On one hand, he appeared remorseful, but past actions pointed to a man who didn't care who he hurt on his quest for vengeance. On the off chance he still cared for his cousin, she remained the only leverage they had to use against him.

"It's not up to me. Her safety and freedom depend on whether you live up to your end of the bargain."

Whatever regret Jeff might've been suffering vanished. "Becky was right," he stated coldly. "You are sorrier than ever."

Tom held onto a straight face and motioned for his guide to continue. He would die before letting anyone harm a hair on Becky's head, but he didn't owe Jeff an explanation. Besides, he had to make the rebel believe the stakes were high or he might not cooperate.

Lightning flashed behind dark clouds in the distance. Thunder grumbled and rumbled down the river.

"How much farther?" Tom asked.

"Not far."

Fat drops struck Tom's cheek. Then a hard rain pelted them.

Jeff vanished into a canebrake. Tom followed his guide. On the other side of the cover provided by the cane, someone had hidden a two-person skiff.

Jeff untied a rope securing the boat to a dead branch that poked up out of the water and used an oar to give a hard push that launched them. As they glided out onto the river, the storm took a breath.

Tom slicked water off the brim of his hat and hunched deeper into his coat while his guide rowed. They were headed for a sand bar at the north end of Jackson's Island, close to a mile away. He could chart the course blindfolded as many times as he'd made the journey as a boy. The last time, he'd taken Becky with him. He was damn glad she wasn't with him this time.

Federal boats routinely patrolled the island for rebels, but a stealthy crew could sneak ashore. The conspirators might be using the strip of land as a pickup point.

A while later, the bottom of the skiff scraped sand and Jeff clambered over the side. Tom shifted his carbine to his back and hopped overboard to help Jeff drag the boat ashore.

The call of a whippoorwill came from the darkness of the forest.

Jeff hesitated.

Tom remained behind him to make sure the rebel took the first bullets. "If you're leading us into a trap, that's not going to help your uncle or Becky."

"I know what's at stake," Jeff said in a low voice.

The storm clouds hurled a bolt of lightning and it exploded in the trees with an earth-trembling roar. Tom's nostrils flared at the smell of scorched wood.

Within seconds, sheets of rain swept the island.

Jeff made for a cottonwood grove and Tom stayed on his heels with the thunderstorm right on top of them. He squinted to see in the wooded darkness through heavy rain.

Lightning flashed. A photographic image of the trees embedded itself on the inside of Tom's eyelids, helping him to avoid running into them.

Jeff ran on ahead, on instinct if not sight.

Another glowing flash revealed a hut cleverly fashioned out of slender branches covered with an oilskin.

Jeff threw back a flap and disappeared inside.

His contact might be waiting for them or it was an ambush.

Tom shifted his rifle over one shoulder and drew a revolver before following Jeff into the dark interior. The dirt floor remained dry, an improvement over being out in the rain.

Something scraped, then a match flared, illuminating the interior of the hut. Hunched over on his knees, Jeff lit a candle stub and stuck it through the hinged door of a lantern. Holes in the tin gleamed like tiny stars, shedding enough light to see inside the shelter but not so much it would leak through to the outside and be noticed.

Jeff shifted to a crossed-legged position and put a pack in his lap.

Tom eyed the bundle nervously. "You got a gun stashed in there?"

"Have a look if you're curious." Jeff set the bag between them.

Tom shifted into a sitting position with the rifle across his lap then picked up the canvas bag. Inside he found a box of matches and a few candles, along with tins of medicinal supplies and bandages. No guns.

The hut wasn't large enough to house troops or very many weapons. Those must be elsewhere. "Is this where you and your contact rendezvous?"

Jeff laid his hat aside and shook like a dog, flinging water into Tom's face. "Sometimes we meet here. Mostly it's a shelter."

"For you?"

"For the runaways."

Tom dashed the water from his ears so he could hear better. "Runaways?"

"You know. Escaped slaves." Jeff spoke as one might address a simpleton. "I told you I'd show you where I take them. Don't ask where they come from or where they're going, because I don't know and don't care. I just deliver them."

Jeff might as well have been speaking French for all the sense he made.

"What the devil does runaway slaves have to do with anything?"

Tom's question was met with a look of surprise. "You were the one that brought it up."

"The hell I did."

Jeff propped his arms on his knees and leaned forward. "You said you wanted to know details about the delivery."

Tom had said that, but he wasn't talking about human traffic. "You must take me for a halfwit if you think I'll believe that fish story. It's not going to help, you know."

Jeff huffed. "You asked and I told you. Whether or not you believe me doesn't change the answer."

"What's the real cargo being transferred off this island?" Tom demanded.

"Well, you tell me, because I'm sure I don't know."

Tom restrained an urge to wrap his fingers around Jeff's thick neck. The oaf had taken him on a wild goose chase and wasted precious time. Exactly the kind of thing a traitor would do. "Stop playing games. You know what I'm talking about."

Jeff braced his hands on his knees and leaned forward with a snarl on his face. "If I knew anything more, I'd tell you. Heck, I'd give you Jesus himself to save my family."

"He's not the man I need to find."

"Who are you looking for?"

"Your contact."

Jeff sat back with a grave expression. "Then you'll have to wait."

The call of a whippoorwill broke through the sound of steady rain.

Jeff sat up and cupped his hands to his mouth. "Hoo hoo, hoo hoo hooahh."

He'd given a fine imitation of a barred owl.

Tom gripped his gun. "Who're you answering?"

"You'll see. I wasn't sure he'd show up."

The flap opened and a tall, slender man with skin as dark as midnight ducked inside. When he spotted Tom, he remained poised at the opening. The light coming from the tin lantern reflected surprise in his obsidian gaze.

He wasn't the only one surprised.

"Who the hell are you?" Tom blurted.

"It's all right." Jeff gestured for the stranger to enter. "You recall this cussed fool?"

"Indeed, I do. Don't look like he recollects me."

Tom didn't like being called a fool. He disliked being made to look like one even more. He studied the stranger's face, which was vaguely familiar. Couldn't be, yet... "Little Jim?"

The flash of white teeth confirmed it. The man folded his long legs as he sat. His knees almost touched his nose. "Not so little anymore."

Jim had been a childhood playmate, and also a slave. Aunt Polly had freed him upon her death, and that was the last Tom had heard of him.

"What are you doing here?" Tom asked.

"Jim is my contact," Jeff explained. "I deliver the runaways. He guides them to freedom. Now that you know, what do you plan to do?"

The men waited for an answer.

Tom couldn't give them one. He was downright perplexed by the turn of events "You...you expect me to believe you've been ferrying runaways to freedom? You're a Reb, for God's sake. They don't cotton to such things."

Jeff picked up a pebble from the dirt floor and rolled it between his fingers. "I didn't pick sides because I wanted to protect slavery. Federal soldiers murdered my father. They beat him to death because he tried to stop them from looting. I hated them. I wanted to drive the whole lot out of the state. That's why I fought —for a time."

"What changed your mind?"

"Woke up, more like." Jeff flicked the pebble and it struck the star-spangled lantern with a ping. "What do you know about Asa Lawrence?"

"Becky told me he led a loyalist militia, and you're wanted for his murder."

"I didn't give the order. But I can't say it wasn't my fault."

Jeff fixed his gaze on the light. "About a year ago, I was sleeping out in the woods when Asa surprised me. He could've shot me before I ran. For some reason, he didn't. I didn't mention it to anyone because I was embarrassed to be caught napping. 'Bout a week later, some of our men ran him down while he was helping two runaways escape. He fell off his horse. They strung him up by his broken arm and shot him."

Even as jaded as Tom had become, the story horrified him. It was an act of pure evil.

"I still ponder over it. If I'd told the men that he'd let me go, would they have spared him?" Jeff continued to stare at the lantern.

He didn't need an answer he'd already figured out, but Tom gave him one anyway. "Not likely."

"Perhaps not. I'll never know."

Tom leaned back, awash in amazement. He understood guilt. It launched religions and revivals. He couldn't say as it had done much to improve the human race, in general. But Jeff implied that guilt had affected a turnaround, he'd been paying penance for his sins. "That's why you took up Asa's work?"

"As best I could." Jeff motioned to the other man. "With Jim's help. Couldn't do it without him."

"Why do you want to stop us?" Jim asked Tom.

Was that what they thought? Lincoln's emancipation act freed slaves in states that were in rebellion. Missouri, having not officially separated, fell into a shadowy middle ground. Most federal commanders didn't care if slaves ran away, but they opposed any coordinated efforts to aid them. Personally, Tom was all for it.

"I don't care if you two ferry every slave west of the Mississippi to freedom. That isn't what I'm here to investigate. It sure as hell can't be the sort of delivery those men were talking about."

Jeff rubbed his eyes. "Confound it, Tom. What men?"

"Sid says they're mercenaries."

"The ones you got into a shoot-out with?" Jeff asked.

Tom narrowed his eyes. He hadn't mentioned the shoot-out. "Were you with them?"

"With them? No. I was keeping an eye on you."

"Why me?"

"I wanted to know what you were up to."

That would mean Jeff was the mysterious gunman, the one who had provided cover, which was just as puzzling as him running slaves. Possibly, further proof that Jeff had done a turnabout. Or maybe he just didn't like seeing one man take on three.

"You saved my skin."

Jeff's mouth turned down. "Something I'm thinking now was a mistake."

"All righty then. Glad we got that settled. Let's move on." Jim clapped his hands on his knees. "What'd you expect to find out here, Tom?"

Not this.

Tom drove his fingers through his wet hair. He didn't have time to go into all the details about plots and conspiracies. "Weapons, stolen goods, I don't know. One of the men talked about getting a message and making a delivery. I reasoned that's why they used this island."

Jim put his finger to his chin. "Hm. Maybe they did. Early on, before dawn, I saw lights at the other end of the island. Thought it might be slave hunters, so I went closer to check it out."

Tom leaned forward. "What was it?"

"Some bluecoat soldiers loading barrels onto a ferryboat...all except for one man. He stood to the side like an overseer."

"Was he a soldier?"

"Don't think so. He had on buckskin and a big floppy hat. Wore his hair in a braid down his back—"

"Like an Indian," Tom finished excitedly. "It's him. Injun Joe's lookalike.

"Who?"

"The man I'm looking for." Tom gathered his weapons and opened the tent flap, turned to Jim. "Come on. Show me where you saw him."

CHAPTER NINETEEN

As the afternoon stretched on, Becky peered through a broken window pane three floors above the freight yard, hoping to catch sight of Tom. He'd marched off with Jeff past the levee and they hadn't returned. If neither of them made it back alive, whose fault was it?

Guilt gnawed at her conscience. She'd done nothing wrong. Jeff had contributed to his downfall and taken his family with him. Tom wouldn't listen. He was determined to take a prisoner. If not her father, he'd settle for Jeff.

Down at the landing, thunder and lightning interrupted workers unloading a ferry. Moments before the deluge, tarps had been hastily secured over rows of hogshead barrels sitting at the wharf.

Possibly, the storm had kept Tom and Jeff holed up somewhere, which would explain their delayed return.

A lone steamboat had managed to weather the storm. Atop a pole, the Stars and Stripes gave an occasional weak flutter in between torrents of rain. Eventually, the downpour became a drizzle. Dockworkers removed the canvas over the barrels and rolled them up the stage plank, under the supervision of several soldiers. What was the army taking away? They'd already confiscated everything of value, including her father.

A tear escaped and slid down her cheek. How could she save him if she was locked up?

The sound of a key scraping in the lock sent a thrill through her. Had Tom returned? He'd instructed her to wait for him. As if she had any choice in the matter.

The door creaked open and a sandy-haired man stuck his head inside.

Her anticipation took a tumble.

"Alfred!" She ran and threw her arms around his neck, determined to show her happiness and gratitude to a true hero.

"My darling girl. Are you all right?" He hugged her, a little too tightly to be considered proper. Her too-effusive welcome was to blame, not his impropriety.

"I'm fine. Just very relieved." Becky extracted herself and took a demure step back. She smoothed her hair and fretted over her disheveled appearance.

She still wore a faded work dress, and he looked so handsome in his crisply pressed uniform. Well-groomed, with no scruffy beard, only a tidy mustache the same fawn color as his hair. Any woman in her right mind would consider him a good catch. For her, he was a godsend.

"I'm so happy to see you. I wasn't sure you'd received the message."

"The message?" Alfred blinked. "Ah, you mean the telegram, yes. I came as soon as I could."

She couldn't hold back a rush of grateful tears. "Oh, Alfred. I was so afraid you might decide I wasn't...worth the risk."

He circled her waist with his arms and bent his head. "You are worth a great deal to me," he whispered before his lips touched hers.

Becky waited for something to happen. His kiss brought on no tingling rush of pleasure. Only a wave of disappointment. She put her hands on his arms to prevent him from crushing her against him for a second kiss. "Have you talked to Sid? Will he release my father?"

Alfred's crystal-blue eyes chastened her. "Becky, we haven't seen each other in ages. I promise we'll have plenty of time to discuss your father's situation on the way to St. Louis."

Faith, he was right. She had to calm her nerves. He had risked censure to come to her rescue. She ought to be kissing his feet. "Forgive me, I am not myself."

"There's nothing to forgive. And to answer your question, yes, I've spoken with the provost marshal. He said Tom Sawyer wanted you locked up for your safety while he went off with your cousin to find a traitor. I'd say he's found one already and is wasting his time."

Alfred's wry remark echoed her doubts. Jeff had denied knowing the mercenaries, but why would he be hanging around if he wasn't involved? What was he doing that her father couldn't tell her about?

"You are to come with me." Alfred offered her his arm. "You'll be much safer."

"What about my father?"

"He'll be coming along, too. General Rosecrans gave me the orders for his transfer."

Becky balked at the top of the stairs. "Transfer? Do you mean, as a prisoner?"

"Yes, I am sorry to say. He has to remain behind bars until his trial. But he will be in better quarters in St. Louis, I promise." Alfred took her hands and kissed both palms. "My darling, if I could have stopped the investigation, I would have. I did try. The reports filed by the provost marshal cinched it."

"What reports?"

"About the judge's association with your cousin. Did you know about that?"

If she said yes, it was an admission that could be used against her father. As much as she trusted Alfred, she could not afford to let anything slip that might be repeated, however unwittingly. "My father is loyal to the Union. He had no part in any conspiracy."

"Then he will have nothing to fear." Alfred urged her to move.

She started down the stairs. "His very character exonerates him. He shouldn't be in jail at all. Besides, we have evidence that proves his innocence."

"We?"

He might not be too pleased to find out she'd been roaming the streets with Tom. "I mean Tom. He has proof that those traitorous pamphlets weren't even printed here."

"Has he?" From behind her, Alfred sounded surprised. "By all means, he should produce it. In the meantime, I've come to do what I should've done months ago. Bring you back to St. Louis where you'll be safe."

If only she could be certain of her father's well-being.

Alfred followed her down the stairs. "Be patient, Becky. I know it's difficult, but these investigations take time. In the meantime, you'll be far safer and more comfortable with me in St. Louis."

Becky chided herself. Alfred had only just arrived. What did she expect? A miracle?

When she reached the bottom, she curled her hand around his arm. "Yes, of course, you're right, and I am grateful for your help."

He bestowed an adoring smile. "It is my responsibility and my privilege, as your future husband."

She stopped her tongue before reminding him she hadn't formally accepted his proposal. That was something else they would need to discuss after they were on the boat. Given all that would happen over the next weeks, possibly months, an extended courtship wasn't a bad idea.

The dark interior of the freight house gave way to bright sunlight. Squinting, she searched the freight yard for any sign of Tom. He had asked her to wait for him.

As if she had any choice at the time. He hadn't kept his promises.

The military police guarding the front door chatted with other soldiers who had come in on the steamboat. No sign of Sid.

"I'm surprised the provost marshal gave his approval for my release."

"Why wouldn't he? He agrees that you should go along with your father." Alfred took her arm and guided her toward the wharf where an ironclad side-wheeler was docked.

Black smoke billowing from twin stacks formed ominous clouds in the overcast sky. She was reading too much into it. Her unease could be explained, given the fact that her father would have to suffer through a trial. Unless Tom returned with evidence that would clear him.

"Is the boat readying to leave?" she asked.

"Yes, we need to hurry. My orders are to pick up supplies and return immediately."

"Surely, they'd understand a short delay. I don't doubt Tom will have important information. We should wait." She hung back at the gangplank.

Alfred circled her waist and pulled her along. "Sid will let him know we've gone ahead."

She didn't feel right about leaving. Not yet.

"What about my things? I'll need clothes to wear."

Alfred's smile remained, but his hand moved to her back, applying pressure. "The boat is about to set off. Your father is on it. My orders are to return to St. Louis posthaste. I can *buy* you new clothes."

As soon as they stepped onto the deck, a bell sounded and the plank behind them started to rise. Her anxiety ratcheted up.

She'd forgotten to tell him about Mrs. Bent's murder. What if someone found the letter she had dropped? She could simply deny knowing anything about it and no one would be the wiser. Nothing linked her to it, except Tom's suspicions. Then again, if Anne's correspondence was material to the investigation, she had a duty to report it. Which could get her in trouble. Worse, it would make things look bad for her father.

First, she would consult with the judge and then talk to Alfred. "You said my father was on board. Where is he?"

Alfred patted her hand and smiled. "He's doing fine. I've already told him I'll take good care of you."

His declaration, meant to reassure, rubbed her the wrong way for some reason.

"I appreciate your concern, but I'm not the one who needs it. I am capable of taking care of myself. What I'm not able to do is help my father, not without your assistance. He needs someone with influence who can argue for his release."

"We can discuss it after we're underway."

They ascended a wide stairway to the second level and entered a lavish dining room with glittering chandeliers. The tables and chairs had been pushed against the walls and the space was filled with stacks of crates marked as medical supplies.

Alfred led her out a far door and up another set of stairs to the third level where the pilothouse was located. These cabins were reserved for the boat's senior crew, not passengers or prisoners.

"Are you taking me to see the judge?"

"Later. After we're underway." He opened the door into a well-appointed cabin.

A desk dominated the center of the paneled room, which also had a sitting area. Opposite, another door opened into the bedchamber.

Confusion slowed her steps. "This is where my father is staying?"

"No, this is where you're staying." From behind her, Alfred cupped her shoulders and turned her to face an oval mirror mounted on the wall. "You might want to freshen up."

Her dazed reflection stared back at her. She'd forgotten her bonnet, her hair was a fright, and were those smudges on her face? "Oh dear. I'll need a basin and some clean water."

"I've already thought of that." The Alfred in the mirror smiled. "You'll find both in the bedroom."

A warning bell sounded in her mind. Something wasn't right. She didn't want to be in this cabin alone with him. She needed to see her father. She wanted to talk to Tom.

"This is a mistake."

"I don't make mistakes," the man in the mirror whispered directly behind her right ear.

She whirled around to make certain she hadn't entered the room with a stranger who only resembled Alfred.

He straightened and his well-groomed mustache lifted upward with his lips. "You should find the captain's quarters suitable. He was gracious enough to give it up for your comfort."

"That wasn't necessary."

"Only the best for my bride-to-be." Alfred's indulgent smile didn't calm her nerves. He put his hands around her waist. They were pale and rather small, compared to Tom's. "Finally, we will have a chance to be alone..."

He dipped his head, aiming for her lips.

Becky turned her face away and the kiss ended up on her cheek. "I-I'm not ready for this."

"You're shy, that's understandable for an innocent maiden," he murmured, forging a trail toward her mouth. He wasn't getting the clue.

She put her hands on the front of his coat. "Stop. This isn't appropriate."

He pulled her roughly against him. "That's what makes it more fun," he replied in a husky tone. "I like it when you struggle."

"Why would you find my resistance attractive? Alfred, please..." She pushed at his shoulders. "You're scaring me. Let me go."

He licked her neck, followed by painful little bites. "Ah, Becky," he murmured, "You are as sweet as a strawberry. Meant to be savored. You'll enjoy this, I promise..."

Her stomach knotted with revulsion. What in God's name had she gotten herself into? He had conducted their courtship through letters that were romantic and respectful. She hadn't guessed he would assault her at the first opportunity. He was intent on bedding her before their vows were spoken, and she was no longer certain she wanted to marry him. She wasn't even sure she *knew* him. "Alfred, please. Don't shame me."

"Darling, there's nothing to be ashamed of. You belong to me," he whispered in her ear. "We'll make it legal when we reach St. Louis."

She wrenched out of his hold and took a step back.

The frown on his flushed face warned her that he was losing patience. He might decide not to help her gain her father's freedom if she thwarted his will.

Trying to appear calm, she smoothed the hair he'd mussed back into place. "Alfred, as a gentleman you must understand that I cannot grant you liberties. We are not wed. I wish to see my father now. He will act as my chaperone until we reach St. Louis."

"Don't tell me what to do." Alfred captured her arms and shook her. "The problem is Tom, isn't it? He's seduced you."

Fear banded her chest, making it hard to speak. "N-no, he's done nothing of the sort," she rasped. "This has nothing to do with him."

Tom would never force himself on her. He treated her with respect.

Alfred tightened his hold, his fingers digging into the tender flesh of her arms. "That worthless cur. He shouldn't have gotten anywhere near you. If he continues to sniff around, I'll have him arrested."

Jealousy might explain this antipathy toward Tom, but Alfred's eyes gleamed with something deeper and more primitive. A burning drive to triumph, over her, over Tom, over anything and everything that stood in his way. She'd known men like that. They were the ones who'd started this godforsaken war.

Was this his true nature? How could she have been so blind? She'd wanted so badly to believe in his promises. Just as she had at one time believed in Tom.

Honestly, she should've known better. Both men had done whatever would get them what they wanted. Freedom, in Tom's case. Control, in Alfred's.

He had no intention of reuniting her with her father, at least not until after she succumbed to his seduction. Even then, he might not keep his word. She had to stop this before Alfred ruined her and destroyed any remaining affection between them.

Cradling his flushed cheeks, she spoke softly to soothe him. "Listen to me, Alfred. I have not fallen under Tom's spell. You have nothing to worry about in that regard."

His painful grip on her arms lessened, the fire in his eyes cooled and he appeared to come to his senses. "Of course not. You know we are meant to be together. Your future is secure with me."

No, her future would not be secure until she took control of her own life.

"May I beg a boon? Allow me a moment of privacy so that I can collect myself, and, as you suggested, freshen up. Then I'll be ready to...to receive you. As a lady would a gentleman."

He grazed her lower lip with his thumb. "Forgive me if I've frightened you. I admit to being overly eager to consummate our union. I have longed for you since we were children."

"I understand..." She was an obsession. Love had no part in this.

She gave him one last opportunity to redeem himself. "When you return, will you bring my father to be with me for the remainder of the journey?"

"Darling, you won't need a chaperone. I protect what's mine." He brought her hands to his lips and kissed each knuckle.

It was all she could do to hold onto a pleasant expression. She would not willingly become his property for him to do with as he pleased. Indeed, she would rather remain a spinster for the rest of her life than wed a man who viewed her as a possession.

At last, he released her hands. "There's water in the bedchamber. I'll return after I take care of some important business."

"Take your time." She would prefer forever.

Alfred's friendly smile returned. "Help yourself to whatever is in the wardrobe. The captain's companion left behind some interesting items."

The door clicked shut behind him.

A key scraped.

She rushed over and twisted the knob, then bit back a frustrated cry.

He had locked her in!

CHAPTER TWENTY

The storm hammering the island spent itself, a last, settling into a drizzling rain. Slogging through the mud made running impossible for Tom and the two men with him. An excruciating lope was the fastest they could manage, as they made their way to the place where Jim had seen the black-haired man.

Not Injun Joe or a ghost. It had to be the mysterious mercenary, as human as any other man. He would hold the key to discovering who was behind a plot to frame the judge for treason. With any luck, the storm had delayed loading the ferry and the man would still be there.

Tom's boots squished into the saturated ground. The rifle and extra ammunition weighed him down, and running made his side hurt.

Jeff, unarmed and unencumbered, still lagged.

"We'll run out of daylight if you go any slower," Tom called out.

Jeff lumbered past. "Then don't wait."

"You aren't off the hook yet."

Jeff gave a dismissive wave. "You got bigger problems than worrying about my whereabouts."

"What do you mean by that?" Tom stayed close to Jeff so he could keep an eye on him. The wily Reb knew more than he was letting on.

They emerged from the forest at the other end of the island.

Jim pointed to a quiet cove at the base of a bluff. "They were right over there."

Not anymore.

Tom cursed his bad luck. He remained one step behind the scoundrel. "Let's have a look around and see if they left anything."

While Jim combed the shore, Tom took Jeff with him to explore a cavern beneath the bluff. Under a rocky overhang, he spotted several sets of footprints. Farther back, something larger and heavier had left circular indentations in the sand.

Tom squatted to examine the marks. "Barrels, like Jim said. Must've stored them here."

Jeff hovered. "What do you think is in them? Weapons?"

"Could be." Tom dug up a black rock, half buried in the sand. "What's this? Looks like coal."

Fuel was in short supply, so maybe the Rebels were getting coal from their Copperhead contacts in Illinois. Were they planning to invade using steamboats? They couldn't transport thousands of men across the river before Union artillery gunned them down.

Odd. The lump didn't feel like a chunk of coal.

Tom rubbed the surface with his thumb and a sprinkle of black dust rained onto the sand. Underneath the dust, something sticky... He sniffed. Smelled like tar. With his thumbnail, he scraped off the residue. Wasn't coal. It was a casement made of tin disguised as coal.

Tom used his knife to pry it open and examined the substance inside, touching his tongue to it. *Gunpowder.* His mind raced through the implications.

"Well? What is it?" Jeff asked.

"I'd say it's a homemade bomb coated with tar and coal dust."

"Grenades bound for the Confederate forces?" Jeff suggested.

That might make sense, except, why disguise them?

Tom turned the explosive over in this hand, pondering the significance. "These would be virtually undetectable in a shipment of coal if you weren't looking for them. But why would they go to all that trouble?"

Another possibility made Tom's heart stop dead in its tracks. What if it wasn't meant for the Confederates? If an unsuspecting Union crew shoveled this fuel into their boilers...

"By all that's holy! That delivery isn't going to the Rebels. It's intended for our steamers."

Tom's clothes, still damp from the rain, fairly steamed from the heat of his exertions as he rowed for all he was worth. He had to get back to Sid's office and telegraph the commanders of the District, stop the boats until they located those coal-encrusted bombs. If the plan was to create havoc on the river, the traitors were closer to success than anyone imagined.

Jeff sat near the bow, the brim of his hat shielding his expression as he peered out over the water, with the slack posture of a man who was resigned to an unfortunate fate.

What would motivate him to come clean?

"It would help Becky and your uncle if you'd just tell me who's behind this."

"I don't know," he said sullenly.

"You knew enough to kill those scoundrels in the woods."

"Before they killed you, you mean?"

"You didn't do that to save me."

"If you say so."

Tom grew uncomfortable with the direction of the conversation. Jeff Thatcher refused to fit into a neat profile that would make it easier to hand him over to be hanged. "I say you aren't as innocent as you pretend to be."

Jeff shifted forward to rest his arms on his knees. "Look here, Tom. Use that brain that Becky credits you with having. The judge was stripped of his authority and influence. He's in no position to mastermind a strategy like this one. Whoever is running things has to have access to information about when supplies are picked up and where. He's someone who can issue credentials, forge documents, seize a boat without causing alarm, and arrange to deliver fuel to other steamers. Do you think I can do that? Or the judge?"

What he said made sense, still...

"You aren't telling me anything I haven't already considered. I know the mastermind has to be someone who can infiltrate the Union chain of command. That doesn't mean you weren't in on it."

"Oh, for God's sake..." Jeff shook his head in disgust. "You wouldn't believe the good Lord if he appeared in front of you."

"You aren't the good Lord."

"Yeah? Neither are you, my friend. Like I told you, the men you described aren't locals. Somebody hired them and sent them here. I did hear talk about a scheme being hatched, but I didn't care to know about it. I had my hands full providing supplies, ferrying runaways to Jim, and keeping anyone from finding out."

"Does anyone other than Jim know what you were up to?"

Jeff's silence was answer enough.

"Who are you protecting?"

"The judge caught me in the house stealing blankets. I told him what I was doing and why. After that, he made sure I got the food and supplies I needed. He didn't tell Becky because he didn't want her involved. I agreed it was too dangerous."

Keeping Becky ignorant wouldn't keep her safe.

"Well, she's involved now."

"And whose fault is that you reckon?" Jeff held Tom's gaze for a lengthy moment.

Guilt occupied more space in a man's conscience than all the other emotions combined. In Tom's case, it had grown to the size of a boulder. He hadn't done such a great job of keeping Becky out of trouble either. Fortunately, she was locked in a storeroom at the freight house. Sid would see to it that she remained there, safe.

"You told her I'm a spy.

Jeff removed his hat and mopped his forehead with his sleeve. "It's no secret. Someone put out the word you're a double agent with a price on your head."

Sweat trickled down Tom's face, as he dug his oars into the water. He'd have a hard time tracking down the source of the rumors, which painted him, ironically, as a traitor. "If I was, I wouldn't be hauling your sorry ass back to jail."

"What about Sid?" Jeff asked.

"What about him?"

"He might be the one you're looking for."

Sid might be smart enough, but deception didn't fit his personality. He liked being righteous too much.

"Anything's possible, but I'm not inclined to believe the mastermind is Sid, given what I know about him."

Jeff responded with a slow smile. "Blood is thicker than water."

"Sid isn't acting out of brotherly love."

"I wasn't implying he was. You're the one who doesn't want to believe it. Think about it. He doesn't want you to get too close to the judge, so he arrests him. Then he gets Becky. Then he points you in my direction and sets everything up so it looks like we're the guilty ones."

There were a few holes in Jeff's theory, but Tom couldn't completely dismiss his reasoning. Sid had deftly planted seeds of doubt about his superior, Colonel Sanderson. Sid was aware of things about Injun Joe that Tom hadn't told everyone. As the ranking officer in charge, Sid could easily hire mercenaries. If Jeff could change for the better, who was to say that Sid couldn't change for the worse?

Tom gave another hard pull on the oars. Rowing against the current was making the return trip take twice as long. Desperation drove him to row harder and faster until his hands were blistered and his lungs burned.

Why had he left Becky behind in Sid's clutches? He should've taken her with him.

Jeff stripped off his coat. "Here, let me row awhile. We'll get there faster if we take turns."

"So long as you row faster than you walk."

The big man bent to his oars with powerful strokes and the boat shot ahead. He could go fast when it suited him.

A crack resounded. Something kicked up a splash near the boat.

Someone from the shore was firing at them.

Tom swung his rifle around, sighting two men near the water's edge, who dived into the tall grass just as he took a shot. "Get down!" he yelled at Jeff while he dove for cover.

Bullets peppered the side of the boat.

Jeff jerked to one side, then toppled overboard and sank out of sight.

Tom vaulted over the edge, splashing into the water while keeping his rifle dry. He turned the skiff sideways to use it as a shield. Bullets might pierce one side but not two.

Anxious, he scoured the black water for any sign of Jeff. If they hadn't switched places, he would've taken that bullet.

Tom thrust aside the tormenting thought and leveled his rifle to fire at the men who were hiding behind trees and in the tall grass. He counted four, but there could be twice that many. Best he could tell, they weren't wearing uniforms. Could be rebel guerrillas, loyalist militia, hired killers...

Jeff's head bobbed up. Tom dropped his rifle into the boat, then lunged, grabbing the other man by the collar of his coat. He dragged Jeff over to the side. "Hold on."

With a grunt, Jeff grasped the gunwale. "Give me a gun," he gasped. "I can pick off a few of them scoundrels."

Tom snaked an arm around him and wedged the wounded man up against the hull to keep him from going under. "You can have one of mine soon as I can get it out of the boat. Current is taking us downriver. We'll float out of range of those guns then go ashore."

"They'll follow," Jeff murmured.

Another shot plunked into the opposite side of the boat.

Sure enough, the attackers were moving to keep up with them.

Tom swore. "How bad are you hurt? Can you swim? If we go under and let the current take us, we can make it. I'll help you."

Jeff shook his head. "Don't worry about me. Go. Get Becky. Save her. It's up to you..."

"Damn you, hang on! I'm not letting go."

From the shore came a shout, followed by crashing sounds.

Tom peered over the edge of the skiff to assess the situation.

Flashes of blue appeared in between the trees amidst crackling gunfire. The men who'd been shooting at the skiff fled amidst the blistering attack.

"Looks like we got lucky. Those soldiers showed up just in time."

Jeff released his grip on the gunwale and slipped Tom's grasp, sinking below the surface.

"Wait! Don't let go!" Tom plunged his hand into the water to snag Jeff's coat but came up empty. He couldn't see a thing in the murky depths.

He plunged in and swam, sweeping out with his arms, finding only a strong current that tugged and pulled and tried to take him under. Jeff, being injured, couldn't have fought for long. It had likely swept him away.

Tom resurfaced for air, coughing. He had to swim hard to catch hold of the boat. *Why?* Why had he let go? They'd been on the brink of salvation.

Not Jeff. Once returned, the best he could hope for was imprisonment. His more likely fate would be a public hanging.

Tom rested his forehead on the boat and heaved a broken sigh. If faced with the same choice, he would've let the river take him too. "God rest your soul, old friend."

The troubled man who'd sought redemption would, at last, find peace. Tom suspected he wouldn't be half as fortunate when his time came.

"Tom! Captain Sawyer!"

He peered cautiously over the skiff at the man on horseback hailing him.

Sid. Had he led the charge? Why wasn't he looking after Becky?"

He dismounted at the edge of the water. "Captain? Are you out there?"

"Careful," Jeff's voice whispered.

It wasn't real, only in his mind.

But it would be just like sneaky Sid to act all concerned, then, when his nemesis least suspected, have someone ambush him as he exited the water.

Tom retrieved his rifle from the bottom of the boat. He aimed at the center of the provost marshal's brass-buttoned coat. Someone had started a rumor, put a price on his head, and led him on a merry chase, all the while laughing at him. It was something Sid might do.

Sid splashed knee-deep into the river. "Hey, Tom? Are you all right?"

Less than a second later, Sid tossed his hat and guns on the shore, threw himself into the water, and started to swim toward the boat.

Why would he do that, make himself an easier target? Was he just trying to get close, lure his prey into complacency, then have some sharpshooter kill him?

Tom frowned with confusion as Sid swam directly at the skiff. When he reached the other side, he grabbed hold and slicked his hair back. His eyes widened at the gun pointed at his head. "Don't shoot! It's me!"

A low buzzing started in Tom's ears before a jumble of images flashed through his fevered brain. *Old men in resplendent uniforms seated around a table, a map of the river like the one in Sid's office, Except the man standing in front of it wasn't Sid, it was...*

Tom eased the hammer down. He needed Sid alive. If by some chance, his brother did turn out to be a traitor, he could lead them to the bombs and the others involved.

"I'm fine. Jeff got shot. He's..." Tom struggled to sound normal, but he couldn't mask the roughness in his voice. "The river took him."

A flash of sympathy crossed Sid's face before he wiped all emotion from his expression. That's how he managed the soft part of him he feared others would see. He pretended it didn't exist. It was a trick Tom had learned too. They weren't as different as he liked to believe.

Tom turned the skiff and together they swam toward the shore.

"Those men shooting at you, dressed like bushwhackers," Sid observed. "They might've been trying to free Jeff and hit him by mistake."

"I'm inclined to think whoever sent them didn't want either of us to return."

Sid made no further comment until they reached the shore and dragged the skiff onto the bank. "I got worried and was coming to find you when I heard the shots. Captain Temple arrived on the Athena and showed me an order from General Rosecrans assigning him responsibility for transporting the judge back to St. Louis. Becky went with him."

Shock struck Tom square in the chest. Becky was gone?

He grabbed Sid by his soaked coat. "Why did you let him take her?"

With a muttered oath, Sid broke the hold. "That's what you wanted."

It was what he *said* he wanted, and he should be glad she was headed for St. Louis where she would be safe, even if it meant she would be with Alfred. Besides, her absence would make it easier to focus on finding the traitors without worrying about her getting hurt.

Tom thrust her from his mind. He couldn't hand over the evidence to Sid without being certain his brother wasn't involved. The best way to determine this would be to offer Sid the opportunity to provide assistance and see if he balked. "A ferry picked up a shipment of coal off the south end of Jackson's Island. Did one come in at the docks?"

Sid snatched his hat up from the ground. "Is that what Jeff was up to?"

"We didn't have it right. About Jeff, I mean. He was delivering escaped slaves."

"What? Why would he do that?"

"Crazy as it sounds, he did it because of what happened to Asa Lawrence. No time to explain. We have to find the mercenary I told you about. He loaded those barrels onto the ferry."

"Did you see him?"

"No. Little Jim did."

"Little Jim?" Sid shook his head as if he was having trouble following what was a pretty straightforward explanation. "*Aunt Polly's* Little Jim?"

"He's not anybody's Little Jim anymore." Tom tromped up the bank toward his brother's mount, intending to take the horse and ride like a demon to the docks. "Will you focus on the ferry, please? It's loaded with barrels."

Sid stayed abreast with long strides. "A ferry dropped off a coal shipment earlier today." "The deckhands from the Athena were loading barrels when I left."

"The *Athena*? Is that a Union steamer?"

"No, a civilian boat, conscripted by the army. The senior officer on board was Captain Temple. He signed for the barrels."

Tom's brain was stuck on one fact. "*Alfred* picked up the shipment?"

"That's right. He indicated he'd come up here for that purpose. Why? Are the rebels planning to steal our coal?"

Pieces of a puzzle arranged themselves. A chill went through Tom. Alfred, the general's adjutant...in that position, he would have the influence and authority to pull off the devilish scheme. His motivation? Power. Control. Adulation from half the country. The same things that had driven him as a youth.

And now he had Becky.

"We have to stop that boat! Arrest everyone, including Alfred." Tom reached for the reins held by a private.

Sid grabbed his arm. "Hold on, Tom. Are you sure about this? We can't disrupt traffic on the river and arrest a general's aide without any evidence he's involved. For all you know, Jeff is the one who's lying."

Tom jerked his arm free. "If that were the case, Jeff wouldn't have let me off that island, much less helped me row back at risk to his own life."

"It's too late to stop the Athena. There she goes." Sid pointed at the river.

Tom could only watch helplessly as the steamboat chugged past. Even if he fired shots, a boat manned by federal troops wouldn't stop. They would assume it was an ambush and return fire. And he couldn't risk setting off an explosion if his shots hit one of those barrels. He would have to catch the boat and take control.

He ran down the bank and pushed the skiff back into the river with the clock in his head ticking ominously.

Sid stayed on his heels. "What are you doing?"

"Going after them." Tom shoved off and took up the oars.

Sid grabbed the gunwale and hoisted himself into the boat.

"What are *you* doing?"

"I'm going with you." Sid settled onto the bench facing Tom. "You'll need my help if you intend to board a steamer under Alfred's command."

This was no time to argue, and it might be best to keep Sid close for the time being. If he was part of it, he'd soon play his hand.

Tom glanced over his shoulder and gauged the distance. He had the current with him, but the steamboat would be benefiting, as well. Soon, they come to a shallow bend where the pilot would have to slow down, and that's where he could catch them.

He turned and met Sid's speculative gaze.

"What else, besides coal, is in those barrels, Tom?"

CHAPTER TWENTY-ONE

Becky pressed her ear to the door to listen for Alfred's footsteps. It wasn't likely to be long before he returned, considering the lascivious look in his eyes when he'd left. She propped a chair beneath the knob. It would keep him out, temporarily. Long enough for her to escape.

If she gave him what he wanted, it would leave her little to bargain with, and if she made the mistake of marrying him, she would, for all practical purposes, become his possession and forfeit what few rights she possessed. Neither option appealed to her.

She knelt to roll up the bottoms of the trousers she'd found. Alfred had wanted her to make use of the captain's wardrobe, although she doubted this was what he had in mind. She tucked in the white shirt and stuffed her hair inside a cap. Dressed like this, she could move about the boat without attracting much notice.

She would find her father and formulate a plan. The judge would know what to do.

Becky cranked open the transom window. Alfred hadn't reckoned she had either the sense or the nerve to escape. Tom wouldn't have underestimated her.

Letting go of the sill, she hit the deck with a thud.

Her gaze tracked upward to where the pilothouse soared above the officer's quarters. Its rectangular windows were usually open to give the pilot a clear view of the river from all sides, but this wary crew had nailed up sheets of tin to protect the man steering the boat from snipers.

The pilot's limited view through the lookout holes would work to her advantage.

She sprinted to the stairway and scampered down the steps. Bare feet made no noise on the metal tread. On the second deck, she entered the main cabin where the spacious dining room had been cleared of tables and chairs to make room for crates, which were stacked shoulder-high. She tiptoed down one row and cautiously peered over the top. Her father might be in one of the passenger suites that lined the perimeter of the cabin.

At the sound of men's voices, she crouched down. Whoever they were, they might not think twice if they mistook her for a cabin boy, but she wasn't taking chances. Her disguise wasn't that good close-up.

The men continued talking as they came closer then stopped on the other side of the row of crates.

"Have you secured the shipment?"

She froze at the sound of Alfred's voice and prayed he couldn't hear her pounding heart.

"Yes sir. It's cordoned off on the main deck. We have two men guarding the barrels and the prisoner."

"We'll make for St. Louis full speed. No stops..."

Becky remained still. She heard the creaking of stairs and peeked around to see the men ascend to the top deck. Then she crawled away as fast as she could.

The prisoner. Her father. Downstairs. She had to get to him before Alfred discovered she wasn't in that room.

On the lower deck, she knelt behind a collection of barrels that had been roped off from the rest of the freight. The shipment Alfred had mentioned.

By peering over the top of one barrel, she could scan the area near the engine room. Two soldiers stood with their backs to her in front of the barrels. The rest of the crew, who weren't in uniform, pointedly ignored the guards with silence bordering on hostility.

Another boon—a civilian boat with a crew that resented the presence of federal soldiers. If necessary, she would appeal to them and make it awkward for Alfred to keep her away from her father.

Her gaze halted at a slumped man, who was seated on a crate next to the engine room.

Dear God. It was the judge. They'd bound him to one of the beams supporting the upper deck in a sweltering spot near the boilers. His white hair hung in damp tendrils. He didn't have his hat or coat. Livestock got more respect.

Her shock reverberated into full-blown anger. Alfred had done this. As the senior officer on board, he was in charge. He could've seen to her father's comfort, but he'd chosen instead to humiliate his prisoner. If she needed further proof that she couldn't trust the cad, this was it. He didn't care about the judge, wouldn't defend him. Once they were in St. Louis, her father would be locked in a jail cell, and she didn't trust a military court to administer justice.

What now? She couldn't leave her father bound to that beam, suffering. At the same time, she couldn't stay with him. What good would that do?

She would sneak past the soldiers and untie the judge without being seen, then get them off this boat while they still had a chance.

Impossible.

Becky fought against despair-inducing stasis. Nothing was impossible. Hadn't she snuck out and fooled the patrols, broke into the newspaper office and found evidence favoring her father, delivered a baby, and escaped from Tom?

Tom. What would *he* do? Take advantage of the first opportunity and brazen it out. He wouldn't lose courage.

One of the bluecoats strolled over to the rail, close enough to the edge that water splashing over the side dampened his boots. "This heat's the very devil. Why do we got to stand out here in the sun and guard a bunch of barrels?"

The second soldier joined the first at the railing. "I'll be ready for a swim soon."

Yes! Over the edge was the fastest way off.

Becky pulled her cap lower and started to move, then hunched down when someone came out of the engine room and started in the direction of the barrels. Coal dust had turned the man's face black, which marked him as one of the firemen who tended the boilers.

The rope around the barrels fell.

"Hey, you!" one of the soldiers called out. "Leave that be. Them barrels ain't to be touched."

The sound of the barrel being rolled stopped.

"Wha'dya reckon we orter use to fuel this here boat? Our turds?"

Rumbling started up again.

The taller of the two guards lifted his rifle. "Use your own fuel."

"We have," the fireman shot back. "It's all used up, thanks to your cap'n. He ordered us at full speed. Didn't bother to find out whether we had fuel enough to race the wind."

"Well, you can't have *that* fuel."

Becky peeked around the barrels in time to see the fireman

draw up straight with a belligerent scowl. "Just try and stop me," he told the soldier.

One of the other firemen walked out of the engine room wielding a shovel. A strapping deckhand stopped coiling a rope and picked up a wrench. Should a brawl break out, she could run over and untie her father amidst the confusion.

"So? You gonna shoot us? Who'll keep the boat going?" the brawny fireman taunted. "We need fuel or we'll soon be sittin' in the water like a big ol' wooden duck. Is that what your cap'n wants?"

At this, the soldiers looked at each other. The stouter one muttered something to his taller companion before hurrying up the stairs, presumably to alert Alfred to the crew's misdeeds. The remaining soldier followed the fireman into the boiler room.

It was now or never.

Becky raced over to her father and knelt behind him to untie the ropes binding his wrists.

He craned his neck to look at her. His face was the exact shade of a ripe persimmon. "Wh-what? Becky, what are you doing?"

"Shhh, don't talk. I'm getting you out of here. Alfred is... Well, you were right. He isn't the man I thought he was," she said bitterly. "Neither of us is safe."

The heat and humidity had caused her father's arms to swell, making the rope more difficult to unknot. A pained expression twisted his face. "They'll shoot you if they catch you."

"I'd rather die than be married to someone like that." She picked at the stubborn knot until it finally gave way. After jerking the ropes from her father's wrists, she helped him to stand.

He swayed, unsteady on his feet. "I'm a bit lightheaded."

"Here, lean on me." She threw an anxious glance over her shoulder. No sign of the soldiers yet and the crew was otherwise occupied. "Hurry, Papa, please."

She directed him toward the front of the boat to where the

railing ended. It would be easier to jump into the water, and they would be far enough away from the giant paddlewheel to avoid getting sucked in.

The leadsman on the forecastle glanced over and then turned his back as if he hadn't seen them. *Good.* He could care less about the army's prisoner and wouldn't bother her if she didn't interfere with the workings of the boat.

She nudged her father, who stumbled along, clinging to the rail. "Just a few more steps."

"Stop!"

Becky jerked around at the shout.

Alfred came clambering down the stairs leading from the second level. He hadn't spotted her yet, but she could tell in an instant that he was furious.

"Run!" she told her father. As they came to the end of the rail, she shoved the judge overboard.

A roar shook the boat, then a force struck her from behind, like a giant invisible hand, and propelled her into the air.

Borne aloft, arms outstretched, Becky flew. Her thoughts, as well as her body, were held suspended, outside of time. Flashes of color sped past. A burst of radiant light. Then darkness, as she plummeted into the water.

CHAPTER TWENTY-TWO

Tom bore down on the oars, disregarding the ache in his shoulders and the sweat running into his eyes. He'd lost sight of the steamboat after the Athena disappeared around the bend. But the pilot would soon have to slow down and that's when they'd catch up.

Sid held up the homemade bomb Tom had shown him. "Incredible. It could be mistaken for a piece of coal." His expression—part horror, part awe—fit with having no prior knowledge or involvement.

Tom related his experience on the island and his suspicions. "Those barrels Alfred picked up at the dock are laced with bombs disguised to look like fuel. He's on his way to deliver them to the army docks in St. Louis. He's the traitor we've been looking for."

"Captain *Temple*?" Sid shook his head. "Are you *sure* he's the one who planned it? Someone might've tricked him."

The provost marshal's disbelief wasn't difficult to understand, considering Alfred's vaunted position. Unless Sid was in on it, too. Then, he would try to seed doubt and cover Alfred's tracks.

As hard as it was to believe what Jeff had suggested about Sid's involvement, Tom had to consider the possibility, however remote. Either way, he would know soon whether he was dealing with two traitors.

"We'll find out soon enough."

Sid tucked the evidence into his pocket. "No, Tom. We have to go back and report this. Get help."

"Help? From who? I don't know who else might be involved yet, and we don't have time to turn around."

"If what you suspect is true, you can't stop Alfred single-handedly."

Maybe Sid was just a coward.

"I'm not single-handed. You're with me, aren't you?"

A tremendous boom thundered up the river.

Tom jerked around as the sound reverberated in the humid afternoon air along with the alarmed cries of birds shot from the trees. The forested bend blocked his view, but the blast was unmistakable, as was the massive cloud of smoke billowing into the sky.

God no. It couldn't be. Wasn't possible.

His stupefied mind conceived alternative scenarios.

"That's not the Athena." He waited for Sid's confirmation.

Sid stared over Tom's shoulder with his face frozen in a look of horror.

"It's a different boat," Tom insisted. "Not the one Becky was on. If Alfred left after you set out, he would've been long gone by the time you got to me. We're chasing the wrong boat, I tell you. They put those bombs on another one."

Fear gave Tom a burst of strength. He dug the oars into the water. Becky had to be alive. He refused to believe otherwise.

As the skiff shot into the bend, a gray haze rolled over them, and an acrid stench.

"God have mercy." Sid's harsh whisper rasped against Tom's frayed nerves.

He purposely avoided his brother's eyes and used an oar to swing the skiff around. Shock sucked his breath away.

Nothing remained that remotely resembled a steamboat. All that testified to its existence were splintered planks of wood and debris drifting on the surface of the dark water. It looked like the remains of a giant toy ripped apart by some enraged god who'd scattered pieces from one side of the river to the other.

Tom pulled the oars into the skiff. He braced his boots against the gunwales, steadying himself, as he stood to scan the littered surface for any sign of life.

No cries for help split the silence. No hands waved from the water. Nothing moved, except for small waves lapping the beach where a light strip of sand melted into the dark woods.

He sank back on the bench. "It's not the Athena."

"Tom, look at me." Sid held onto the bench and leaned forward as if the problem had something to do with Tom's eyesight. "That explosion came from the Athena. It was the only boat at the dock. Alfred got on it. So did Becky and her father."

Tom's ears rang from the explosion so he only heard half of what Sid was saying. The half he didn't want to hear. "Did you see her board?"

"No. But Alfred told me she would be going with him."

"Maybe she wasn't on the boat."

"They escorted the judge on board." Sid's implication was clear enough. If her father was on that boat, she would be too.

Sid shifted forward and gripped Tom's arm. "Trade places with me. I'll row. We have to go back. Report this. Get a search started for...for anything that's left."

Tom shrugged off his brother's hand and took up the oars. "I'm going after her. She's out there."

"If she is, you can't help her." Sid grabbed the oar.

The heartless reaction shoveled fuel onto Tom's anger. He tightened his grip and pulled hard, tumbling Sid from his precarious perch onto his knees. "It's a trick, I tell you! Alfred wouldn't blow himself up. He's out there and he has Becky. I'll find them and—

"And what?" Sid ground out. "Alfred won't be blowing up more boats. He won't be blowing up anything. He's *dead*, along with Becky and the judge. Nobody could've lived through that blast. This is a fool's errand, Tom. Give me the oars."

Sid fought Tom for control.

"Let go!" Tom punched his brother's arm.

Sid returned a wild swing and clipped Tom's ear.

In a fury, Tom came off the bench and delivered a blow that knocked the mutineer onto his back. "It's not *your* decision, this time. You already screwed up when you let her go."

Sid's face darkened as he rolled to his side. "The hell I did. You told me she was betrothed to Alfred."

"What difference does that make? You were supposed to keep her safe."

"Me? That's your job, not mine."

The accusation struck Tom square in the chest. Yes, it was his job, yet he'd trusted the wrong man to carry out a simple assignment.

The turbulent storm raging inside built to the strength of a tsunami. He stopped resisting and gave himself to the massive black wave, which launched him at Sid.

"You let him take her! You killed her!" Tom got his fingers around the neck of the miserable cur, ignoring the blows to his head and shoulders. White-hot rage surged through him. Someone had to pay...

Sid's rock-hard knee slammed between his legs.

Pain ripped Tom asunder. He tumbled back with a choked cry —couldn't see, couldn't speak, couldn't do a thing except clutch his balls and writhe in agony. He was drenched. His skin, his clothes. The force that had taken hold and washed over him collected in a pitiful puddle on the bottom of the boat.

The skiff rocked and Sid's furious visage swam into Tom's blurred line of vision. He grabbed Tom's coat and shook him. "What the hell is wrong with you?"

Still dazed and in pain, Tom could only blink. Red, ugly marks on Sid's neck came into focus.

Tom shifted his attention to the smoky sky. He had tried to kill his brother. Like Cain. He owed Sid an apology. After he dredged up the strength to forgive himself for a lapse in judgment.

"Where did you learn to fight dirty?" he rasped.

Sid pushed Tom aside and took up the oars. "You taught me."

"My mistake." Tom crawled to the opposite bench.

He might never father children, which was a good thing. He'd make a lousy father if he couldn't even protect a vulnerable woman. But he wasn't ready to accept that she was gone. Not as long as there was a chance she could be alive.

"We've got to go ashore and search for survivors."

Sid dipped the oars into the water. "If you're so sure about it, we'll take a look."

"Thanks."

"Don't thank me yet." Sid's gruff retort made his expectations clear enough.

Tom gingerly perched on the edge of the seat and leaned over, breathing heavily, his heart aching worse than any other part of him.

Sid wasn't to blame for what happened to Becky. He hadn't put her on that boat. She hadn't depended on him to rescue her. The person responsible was the one she had trusted to protect her.

If she was dead, Tom prayed he would soon follow her. But not until he caught Alfred. Snakes had a way of escaping fire when other creatures perished.

When the bottom of the skiff scraped sand, Tom helped Sid

drag the boat onto land. He nearly tripped over a soldier, who lay sprawled in the high grass in an unnatural position that couldn't have been accomplished while still living.

Further up the shore, something bobbed beneath an overhang of willows. Whoever it was appeared to be moving.

"Look there," Tom called out. "Someone's in the water."

As he splashed closer, reality blew his hope to bits. Waves made the person tangled in the branches appear to be moving. Whoever it was, they were dead.

Working together, Tom and Sid extracted the corpse and laid it out on the grass. The form was too large to be a woman, but it was difficult to tell anything else. Everything had been burnt away— clothes, hair, even flesh.

If they found Becky would he recognize her?

Bile surged up the back of Tom's throat. He twisted around, swallowing hard. After he had his stomach under control, he straightened and avoided looking at the desecrated corpse. Instead, he scanned the area around them.

This section of the river, guarded by high bluffs and dense forests, was sparsely populated. A few remote cabins. Bat-infested caves—so many it would take years to search them.

"If they made it off the boat, they came ashore and fled through the forest," Tom surmised.

"Or got swept under by the current."

Trust Sid to offer the least hopeful prediction.

Tom staunched the moisture in his eyes with his thumb and forefinger. He had a task to finish. Find Alfred. Kill him. Rescue Becky. "You go on. I'll stay here and keep looking. For all we know, they loaded mostly empty barrels and blew up this boat to throw us off course."

"It is possible." Sid finally conceded. "Thus far, they've been crafty as hell. We never suspected this."

"No, but we should have." Tom reached into the tall grass by the water to retrieve a leadsman's pole, then used it to push away debris and reach another body floating face down. Smaller than the others, the clothing on the back seared away with the flesh.

Rolling it over, he released a sigh of relief mingled with guilt. If they had caught up sooner, this boy might still be alive and his mother wouldn't be weeping tonight.

Tom brought the youth to shore, being gentle with him.

Sid's features were fierce as he knelt to smooth back a fringe of wet hair from the boy's face, as tenderly as a father might. "My men will do a thorough search of the area. We'll dredge the river for more bodies."

Would they find Becky? Powerful currents coursed beneath the deceptively placid surface, carrying away the dead, as well as those who might still be alive.

Tom rose to his feet, feeling far too hopeless for someone who professed there was still hope. "What are the chances she survived?"

His brother stood up. Although his arms hung at his sides, his fingers twitched, giving the impression he was on the verge of doing something he would never do—offer a hug. "If you believe Alfred is still out there and Becky is alive, go look for them."

Tom left Sid with the skiff and slogged through the canebrakes toward the trees. He had always bet against the odds, Usually, he won.

Up until now.

CHAPTER TWENTY-THREE

"Rebecca, wake up!"

Becky struggled to prop open her heavy eyelids. Her father's urgent command sounded far away, yet someone stroked her hair, which meant he had to be right next to her.

"Dear child. We must find a place to hide."

He wanted to play hide-and-seek, her favorite game. As a small child, she would duck behind the judge's desk, and while she giggled, he would walk around, swearing he had no idea where she'd gone.

She didn't feel up to playing today. Every muscle resisted movement, and every joint ached. "Umm," was all she could get out.

"You must wake up," he insisted.

She wanted to do as he asked to please him. As she shifted to rise, the achy discomfort erupted into points of pain along her back and legs, which brought her fully awake.

Awareness took another moment.

She pressed her arms into the wet sand to leverage herself

upward and twisted around to get into a sitting position. Gravel poked her hip.

By some miracle, they'd gotten to shore.

Her trousers and shirt were soaked. Had she been in her skirts, the weight of them in the water would've taken her under.

Her father, who knelt beside her, began to cough. A bruise marred his cheek, his wrists were red from the rope they'd used to bind him.

She touched his cheek with concern. "Are you all right?"

He gave her a wan smile. "I am alive, thanks to your quick thinking."

She had freed him and had pushed him off the boat. "What happened?"

"What do you remember?"

"Rushing to the front of the boat, past the railing, so we could jump off." She rubbed her forehead. "I don't recall after that."

Her father helped her sit up. "If you hadn't insisted on going overboard, we would've died in that explosion. It ripped the boat apart."

"Explosion?" She looked around, still dazed. Her mind went blank except for... "I saw Alfred running down the stairs after us. Have you seen him?"

"No. I was more concerned about getting you away from that burning boat. The force of the explosion knocked you unconscious. I managed to catch hold of a piece of siding and hoist you on top. The current aided my efforts and we ended up here."

"Where is here?"

"I'm not sure." The judge grasped her arms and helped her to her feet. "But we need to find shelter before it gets dark."

Pain shot through her right ankle and her leg gave way. Her father caught her before she fell then steadied her with his arm around her waist.

"I must've twisted my ankle." She bent to pick up a piece of driftwood long enough to use as a walking stick. With it, she could support her weight and not burden her father. "This will come in handy."

They made slow progress from a sandy point to a rockier strip of land where scrubby bushes grew at the base of a high bluff.

Her ankle throbbed.

The judge had another coughing fit.

"You must've gotten water in your lungs. Let's sit here for a moment and rest." Becky collapsed onto the trunk of a fallen tree, which appeared to have tumbled over a rocky ledge behind her.

The towering limestone bluffs lined the western shore, which meant they had ended up on the Missouri side of the river.

"How far are we from town do you think?"

Her father ran his hand over his damp hair and sighed. "Several miles I'd guess. Too far for you to walk with that bad ankle. Let's find a place to stay for the night, I'll go for help in the morning."

Help from whom? If Alfred had made it off the boat alive, he certainly wouldn't be in the mood to assist them. Neither would Sid. As for Tom, she couldn't put her faith in a man who'd been sent to spy on them.

A flood of emotions threatened to overwhelm her. She squelched the urge to cry. It would only upset her father. "You can't go back. You're wanted for treason. The soldiers will arrest you—or shoot you."

He wrapped his arm around her shoulders and drew her close. "We'll have clearer minds and can decide what to do after we get some rest."

Dusk had settled over the river, so seeking shelter did sound like the best plan at the moment, although the options were limited. Scaling those limestone bluffs would be impossible, as would reaching the woods before nightfall. Even if she could even manage to walk that far.

"Where can we go?" She tried not to sound miserable.

The judge pointed to a crevice in the rock wall behind them. "That looks promising."

Along this stretch of the river were innumerable caves, most of them unexplored. The entrance to the one her father had indicated might be large enough for a man to fit through, but there was no telling what they might find inside.

"Ugh." Becky shuddered "It's probably inhabited by bats."

Despite her warning, her father went off to explore. He vanished through the opening, and soon after came the sound of tumbling rocks, distant coughing, then silence.

Had he fallen? Tumbled into a pit?

She limped over. "Papa? Are you all right?" she asked anxiously.

"Fine. Give me a moment."

His disembodied voice echoing out of the dark hole gave her shivers. As a child, she had once spent several days inside a cave, lost and without food. The only light, a single diminishing taper, had burned down to nothing, as hopelessness and despair filled her mind to breaking point. Had Tom not been with her, if he hadn't found a way out, her lifeless body would still be there.

"Please come out," she pleaded.

"Why don't you come in? It's rather pleasant."

Pleasant was not a word she would use to describe a cave.

He put his hand out of the opening. "Join me, my dear."

So said Hades when he brought Persephone down to his unholy kingdom. Her father ought to know better.

"Are you sure? Isn't there somewhere else—"

"I'm staying here."

If he refused to leave the cave, then she had to go in to make sure he was all right. But she would not go more than a few feet from the entrance.

Taking hold of his hand, she allowed him to help her over

loose rocks and into the space he'd discovered. "Have you thought about the possibility of a cave-in?"

"It looks secure enough." Her father held up a lit candle secured in a reflective holder. "And I found some useful supplies, this miner's lamp for one."

Who would leave useful supplies behind? Men who lived in caves because they didn't want to be found.

She glanced around fearfully. "Are you sure the previous occupants aren't in here?"

"It appears to be deserted."

He handed her the miner's lamp and busied himself with unpacking a wooden crate.

She held up the faint light to examine the interior. It was at least dry in here, if not *pleasant*. Both of them could stand up without hitting their heads. Although it was impossible to tell the height of the ceiling or whether bats clung to the crevices and would swoop down on them at any moment.

"I haven't gone through everything yet." Her father drew out a blanket. Dust flew as he shook it. "Army issue."

"Likely stolen."

Next came a rusty knife.

"Mm, that's helpful," she said dryly.

"We aren't finished..." He pulled out a belt with a gun still snug in its holster. He checked the cylinder. "Excellent. It's loaded. Might come in handy."

Forget the bats. They had bigger problems.

"Papa," she said in a whisper. "We've stumbled into a guerrilla hideout. We should leave before they return."

He appeared nonplussed and dropped the gun belt onto the blanket. "Look around. Everything is covered in dust. Whoever left this stash hasn't been in here for some time. I say we take the risk. Much better than trudging through the woods in the dark."

"I suppose." She remained uneasy but couldn't offer a better plan, so she limped over to a ledge to sit down. Behind her, the candle's reflection appeared on the surface of a small pool.

Becky tested the water. "Tastes fresh." She quenched her thirst. "They picked a good spot to hide. I wonder where they've gone?"

"With any luck, they'll stay gone." Her father cupped water in his hand and took a drink.

Perhaps the outlaws wouldn't return, but soon the authorities would be crawling the river and shoreline, searching for survivors. She and her father had few options. If they were found, the judge would be arrested and taken to trial. She didn't have much faith in his chances before a military tribunal. "Anyone who isn't found will be reported as perished. We could start over somewhere with new identities."

"Perhaps." Her father's cough crackled. It didn't sound good. If he required a doctor, where would they find one out here?

He propped the miner's lamp in a niche and stretched out on the blanket. "I'm exhausted. Let's talk about it after we get some rest."

Becky remained by the pool, immersed in her troubles. They could trust no one. Not even Tom. He'd betrayed her, lied to her. Granted, he had nearly died trying to protect her, but then he had locked her up, all the while promising safety. It wasn't logical. But with Tom, when did anything make sense?

She heaved a sigh.

"My dear, come get some sleep." Her father motioned to a spot on the blanket next to him.

"You rest. I'll keep watch. My ankle hurts too much for me to sleep."

Her father rolled over. The coughing started up again.

She dug through the crate and found a tin cup, which she filled with water and took to him. "Here. Have something to drink."

He propped up on one elbow and drained the cup.

She placed her palm on his forehead and frowned with worry. "You're burning up."

"I'll feel better tomorrow," he mumbled and flopped onto the blanket.

God willing, he would be well enough tomorrow to strike out for parts unknown. In the meantime, she had to make sure no one could find them.

"Yes, you rest. I'll go outside to erase our tracks."

"Take the gun. In case you meet with predators."

She understood he wasn't referring to the wildlife.

Becky used the rusty knife to hack off the bottom of the wet trousers and used the fabric as a wrap for her swollen ankle.

They would soon need something to eat. Before trying her hand at hunting, she would search through whatever might've washed up along the shore.

By the time she crawled outside, darkness had descended. Fortunately, a bright moon provided ample light. Using her makeshift cane, she made her way toward the clearing at the water's edge.

Above the chorus of frogs and insects, the sound of human voices drifted over.

Alarmed, she crouched behind a bush. It could be searchers or the previous occupants of the cave. Either way, she didn't want to be found. From her hiding place, she could see the shore while remaining in the shadows.

Two men pulled a skiff onto the sand. The taller one wore the uniform of a federal officer. He removed his hat and as he shook it, droplets glinted. When he turned, the moonlight illuminated his face, and Becky's heart tripped.

Alfred.

Was he searching for her?

She wasn't interested in being found. Not by him, at any rate.

The other man wasn't in uniform and wore a slouch hat. He

dragged the rope to a dead branch and tied it to hold the skiff in place. A dark braid swung between his shoulder blades.

She bit her lip to stop a gasp. It had to be the mercenary Tom was looking for. How had that evil man come to be with Alfred?

"What the hell happened?" the man asked Alfred. "I thought you had everything under control."

"Everything *was* under control." Alfred's voice vibrated with anger. "Until those idiot firemen stole one of our barrels. I'd told the crew it was off limits and put soldiers in place to guard it."

"Should've had our men guarding it," the mercenary grumbled.

"I couldn't risk bringing any of you aboard. The provost marshal put out a warrant for your arrest after you had that run-in with his brother."

"Yeah. He's a hard one to kill. Like a damn cat. Already tried three times." The mercenary retrieved a knapsack from the skiff. "We both better hide out until things calm down. There's a safe place nearby."

Panic spurred Becky to grab her cane. If he was talking about the cave, she had to get back to warn her father. But if she moved away from the bushes, she might make noise and alert them to her presence.

"No! I can't stay here. I have to get to St. Louis. Take command of the search for the remainder of those barrels. Before someone else finds them." Alfred grabbed the other man by his arm when he didn't respond. "We're not calling it off. Not now. Not when we're so close to victory."

The mercenary jerked free. "Victory? You're crazy. Whatever barrels didn't blow up are at the bottom of the river, and the federals are onto us. Do whatever you want, but I'm not in anymore—and you owe me five hundred in gold."

"For what?" Alfred bellowed. "You didn't get rid of Sawyer like you were hired to do, and you drew too much attention when you killed the old lady."

Becky put her hand to her mouth, horrified. Alfred had *paid* this murderer to kill Tom?

The mercenary untied the rope. "What fool funnels his communications through women? You never sent the final message. That's what the old lady said. How was I to know whether she was telling the truth or planning to betray us? It's not my fault you lost the shipment. The Knights of the Golden Circle will hold you responsible for that, not me."

The stream of revelations sent Becky reeling. Whatever treachery was afoot, Alfred was right in the middle of it. For that matter, it appeared he was one of the ring leaders.

Alfred leaned over to pick up something out of the boat. "Who's to blame is a matter of perspective."

Moonlight glinted off a blade as he thrust it into his companion's midsection.

The other man grunted. His legs buckled.

Terror paralyzed Becky as the awful scene played out in front of her eyes.

The mercenary fell to the ground. He put his hand up and made a garbled plea for mercy. Without a word, Alfred bent down, the blade flashed again, and the pleas stopped.

He stood and wiped the blade on his trousers before sheathing it, then bent to drag the dead man into the water.

Afterward, he retrieved the skiff and shoved off. The rhythmic splash of the oars became fainter until the sound faded.

Alfred wasn't just a cad. He was a traitor and a cold-blooded killer. He had lied to her, manipulated her, and used her in some mad scheme that involved Mrs. Bent, which had resulted in the old lady's death. Tom might be closer to figuring it out, but he didn't know half of it, and someone had to warn him.

Drenched in sweat and trembling, Becky hobbled back to the

cave. Alfred was mad or desperate or both. He'd let nothing stop him. He had killed a comrade to silence him. If he found her out, he would do the same to her and her father.

She was in no position to warn Tom.

But if she didn't, who would?

CHAPTER TWENTY-FOUR

W hile Sid's men searched the river for victims, Tom combed the shore. Every dock and outpost and broken-down shack. He found no sign of Alfred or Becky.

After a sleepless night, he headed for Sid's office to request that more men be assigned to help him throw a larger net for the missing couple. Every instinct he'd developed from years of impersonating conspirators and scoundrels assured him Alfred would've gotten off the boat and taken Becky with him.

She was out there, somewhere.

On his way up the stairs to the second floor, lightheadedness struck. Tom grabbed the railing. He waited for the dizziness to pass before entering Sid's office.

Sid sat behind the big desk engrossed in paperwork and wearing a frown. Considering how poorly things had gone thus far, a bad mood could be excused.

"I need help," Tom stated.

Sid glanced up without breaking the scowl. "Sleep might help. You look like hell."

What difference did it make? He'd grab something to eat before he left. Rest would have to wait.

Tom shoved his fingers through his untidy hair and straightened his rumpled coat. "There. I don't look worse than any soldier in the field."

"You smell worse." Sid came out from behind the desk. He took his favorite spot, resting his hip on the edge. A posture perhaps intended to put his visitor at ease, which didn't bode well. "Did you find anything?"

Didn't he mean *anyone*?

"No, that's why I'm here to ask for additional men to be assigned."

"Have you been to the schoolhouse?"

"Yes." Tom didn't add the part about losing what little food was in his stomach after he'd inspected the remains of those poor souls.

"Then you'll understand why we haven't found but a few survivors," Sid continued in a soft tone. "Most of them were too badly burned to identify. One survivor, a deckhand, was lucid enough to tell us about the explosion. It occurred shortly after two firemen filched a barrel from a shipment of coal that was supposedly off limits."

The story was more horrible than Tom had imagined. "Merciful God. The crew didn't know what they were transporting."

"We still aren't sure exactly what they were transporting."

"You have the evidence. I gave it to you."

"I have what appears to be a homemade bomb that you brought back from the island and a lot of theories. No other barrels have been found yet. Our resources were focused on recovering bodies and locating survivors. We'll start the process of searching for any remaining barrels later today." Sid reached for something on his desk, a piece of fabric."

Tom's heart skilled a beat. "What is that?"

"My men brought it back It was caught in some debris along the shore." He held out a torn piece of cloth the same blue color as the dress Becky had worn.

They'd found Becky. No, not *her*, just a piece of her dress. The rest of her was gone.

Goosebumps prickled along Tom's arms before a strange numbness took hold. He swayed as he grabbed for the precious scrap.

"Tom!" Sid caught hold of his upper arms. "For God's sake, sit down before you fall over."

Had he been falling? Felt like floating. He broke his brother's hold and dredged up anger to preserve his thin hold on sanity. "Keep looking. She's still out there."

"No," Sid replied, too softly to be considering arguing. "That blast took out all four boilers and tore the boat apart. We have no evidence that either Becky or her father survived."

Tom fisted the fabric. The only physical thing connecting him to Becky. His talisman. "She's a good swimmer. She could've torn her dress while getting away."

Sid distractedly moved papers on his desk. "The church is holding a service today at noon to honor the victims. General Rosecrans and Colonel Sanderson arrived an hour ago, to pay their respects."

"We're not holding a funeral yet," Tom ground out.

"When should we hold it, then?" Sid asked in an irritatingly calm voice. "Next week? Next month?"

"I don't care if they never hold the damn service."

"So, what you're saying is, you want everyone else to put their grief on hold because you can't handle yours?"

Tom longed to slam his fist into his brother's face, but that wouldn't make him feel better, and it sure as hell wouldn't bring Becky back. Instead, he swallowed his rage, letting it burn in his belly. "Why are you in such an all-fired hurry to bury her?"

"You know I'm not." Sid's tone and expression conveyed an earnestness that was even more enraging.

Tom moved to the window before he gave in to his desire to do violence. He stared out at the river, unable to accept that Becky could be gone and he would still be alive. "How can we bury her? There isn't a body to put in the coffin."

"We've recovered all the bodies we could find." Sid's heavy tone conveyed weariness. "You know as well as I do, the current sweeps them under and carries them downriver. Sometimes they turn up. More often they don't."

An awful image formed in Tom's mind: Becky's face, barely visible through the dirty water, her gaze open and fixed, the clear blue turned opaque like the eyes of a dead fish, ribbons of pale hair wrapping her charred body like a shroud.

Regret hollowed him out. His mind replayed the same recriminations it had repeated over and over. If only he'd taken Becky somewhere safe. If only he had stayed with her. If only he had come home and married her years ago.

If only...

"There's something else you need to know before you go over to the church."

"I don't give a damn about anything else."

"Alfred has turned up."

Hearing the name spun Tom around. "Dead?"

Sid stood stiffly, almost as if he were bracing himself for a strong wind. "No. He's very much alive."

Disbelief held Tom motionless. Alfred had survived, yet he'd left Becky to die. He had consigned her to a hellish end while he walked away.

Tom jerked his revolver out of the holster and checked the cylinder with cold precision. "Six bullets ought to be enough to send the bastard to hell."

Before he could reach the door, Sid got in front of him and put his hands out. "Hold on. We need to talk."

"I'm done talking" Tom fingered the trigger. "He's a lying snake, a traitor. I'm going to do what I should've done the minute I laid eyes on him in that damn—"

Prison.

The maddening puzzle in Tom's mind came together with the missing pieces. An officer he'd dreamed about, the one at a fortress, had been Alfred. They'd met there to...to do what? Who else had been there?

"Tom? Tom! Put the gun away."

His brother's command snatched Tom into the present.

"I just recalled something." He holstered his gun. He had no reason to threaten Sid or argue with him, and it wouldn't change a thing. "Doesn't matter. Alfred's a dead man."

Sid gripped Tom by the shoulders. "Will you listen to what I'm trying to tell you? Alfred returned with the general. With orders to take over the search for the remaining barrels."

Tom knocked Sid's arm away. "What the hell? Have they all gone mad? Alfred's a traitor, for God's sake. He deserves to hang!"

Sid transformed from brother into provost marshal, who faced Tom with a stern frown and crossed arms. "He claims *you're* the turncoat."

CHAPTER TWENTY-FIVE

The ferryboats fired off cannons all night, which meant the authorities had given up on finding survivors and were setting off charges to bring the remaining bodies to the surface.

Becky stationed herself near the cave's opening with a loaded pistol, in case Alfred or one of his cronies showed up. Her father's coughing and fevered restlessness would've kept her awake even if fear hadn't. Then, there was her conscience, which nattered nonstop like a carnival monkey.

Tom didn't know about Alfred's treachery. What other fiends might be out there with orders to kill him? His luck wouldn't last, especially now that things had gotten desperate for his enemy. She had to go back and find him. Warn him.

If he was still alive.

Her throat tightened and tears stung behind her eyelids.

Jeff might've led him in an ambush. Her cousin and Alfred might even be working together. She could scarcely believe Jeff would betray her and her father in such a foul manner.

Hadn't she been just as guilty in bringing this about through her ignorance and pride? She'd embraced a false notion of security with a man she hardly knew, yet someone she imagined would be the opposite of Tom.

How true that turned out to be.

She buried her face in her hands, crushed by soul-wrenching despair. No white knight would ride in to save her. She had to dredge up enough courage to go out and do whatever she could to right a terrible wrong, and save Tom if she could find him.

Whatever task she'd done by delivering those letters had resulted in tragedy, for which she would have to pay as Alfred's accomplice, however unwitting. She would claim sole responsibility, and by turning herself in might be believed. Would it be enough to save her father? Tom had promised her he would speak on the judge's behalf with the evidence they'd gathered. He would keep his word.

Her father didn't stir when she touched her palm to his forehead and grizzled cheek. His dry, papery skin radiated heat. If he didn't get medicine and nourishment soon, he wouldn't leave this place alive. She also had to find help. Convince someone to come back and take him to safety.

Gently, she shook his shoulder. "Papa? Can you hear me?"

His eyes opened slowly, the effort almost too much for him. He was in no condition to make the journey to town. But if she revealed her intentions, he would attempt to rouse himself. "I'm going to look for supplies that might've washed up. I'll be gone awhile, so don't worry."

"Be careful," he rasped. "Take that firearm with you."

"I will. You stay here and rest." Tears stung her eyes as she smoothed her hand over his thinning hair and kissed his heated forehead. All her life, he had bravely served as her protector and champion. It was her turn to be brave. "I love you, Papa."

As he muttered in fitful slumber, Becky prepared to leave. She rubbed dirt on her cheeks. Tucked her hair beneath a felt hat she'd found in the crate. A rope worked as a belt for the filthy trousers, and the shirt hung loose enough to conceal her breasts. A good disguise. If she were taller and skinnier, she'd look just like Huck Finn. No one had ever paid him any mind. Come to think of it, that might've been his intention all along.

She located a road leading north and followed it, avoiding contact, not sure of who she could trust. At one point, she managed to crawl into the bed of an old wagon and hid in the hay until it came to stop outside a saloon.

The sun had moved high overhead by the time she reached the center of town. Being on her feet made her ankle swell up again. She stopped to tighten the wrapping, then leaned on the stick to rest a moment and let the throbbing subside.

On the busiest thoroughfare, few people were out. Even stranger, local businesses were closed. Soldiers patrolled the streets in packs.

Had the authorities figured out the explosion wasn't an accident? If so, they might've arrested Alfred. She prayed that was the case.

A sergeant left his men and crossed the street to approach her.

Becky scratched her neck, like a boy might do, while reasoning with herself. If she walked away, it would look suspicious. Even if she were arrested, the soldiers would take her to Sid, who would know what had become of Tom.

"What are you doing out here, boy?" the sergeant asked.

"I come to town to pick up a few things for my aunt," Becky replied in her best imitation of Tom's boyhood accent. "Where'd everybody go?"

"The stores are closed down to honor our dead. Everyone went to the funeral."

Not Tom's. God forbid.

"Whose funeral?"

The soldier gave a huff. "The one for them folks who died in

226

that steamboat explosion. Where have you been these past two days? In a cave?"

"Seems like it." Becky kept her eyes on the pavement to avoid eye contact, which might give her away. "I live aways up the road and don't get out much."

"Well, don't be loitering around here. Go over and pay your respects then get on home."

"Yes sir. I sure will."

She hobbled off, her head down, and with some difficulty made her way up the hill in the direction of the church.

Those poor men on that boat. If only she'd known enough at the time to prevent their deaths.

Her ankle pulsed. Having nothing on her stomach made her feel faint. She fixed her eyes on the towering steeple and ignored the weak, whining voice that begged her to stop.

If Tom made it back alive, he would be at the church along with the rest of the community. She would find him and take him aside to warn him about Alfred. Report what she'd seen and heard.

At the church steps, she hesitated. A ragged urchin in dirty clothing was bound to attract attention inside, where other folks were dressed in their Sunday best. One way to avoid the stares would be to go up to the gallery where the colored folk sat. They were ignored, for the most part.

Stairs posed another challenge.

She opted for a bench overlooking the sanctuary that wasn't occupied. A few of the older women eyed her curiously, but no one stopped her. About the time she got seated, everyone stood to sing a hymn.

With a pained sigh, Becky struggled to her feet using the cane. Much as she preferred to sit, standing gave her a better view of the main sanctuary. She scanned the downstairs pews for Tom.

All of her friends were in attendance. Sally Rogers and her mother held handkerchiefs to their faces as if they were weeping.

Someone else slid onto the pew. A skinny man with skin the color of maple syrup. He wore the type of loose-fitting shirt favored by those who worked the docks and held a floppy hat similar to the one she wore. His frown might mean she should remove her hat. If she did that, everyone would know she was female, not to mention blonde.

She pretended a great interest in the service.

The pastor's booming voice echoed in the sanctuary in a recitation of the twenty-third psalm. On the platform behind him sat three uniformed officers. Two of them she'd never seen before. The third man—merciful heavens, it was Alfred!

How was this possible? Had no one yet figured out that he was a low-down varmint? Or were his superior officers as crooked as him?

Becky hunched her shoulders and lowered her head. Good Lord, she couldn't stay here and risk being seen. "Excuse me," she whispered to the man seated next to her. When he didn't move, she tried being more assertive. "Let me pass."

"Sit down," he hissed. "Lessen you want to get caught."

Becky sat stiffly. She slid her eyes sideways at the young man who'd warned her. He looked close to her age, but she'd not seen him around before. He might be a member of a crew or a dock worker. Had he recognized her or just the fact that she was white and female, and thus likely to be called out?

"We shall now hear from Captain Temple," the preacher announced. "Who miraculously escaped a fiery death."

Miraculous, indeed. Alfred must've dived off the boat to save his own skin.

"He will read the names of those who perished, then I will lead a prayer for their souls."

The hall went silent as Alfred approached the podium. He

paused, giving the appearance of someone who struggled to find words, before clearing his throat. "Thank you, Reverend. I am grateful and humbled to be alive when so many others are gone. Let us stand as I read their names to honor their memories."

The devil pretending to be a saint.

Becky ground her teeth to keep from shouting out an objection.

"Captain Gregory Ives...First Mate Liam Shanahan," Alfred intoned.

She fought a wave of lightheadedness that couldn't wholly be blamed on hunger or fatigue. How many men would still be alive if she hadn't inadvertently aided Alfred?

"The Honorable James J. Thatcher, Miss Rebecca Thatcher..."

Hearing their names read out sent a cold shiver over her skin.

The Negro man next to her leaned over. "Glad to see you ain't dead. Somebody you know is still alive too. Follow me. I'll take you to him."

She swiveled her head in astonishment. Tom must've sent the man. "Where is he?"

"Get outside first." The stranger slid off the pew and made for the back stairs.

She tried to move quietly, yet quickly. It was difficult to keep up with a bad ankle, having to take every stair carefully to avoid slipping and falling.

In the vestibule, she dodged a gaggle of women who had crowded inside. Daylight shone through one of the front doors, outlining the departing man's form as he passed through.

Becky almost made it to the door when a large dark shadow blocked the exit. She put her hand out to open a space to slip past him, glanced upward, then came to a startled halt as a man materialized.

Inky whiskers concealed half his face. Dark half-moons deepened his eye sockets, making him look ten years older and twice as weary.

"Tom?" she whispered.

His forest-green gaze raked her and then widened with shock.

"Not safe..." was all she could manage, before another wave of dizziness struck.

Tom's startled expression blurred into shadows.

Tom caught Becky an instant before she hit the ground. As he lifted her, the floppy hat fell off and her golden hair spilled out, confirming her identity.

His heart started up again like a rapid-fire repeater. Becky hadn't died in that awful explosion. It wasn't a ghost in his arms. He held her warm, limp form.

She came around, looking dazed. "Tom? That man said..."

"What man?"

"Is that Miss Becky?" one of the women nearby asked in an awed tone.

"Praise be!" echoed another.

The ripple of rejoicing jerked Tom back to earth.

Not safe, she'd whispered.

Didn't he know it? Jesus himself couldn't have picked a worse time or place to make an appearance after rising from the dead. The minute the authorities got wind of Becky's reappearance, they'd swoop down like vultures and start pecking away with questions.

Sid had shared the lies Alfred had told the general about her and her father. The provost marshal would have to arrest her. In fact, Sid would've arrested Tom, if he hadn't locked his brother in the office on his way out to find Alfred and shoot him.

Tom exited the church with Becky in his arms, hurrying down

the steps to the street in a race to leave the crowd behind them. This would soon turn into a mob scene.

"Where's my hat?" she murmured. "Put me down."

"Can you run?"

"No. I turned my ankle."

"Then I'm carrying you." To where he wasn't sure yet. He couldn't wait until she recovered her wits. He needed to talk to her before anyone else did and warn her about Alfred's perfidy. "I need to get you out of here."

She stopped arguing and wound her arms around his neck. "I came back to warn you. You're in terrible danger. Alfred is a traitor. He stabbed that man...murdered the widow..."

Becky knew Alfred was a traitor. It appeared she knew more than anyone. Tom attempted to follow her halting explanation while fleeing. "Alfred killed the widow?"

"No, he killed the man he hired to kill you, and that man killed the widow."

"Where's the judge?"

Becky rested her cheek against his shoulder as if the effort the speak had exhausted her. Did silence mean her father was dead or hiding?

Tom glanced behind him. The crowd in front of the church had turned into a swarming hive with blue-coated drones. She could tell him later. They wouldn't have much time alone. Thankfully, her house wasn't far.

He thundered up the steps and through the front door, panting from exertion.

"Did Jeff tell you anything?" she asked.

She didn't know about her cousin's fate.

"Jeff isn't...he's..."

"Dead," she said flatly.

Tom swallowed the knot of guilt in his throat. Another person he should've saved. "Far as I can tell, Jeff wasn't involved in the plot, but Alfred claims he is. Says your father hatched a scheme to blow up Union boats on the river, and you covered it up, and I protected you rather than do the job I was sent to do."

Her face drained of color.

Much as he wanted to, he couldn't spare her pain. "Tell me what Jeff and the judge were involved in, no matter how bad it seems. We'll figure something out."

"I-I don't know. Put me down, please. Let me get some medicine for my father and go back to him. We'll disappear."

If only it was that easy.

"It's too late for that."

Someone hammered on the door. "Open up!"

Sid. Of course. Alfred would've shot first, and asked questions later.

Tom heaved a sigh. He could deal with his angry brother. Sid, who was a stickler for rules, hadn't arrested him. Yet.

He set Becky on the stairs. "Don't move."

She gazed up at him with worried eyes. "I trust you."

Her simple statement of faith shook him to the core. He didn't deserve her trust. He didn't deserve her loyalty, either, but she'd risked her life to warn him. He would move heaven and earth to save her.

Tom slipped out the door and shut it behind him.

His brother stood on the porch with his feet braced as if readying for a fight. "Is Becky alive? What the hell is going on? Did you shoot Alfred?"

"Haven't shot him yet, but I might. Now, I'm going back inside. Pretend you didn't see us."

Sid appeared offended by the suggestion.

Tom reminded himself that lying was *his* specialty. He would try, really try, to stick to the truth. "Yes, Becky's in the house. But I need to talk to her before all hell breaks loose."

"Let me talk to her."

Tom resisted the urge to push Sid off the porch and take Becky out the back. Fleeing wouldn't help her and neither would taking action alone. To keep her safe, he needed the assistance of the provost marshal, who had shown himself to be remarkably forgiving and trustworthy.

As Tom opened the door to let Sid inside, Becky reacted with alarm. "What are you doing?"

"Sid isn't here to arrest you. He just wants to talk to you. Tell him what happened."

Her throat worked in an obvious effort to gain control of her fear. "After we boarded the boat, Alfred attempted to molest me..."

As she spoke haltingly about the encounter and her daring escape, Tom's admiration for her grew, and it had already been pretty high. Now he had another reason to kill Alfred. As if he needed more.

"We jumped off the boat before it blew up and swam ashore a few miles downriver. Alfred showed up later in a skiff with a man who had a long, black braid."

"The mercenary," Tom supplied. "They were together?"

She nodded. "I overheard their conversation. Those barrels had something to do with the explosion. They argued about it. Alfred was angry because the man hadn't killed you like he was supposed to. He murdered the widow because she didn't give him something he was looking for. They blamed each other, then Alfred stabbed the man and dragged his body into the river."

It must've terrified her to witness a brutal killing, and by someone she had loved—or at least liked well enough to consider marrying.

Tom knelt at Becky's feet and enveloped her small hand with his. "Alfred doesn't know you were there?"

"No. I hid behind some bushes."

"What about the judge?"

"He wasn't with me."

"Without proof, we have nothing more than her word," Sid stated.

Tom glared at the provost marshal. "You doubt her?"

"What I believe isn't important. How do you think her testimony will be received in court after she escaped with a prisoner?"

Her bottom lip quivered. "He's right."

Tom squeezed her hand. "We'll get proof. Will you tell us where this happened?"

"No, but I'll take you."

Tom turned to his brother and resorted to begging. "Buy us some time, Sid."

"If you try to take her and leave, I'll be forced to arrest you for conspiracy."

"I know," Tom acknowledged. Faced with the choice, he chose Becky. Over his oath of loyalty, over his life, over anyone or anything, he would always choose her. "I almost lost her once. I won't lose her again."

The door flew open with a loud bang, and Alfred appeared, gun in hand.

Tom drew his revolver as he came to his feet. He would've sent the devil's spawn to hell if Sid weren't standing between them and Becky sitting behind him. Only a tight rein on his fury kept him from shoving his brother out of the way and taking the shot, regardless.

"Put your guns away." The command came from someone behind Alfred.

"I found them, sir." Alfred motioned with his weapon before he made way for two older men who'd come up on the porch.

Tom's memory opened like a book. The shorter one with medals pinned to his chest and a reddish beard was General Rose-crans, in charge of the Department of Missouri. The scowling beanpole, Colonel Sanderson, was head of the military police,

Sid's commander. They'd sent a spy to catch a traitor, who had been in their midst all along.

"Captain Temple, holster your gun," the general ordered.

Alfred's expression signaled frustration. "Sir, this man is a—"

"Stand down, captain."

At the general's sharp command, Alfred finally obeyed.

Tom warily holstered his gun. Becky remained behind him, silent. If she could feel safe enough to share what she'd witnessed, they might be able to get the general to look past his blind spot and consider his adjutant as a possible suspect, which would allow for time to build a case.

"Sir, we were about to arrest Miss Thatcher," Sid started.

No need to rush into that.

"General Rosecrans, may we have a private word with you first?" Tom asked politely.

"Don't fall for it, general," Alfred warned. "He'd lie to his own mother if it'd get him out of trouble."

Tom held the scornful gaze of his adversary without blinking. "Your adjutant seems awful worried that I might have something to say he doesn't like."

A flush of anger mottled Alfred's fair complexion. "Sir, you see why he's here—to help Miss Thatcher escape. He knows where her traitorous father and cousin are hiding. Agent Sawyer went off with Jeff Thatcher. Then let him slip our grasp right before they arranged to blow up our boat. The timing is too coincidental."

"What is it you wish to say?" the general asked Tom.

Accusing Alfred of treason before they had hard proof could backfire, and give Alfred enough information to cover his tracks. Worse, he'd find out Becky was onto him. At this point, he didn't know what she'd seen. Tom intended to keep it that way, for now.

"Jeff Thatcher didn't escape. He was shot while helping me return with a crucial piece of evidence. Someone intended to stop us. As you know, general, I'm here because you appealed for help."

Grant had turned the general's inquiry over to Alan Pinkerton and asked if one of his agents could check into it. Tom hadn't been willing to simply accept the judge's guilt. His instincts had served him well, even if his memory hadn't. But now the facts were coming back.

"What makes you think he's not on our side?" The general asked Alfred.

"Look at the purposeful blankness in his expression. He's keeping secrets." Alfred rubbed his chin, playing his part well. "Give him a chance to prove his loyalty. Let him tell us where to find the judge."

"That sounds reasonable," the general acknowledged.

Rosecrans might not be a bad egg. Just misinformed and unwilling to consider the possibility that a snake had slithered into the henhouse right under his nose.

They already suspected the judge and would simply use him as a scapegoat. As for Becky, she wouldn't willingly give her father up, and when she refused, they'd lock her up and charge her with treason. An outcome that would suit Alfred's plan perfectly.

"Well, Mr. Sawyer?" Rosecrans prompted.

What answer would buy some time and keep Becky out of jail?

"Miss Thatcher is fortunate to have survived the trauma. Her father wasn't so lucky."

Becky's fingers tightened on his arm and she stepped off the tread. Or had she slipped off? Tom caught her around her waist to support her weight to avoid further injury to her ankle, and she sagged against him. Now it became clear. She was going along with his fib with an impressive show of grief.

"Is this true?" Alfred's eyes narrowed, sharpening the gaze he aimed her direction. "Your father didn't survive the blast?"

"We made it off the boat before the explosion, but then he..." Not finishing left the others to draw their conclusions, the obvious one being the judge had died, and Becky, left in a state of shock and grief, ought to be pitied and treated with tender care rather than interrogated like a criminal.

Sid snapped his gloves across his hand. The sudden noise got everyone's attention. "It appears that Miss Thatcher has injuries and requires medical attention. We can call the doctor after she's—"

"Tucked into bed," Tom suggested.

"I'll post a guard," Sid added.

An acting troupe couldn't have done a better job.

Tom savored the moment. Sid had come through at the right time. With Becky tucked away safely in her bed, it would free them to search for evidence. Evidence that would clear her and her father and put Alfred in chains.

"Just a moment," the colonel said. He'd stood off to one side and hadn't spoken a word during the exchange. He reminded Tom of a predator awaiting the right moment to spring on unwary prey.

Tom tightened his hold on Becky.

"I agree," said the colonel. "Leave Miss Thatcher here, under house arrest. But I suggest remanding Mr. Sawyer to a jail cell until we learn the location of the traitor he seems determined to protect."

CHAPTER TWENTY-SIX

Two of Sid's guards ushered Tom out of the house while another escorted Becky as far as her bedroom door. The moment it banged shut, she promptly hobbled to the window.

A soldier in the backyard gazed up at her.

She wouldn't be leaving that way anytime soon.

Becky sank onto the side of the bed with her heart throbbing all the way to her foot. She was a prisoner in her own house. Tom had been hauled off to jail for protecting her. Worse, Alfred was still free...and if he found her father...

She fought back an onslaught of tears. What use were they if no one was around to see them? Although her weak-woman act hadn't worked on that awful man who'd ordered Sid to arrest Tom.

A firm knock came at the door.

If someone had sent for a doctor, she could appeal to him for help.

She scooted back on the bed and propped herself up on pillows. Gently, she brought her legs over, grimacing with pain. Her puffy ankle was still wrapped with a dirty cloth. "Come in."

The door swung open. Alfred stepped inside.

"What—" she had to swallow before she could speak louder than a whisper. "What are you doing in here? It's highly inappropriate."

A sly smile crossed Alfred's face. "That ruse won't work again. I'm not going anywhere until after we talk."

God forbid he had somehow found out what she'd told Tom and Sid.

She stiffened her spine and put on a brave front. "There are guards posted outside. If you touch me, I'll scream."

His gaze raked her and his nostrils flared. "Who said anything about touching you? You're dirty and you stink."

Far from offending her, his insult gave her comfort.

"If rolling in filth keeps you at bay, I should ask for a bucket of it to reapply at regular intervals."

He dragged a chair from her dressing table to the side of the bed, sitting down beside her. "Why do you pretend to find me so distasteful?"

Pretend? She didn't have to pretend. He revolted her. He had killed a man in cold blood and ordered the death of another. It appeared he wasn't aware that she'd been witness to his crime, which meant Tom and Sid, bless them, had kept her testimony to themselves. For the time being. Until she could escape, she had to keep up the act.

She pulled the coverlet over her legs to reinforce his misperception that her discomfort stemmed from maidenly modesty.

"You all but forced yourself on me."

He managed an expression of mild chagrin. "I only wished for us to spend time getting to know each other better."

"It wasn't a conversation you wanted."

"Oh, all right. Will you condemn me for being eager to be with you? You didn't have to panic. I can be quite reasonable." Alfred crossed his leg and folded his hands in a posture reflecting easy elegance. If she didn't know he was a scoundrel, she might be fooled into thinking he'd only been a little naughty.

She turned her face away before he could detect her deception.

"Becky, I understand. You were frightened." His voice softened. "I'd scold you for fleeing, but you inadvertently saved our lives when you jumped off the boat and I went in after you."

No, he hadn't cared a whit about her. He had gone over the edge because he knew what was about to happen. She had to be on the alert for anything he said that would give him away and prove his treachery.

"What did you expect? You tied my father to a post like a common criminal. You didn't mean what you said about helping him." With her head still down, she shifted her eyes sideways to see his reaction.

Alfred shifted his foot to the floor and leaned forward with a hard set to his jaw. "The judge and his nephew committed treason. I know that's hard for you to accept, but by keeping his location a secret, you only make it more difficult for those who want to protect you."

He'd issued a veiled threat. Tom would suffer if she didn't cooperate.

Fear beat against the inside of her chest like a trapped bird. She couldn't let on her father was alive or he wouldn't be for long. "Tom told you what happened."

Alfred leaned back and withdrew a silver case from his breast pocket. He removed a thin cigarillo and lit a match. "I'd rather hear the details from you. If the judge is dead, I presume you want a proper burial."

He blew a wave of acrid smoke in her direction, which produced real tears.

She put her face in her hands to make her grief more believable. "I can't speak of it now, I can't..." she whispered in a broken voice. "It's too painful."

"Then I shall return. After the doctor has a chance to give you something to calm your nerves." His casual remark lifted the hairs on the back of her neck.

He would not hesitate to ask the doctor to drug her.

"There is another thing," he said, leaning closer. "It's small, of no particular consequence, but I need you to tell me what happened to the last letter you received. Did you give Anne's note to the old lady?"

Mrs. Bent had been murdered because she hadn't delivered a message, presumably something in Anne's missive. Whatever it conveyed and to whom, Alfred would kill to keep it a secret.

Becky used her shirtsleeve to wipe away tears, thus relieving her from having to look directly at Alfred and possibly give herself away. "Yes, I took it to her." That wasn't a lie. She'd just arrived too late. "Does...does it have something to do with why someone killed her?"

Alfred's smile was too broad and stiff to be sincere. "Of course not. I only worry about the wrong people finding out that you were delivering letters from a *secesh* prisoner to her mother. They might use it against you."

"What about you?"

His eyes took on a flatness that scared her more than his insincere smile. "I'm not the one who delivered the letters. I'll swear I had nothing to do with it. It will be my word against yours. Who do you think they'll believe? The general's adjutant or a woman with a traitorous family?

The fiend. He would let her hang. In fact, he would send her to the gallows with false testimony.

He put his hands on the side of the bed, gripping the covers as if he might tear them off. "Be reasonable, Becky. You know I can't afford to go down with the proverbial ship. But you have nothing to worry about as long as you don't mention the letters. And for my part, I will, as I promised, try to help your father avoid execution."

More lies.

"He's past caring," she whispered.

"If you say so." Alfred unfolded himself out of the chair and walked to the bedroom door.

A moment later, another man appeared. He carried a black bag, but he wasn't the kindly old doc who had treated her as a child. This sawbones had hard eyes and a brutal mouth.

"Doctor, this is Miss Thatcher. She's had a traumatic experience and is suffering from hysteria."

"I am not hysterical."

The doctor gave Alfred a knowing look.

"My poor dear." His countenance fell into false sadness. "She was on the boat that exploded and barely escaped with her life. Sadly, she suffers from a delusion that her father is dead and that she is in danger."

"I *am* in danger," she insisted to the doctor. "And the only thing I'm suffering from at the moment is *that* man's presence."

Alfred sighed. "She and I are to be married."

Her face burned with anger and embarrassment. He made her sound like a nincompoop. "Liar! I cried off. You would have assaulted me if I hadn't escaped."

The doctor shook his head, sadly. Did he believe her or did he think she was mad? He set his bag on the bedside table and lifted the sheet covering her feet. "Hmm," he murmured. "Looks like you've sprained your ankle. Does it hurt?"

Yes, but she wouldn't admit it or take whatever he had to give her. "It's nothing of concern. If I keep it propped up, it feels better."

He straightened. "Are you the expert now?"

Becky gritted her teeth to keep a civil tongue in her head. Insulting him for being a pompous ass wouldn't make him go away. She cast her eyes downward and adopted a meek demeanor. "No, doctor. I just don't wish to bother you. I don't need anything. Only rest."

He withdrew a bottle, uncorked it, and poured some of the contents into a measuring spoon. "A little laudanum will help you relax."

She just bet it would. Then she'd be unable to think straight or to get away when the opportunity presented itself. "Laudanum makes me ill. I assure you, that will be worse than having a sore ankle."

When he offered the spoon, she pressed her lips together.

His thin lips stretched into a humorless smile. "Now you are acting like a child, and you know what that means."

She didn't but wasn't opening her mouth to ask.

He pinched her nose hard, jerked her head back, and when she cried out in pain, shoved the spoon halfway down her throat.

Becky choked and sputtered. Some of the medicine dribbled down the front of her shirt, but most of it burned a path down her gullet.

"There. Now you'll be able to rest." The devious doctor packed his medicine.

Her face, already warm, grew flushed and her eyes watered. Sadistic quack. He had nearly strangled her. In between bouts of coughing, she rasped. "Get...out..."

His grizzled brows drew a sharp V on his forehead. "Young lady, you should be thanking me for coming here. I was tending to men suffering far worse than you.

Had he shown an iota of caring about her, or those men, for that matter, she might've felt guilty. As it was, he behaved just like Alfred, assuming since she was a female, she should be treated like a child.

The doctor snapped his bag shut and exited.

E.E. BURKE

Alfred closed the door with a firm click. "Dearest, don't be angry. It's for your own good."

He sat in the chair next to the bed and reached for her.

She slapped his hand away. "Go away and leave me alone. You are behaving like a beast."

Rather than leave, he settled back in the chair.

She had to get out of there before her thinking got muzzy and she wasn't able to control her tongue. Tom seemed to trust Sid. For certain, she would choose to deal with the provost marshal over Alfred. "Take me to the jail. I wish to confess my crimes to the provost marshal."

Alfred merely smiled. "Becky, you need to calm down. There's no need to confess anything. I told you I'd take care of you."

She would as soon put her faith in a poisonous snake. If he wouldn't take her, she would get there on her own; off went the covers and she swung her feet over the edge of the bed. Someone had confiscated her walking stick. Never mind, she would crawl on her hands and knees.

"What are you doing?" Alfred grasped her around the middle.

"Help! Help me!" She clawed the floor, trying to get to the door.

With disgusting ease, he flipped her over and scooped her up.

She beat him with her fists. "You can't keep me prisoner."

He dropped her onto the bed.

A wave of dizziness struck and her stomach roiled. She groaned and gagged.

"Good grief." Alfred dragged her into a sitting position. Fisting his hand in her hair, he forced her head between her legs. "Breathe deeply. It'll pass."

All his rough ministrations accomplished was to give her a pounding headache.

"Let me go," she gasped.

A moment later, he pushed her on her back. Either he was far

244

stronger than she imagined or the medicine was making her limbs flop about like a marionette.

Her eyelids drooped. She forced them open and licked her lips to rid her tongue of the cottony thickness. "You...can't...get away... with this."

"You and I both know I can. And I will find your father, with or without your help."

Alfred had never liked going with the other children to explore the caves. He'd been too scared. He would have no idea where to search. The only person who might know about that secluded spot was her cousin or Tom.

"You'll never find him," she whispered. "Tom doesn't..."

Alfred leaned forward. "Tom knows where he is?"

Oh, he thought he was so sly.

"No, he doesn't know either...." She started to laugh. It was funny. No one knew where her father was except her, but if anyone might figure it out, it would be Tom. Never Alfred.

Her giggles dissolved into a snort. "You put him in jail. He can't find anyone if he's in jail..." More giggles. She was almost enjoying this game of cat-and-mouse.

"Only Sawyer can find him, and yet, he can't..."

"That's right, he can't."

"If we let him out, he will."

"Nope. He won't." She smiled, knowing she'd won. She could roll over and sink into the soft darkness and forget about Alfred. Forget about everything, except blessed sleep.

"Tom won't betray you."

She shook her head. *No.* Tom had promised he would protect her.

For some reason, Alfred began to chuckle. "Oh, Becky. Thank you for giving me the rope to hang him with."

∽

The jail stank with a mixture of excrement, sweat, and human misery. Tom would've paced, except for the prisoners who were sprawled everywhere. Everywhere, that is, except next to the slop bucket. He stood close to the bars to find a pocket of air that wasn't poisoned.

His discomfort was nothing compared to what Becky must be suffering. He had tried to win a reprieve for her, but things hadn't turned out the way he anticipated.

"You wouldn't have ended up in jail if you hadn't tried to cover for the judge."

Sid's admonishment rang in his ears. In hindsight, he could admit his brother was right, but he'd done his best to protect Becky.

"If you'd let me lock her up, she would be in my custody, not where Alfred can get to her."

Sid's logic could be so damned annoying.

Tom rested his heated forehead against the cool iron. His brother would come back soon and let him out. He'd heard Becky's testament against Alfred. He knew she was in danger.

Across the room, two guards played cards on top of an over-turned barrel. They jerked to attention at the sound of boots on the stone steps.

A moment later Sid appeared, followed by his boss.

Tom wrapped his arms around the outside of the bars. "It's about time," he muttered.

Sid bypassed the guards. He didn't ask for the keys. Maybe he had his own set.

The colonel approached the cell. Sid stood at a respectful distance but close enough to observe and hear what was said. He wore a mask of sobriety.

Tom's confidence in his brother evaporated.

"Agent Sawyer, are you ready to tell us where Judge Thatcher is hiding?" the colonel asked.

Tom had lied, and like most lies, this one had come back to bite him. "What makes you think he's hiding?"

"Miss Thatcher has told Captain Temple that only you know where to find him, which leads us to believe that he is alive and in hiding. As you know, aiding him would make you his ally, and you will be charged with treason if you refuse to cooperate."

Tom longed to reach through the bars and grab the beanpole colonel by the throat. "I don't know a damn thing about where the judge is. Temple no doubt coerced her or threatened her. She told me he accosted her."

Taking an attack on Alfred too far at this point would potentially put Becky in more danger. The timing was everything. But they were running out of time.

He pinned Sid's with a hard gaze. "You know she's innocent. You know her father didn't do anything wrong. It's an obvious setup. Tell him, damn you!"

A dark flush crept up Sid's neck into his face. "Tom, tell us what you know. I'll commit to ensuring Becky's safety."

If he'd cared about her, he would've found a way to retrieve her.

"Your commitment isn't worth squat."

"Do you understand we could hang you for treason?" the colonel asked.

Tom didn't care about his life. It wasn't the one he needed to save. "Here's what I know. There is a traitor among us. One of his henchmen framed the judge as a distraction. I gave Sid evidence to support that. Jeff is a red herring. He's not involved in this scheme any more than his uncle. He's been busy ferrying runaway slaves across the river."

"A rebel? Ferrying escaped slaves?" The colonel chuckled. "Yes, your brother told me what you reported. Ridiculous story. You can't expect anyone to believe it."

Sid did. Or had he laughed, too, when he conveyed the information?

Tom held his brother's sober gaze as he answered the colonel. "If Jeff was involved in seeding coal shipments with bombs, why the hell would he help me get back here? Let me out. I'll give you the evidence you need to find the real traitor."

"Who is he?"

Tom hesitated. He couldn't risk it, yet he couldn't afford to wait.

"Alfred Temple," Sid stated.

"Captain Temple? The general's adjutant? That's ridiculous," the colonel scoffed.

If Sanderson was in on the plan, he'd go straight to Alfred. Sid didn't think so or he wouldn't have spoken up.

"Pardon, sir. Captain Temple is in a perfect position to pull off a scheme of this magnitude."

God bless Sid.

The colonel gave the provost marshal a withering look, then he turned to Tom with narrowed eyes. "Captain Temple told us you might try to pin this crime on him. He had warned the general not to trust you with this mission."

"Hell, he did one better. He hired an assassin to go after me." Tom grabbed the bars to keep himself from reaching for the colonel's throat and getting himself shot. "Tell him, Sid. Tell him what we figured out."

Sid's eyes cut from Tom to the colonel. "Agent Sawyer believes Captain Temple gave the order for that ferry to pick up the tainted fuel off Jackson Island and deliver it to our dock. He did pick it up, but I haven't found the order yet. It appears not to have come through the usual chain of command."

That wasn't what Tom wanted to hear. Still. "He could've put anyone's name on it. He wouldn't use his name anyway. He conscripted a civilian boat to pick up the fuel."

The colonel's pale gaze grew frigid. "Captain Temple wasn't

here to pick up fuel. He was sent down to collect a shipment of medical supplies. He also had permission to transport a prisoner, Judge Thatcher. When he arrived, he was given an order directing him to pick up the fuel as well. That order appears to have been forged by someone here."

Tom stared at Sid. "Who do *you* suppose forged it?"

"We're looking into it," Sid said stiffly.

Meaning what? Stalling?

"Want to know my guess?" Tom said to the colonel. "That mercenary you hired."

The colonel's color darkened. "What are you accusing me of doing, Mr. Sawyer?"

"I'm suggesting that you might've been used, too. But you're intentionally putting on blinders because you don't want to admit you were played."

"And you are good at making up stories. You might be interested to know that Captain Temple also swears Miss Thatcher is innocent and is determined to protect her from the likes of you."

If these idiots allowed Alfred to take Becky, she would be at the mercy of a monster.

"For God's sake, bring her in," Tom pleaded. "Talk to her. Alone. She'll tell you. She doesn't want to go with Alfred. She's terrified of him."

"Will you tell us where to find Judge Thatcher?" the colonel repeated.

"I don't know where he is!"

"We're done here." The colonel motioned for Sid to follow.

Panic flared in Tom's chest. They were leaving without releasing him. Becky would be defenseless.

"Don't let Alfred take her!" Tom yelled.

The two men retreated up the stairs without looking back.

"Damn it, Sid! Get back here and let me out!" Tom banged his hand against the bars. Pain shot through his palm. He welcomed it...anything to distract from the guilt eating him alive.

"If anything happens to her—" Tom's voice cracked. "I'm holding you personally responsible."

They'd gone. He was talking to no one but himself.

CHAPTER TWENTY-SEVEN

R ays of light slanted at sharp angles across a rough-hewn plank floor, illuminating gaps between the boards. Becky stared for at least a full minute in utter confusion. This wasn't her bedroom. It wasn't her bed either—she was stretched out on a cot.

She twisted around and sat up. Her head might've fallen off if she hadn't grabbed it, and her stomach threatened to revolt. After the dizziness passed, she took inventory of her surroundings.

A collection of furniture and crates climbed the brick walls. The storage room where Tom had left her before. Who had brought her here?

The direction of the light shining through a partially boarded-up window would indicate it was late afternoon. She must've slept for a few hours after the doctor gave her that awful medicine. The last thing she remembered was Alfred's malicious snicker in response to something she'd said.

She pressed her fingers against her aching temple. Surely, she hadn't told him where her father was hiding. Tom was the only person who could figure it out and they'd locked him up...

Her breath caught. *No.* Tom didn't know anything.

But Alfred thought he did, and he'd use that information to get Tom hanged as a traitor.

Becky tossed aside a quilt someone had draped over her and hopped to the door, keeping her injured leg bent. The door was bolted from the outside. Using her fist, she banged against the hard wood and yelled. "Help! Someone, please!

She kept banging until the bolt clanked.

The door swung open and the provost marshal appeared. His enigmatic expression told her nothing, as usual. As much as she distrusted Sid, she was frankly relieved that he had come after her and not Alfred. "What is it, Miss Thatcher? Are you in distress?"

"If you call teetering on a single foot distressing."

He offered her his arm.

She accepted it. Would he help her beyond physical support? "I didn't tell Tom where to find my father.

Sid's steady gaze didn't waver. "Yes, Tom said you didn't."

And it appeared his brother believed him.

"Alfred thinks I did."

"He suggested as much."

Becky's stomach dropped. The spider had woven another lie into his web and convinced them to arrest her. "Did he turn me in?"

"No. I insisted on bringing you here for everyone's peace of mind."

She had no idea whether Sid meant it as a favor to her or Tom, but she was glad he'd gotten her away from Alfred. "Thank you."

"You're welcome." His lips didn't betray a smile but there appeared a slight softening in his eyes. He might not be on her side, but it appeared he wasn't her enemy either. "Are you feeling well enough to have a conversation?"

"You mean an interrogation."

"That's up to you."

"Who will be part of this conversation? Tom?"

"Tom has to remain in jail. He will be safer there."

Was Sid saying that to win her confidence? She wished she could trust his intentions, but her judgment had failed her too many times.

"Was it the colonel's idea to punish Tom or yours?"

"Tom has a peculiar way of punishing himself."

Sid's insightful remark took her aback. Indeed, Tom's propensity for finding trouble hadn't ebbed, and his involvement with her wasn't making his life any easier. He risked his life to protect her. One way or the other, she would make sure he didn't get blamed for her failings.

"And Alfred, is he to be part of this discussion?"

"Yes. He said he fears you might implicate yourself to save your father."

Her skin grew chilled despite the stuffy heat in the room. Alfred cared nothing about her or her father. He would be there to make sure she didn't betray him. She had to steel her nerves and think about what she would say and how to challenge his story.

He'd dangled a lure—her father's life, in exchange for her silence about the letters. Only a fool would take the bait. Alfred would throw her and the judge to the wolves if it would benefit him.

Becky straightened her dirty sleeve. She tucked loose strands of hair behind her ear. Would that she could bathe and make herself presentable. They might not judge her so harshly if she appeared womanly and vulnerable. She tried her bad foot and winced at the sharp pain. "I'm sorry. I'm having difficulty walking."

"Come this way." Sid carefully ushered her to the cot where he bent down and pulled a cane out from underneath. "I put this here earlier. It might help."

Sid had put a cane there? And the quilt, too. His thoughtfulness both surprised and touched her.

"Thank you for your kindness."

"I wish I was able to do more, Miss Thatcher."

Heavens. He meant it, and in his way, he was trying to help Tom. Unlike Tom, Sid wouldn't bend rules and break protocol when it suited him. Neither would he step out of his role as provost marshal and spring his brother from jail. No. Only she could save Tom. She must confess to being Alfred's co-conspirator. Throw herself on the sword and pull him down with her.

"Whatever happens, will you promise to testify on my father's behalf, based on the evidence Tom gave you?"

Sid's dark gaze didn't waver. "I will."

She had to rely on someone to help her father. Tom would've told her to trust Sid.

"I will tell you where to find him. He needs medical care. Don't send that awful doctor who drugged me."

"I'll send a qualified physician," Sid assured her.

"Then, I'm ready." She smoothed back the tangles, knowing it was useless. They wouldn't pity her. She'd pray that something would come to her which would erase their doubts and convince them she was telling the truth about Alfred.

The provost marshal secured his hat and offered Becky his arm. "May I give you some advice, Miss Thatcher?"

"Of course."

"Tell the truth. I have it on good authority that the truth will set you free."

Was he serious or joking? He'd said it with a straight face so she assumed he meant it in earnest. She wasn't so naive as to think a truthful testimony would result in her freedom. More likely, she'd be hanged as a traitor. But if in the process she could free two people she loved, it would be worth her life.

The authorities were waiting when Becky entered Sid's office. The colonel sat in the provost marshal's chair and didn't give it up after Sid ushered her inside. The general stood and offered her his chair, one of two wingbacks in front of the desk. Alfred occupied the other one.

Becky clutched her hands in her lap to prevent them from trembling.

"You look pale. Are you sure you're up to this?" Alfred poured from a pitcher on the desk into an empty glass and handed it to her.

A glass of water sounded heavenly. She was parched. Becky started to reach for it, but then stopped. He might've put something in it that would make her thinking muddled.

"It's water." Alfred took a drink. "Cool. Refreshing."

If he was willing to drink it, perhaps it was simply water.

She took the glass and drained the contents.

Alfred leaned back in his chair and smoothed his finger over his mustache. At ease, confident, and sure of his success. He didn't believe she would say anything that might get him into hot water.

The colonel picked up a small container smeared with tar and bits of black dust. "Do you know what this is?"

"No," she said truthfully.

"It's a bomb, Miss Thatcher. Disguised with tar and coal dust to blend in with our fuel. Agent Sawyer says he found it on Jackson's Island. He believes a shipment containing more of these bombs was loaded aboard the Athena. Whatever you can tell us about it would help us identify those responsible for a heinous crime."

Becky stared in horror at the black thing the colonel held out for her inspection. Was that what had caused the explosion? The nightmarish memory suddenly made sense, as did Alfred's conversation on the beach with a doomed man. She didn't dare look at the devil or she would leap to her feet and flee in terror. "I...I don't know anything about it."

"Indeed," the colonel said with obvious disdain. Bald, with a heavy brow over small, round eyes and a sharp beak of a nose, he reminded her of a vulture, waiting to feed on her carcass.

"If I had known there were bombs on that boat, why would I willingly board?"

"To set your father free before he could be implicated," the vulture answered for her.

The general had gone over to the window. To the casual observer, it would appear he was more interested in looking out at the afternoon shadows. Or he had made up his mind.

"Did you see or hear anything while on board that would've made you decide to jump off the boat?" the provost marshal asked in an even tone.

No doubt they had heard some story from Alfred. Sid was giving her a chance to offer a different explanation.

"I left here with Captain Temple because I trusted him to protect me. After I was on board..." She had to be careful to present the facts—the truth, as Sid had advised her—and allow the others to draw their conclusions. "He refused to allow me to see my father. Rather, he pressed his attention on me, and when I rebuffed him, he locked me in the captain's quarters. Out of fear, I decided to escape."

Alfred reached over, took her hand, and squeezed it hard enough to warn her. "We've been through this. You misunderstood my intentions. I locked you in your room to prevent you from doing something foolish."

Becky withdrew her hand from his grasp and turned slightly away from him, continuing her story without commenting on his lies. "While I was sneaking through the main cabin, I overheard Alfred ask another soldier about guarding the barrels. He wanted to press on to St. Louis. He was in a hurry."

"It's standard procedure not to stop while carrying supplies," the colonel pointed out.

The odious man was determined to defend Alfred rather than remain objective. How could she hope to have the truth accepted if they'd already made up their minds?

"Go on," Sid urged.

Becky concentrated on keeping her voice calm. "I found my father tied to a post on the main deck near the boiler room. He'd been treated worse than the animals on board. While I was trying to figure out what to do, a fireman started arguing with two soldiers who were guarding the roped-off barrels. The crew needed more fuel. The soldiers said they were told to guard it. While they were distracted, I ran to release my father."

The colonel's eyes narrowed. "How convenient for you and your father to leap off the *Athena* moments before it exploded. Very few survived the blast."

"Those poor souls. We were all duped." Alfred braced his hands on his knees. "I wouldn't have made it either, had I not seen Becky go overboard. I dove into the water after her."

His pathetic attempt to portray himself as an ignorant hero might convince the colonel. The general continued to stare out the window, possibly disinterested in what was being said. Sid withheld comment.

She had to speak up, carefully. "Whoever planned this has far more power than my father, and certainly more than me. He has to be in a position of influence where he can move soldiers around like players on a chessboard."

Chess was Alfred's favorite game.

Her veiled accusation snagged the general's attention. Perhaps Rosecrans had guessed her implication and decided to pay attention.

Alfred bored a hole through her with his gaze. He would find a way to make her suffer if she failed. Her stomach tightened into a knot and her throat threatened to close up. If she went a step further, there was no turning back.

Tell the truth.

The truth was frightening and difficult to tell. She couldn't control how others might take it. But in the telling, she became responsible for her truth. She would stand up for herself and not depend on someone else to save her.

"My father and I made it to shore and found shelter in a cave. He became gravely ill. We were without supplies so I went out to rummage through whatever had washed up. When I heard voices, I ducked behind a bush until I could see if it was someone I trusted.

"Alfred and another man pulled a skiff ashore. Alfred was soaking wet. The man with him I didn't recognize, but he wore his hair in a black braid down his back. He fit the description of the mercenary Tom encountered in the woods. He demanded his money. Alfred insisted on searching for the lost barrels."

She had better get the story told fast before he stopped her. "The mercenary said Alfred was foolish to trust communication to a woman and would be blamed for the loss. Alfred got angry. He accused his comrade of not killing Tom Sawyer, as he was hired to do, but instead killing their messenger, which he wasn't supposed to do. Alfred stabbed the man and dragged his body into the river before taking the skiff and leaving."

Silence fell over the room, which had grown dim as daylight faded outside.

Sid struck a match and lit an oil lamp on the table. He turned up the flame.

Alfred leaned back and crossed his legs. He rubbed his face with his hand in a gesture that conveyed his embarrassment for her. "Oh, Becky. I knew you had suffered a trauma, but I had no idea how badly it affected your mind. You've made up quite a story. I can see you believe it. You convinced yourself I am a monster because you cannot bear the thought that your father and cousin conspired to undertake such a horrendous scheme."

She flushed with anger. "I did not make it up."

Sid cleared his throat. "We found the body of a man who fits the description Miss Thatcher gave. It appears he died from a puncture wound below his sternum."

"When did this happen? You didn't report it," the colonel accused.

"Earlier this afternoon. I've been so busy I haven't had the opportunity to file a report."

Maybe Sid suspected his boss would attempt to hide it?

Alfred directed his reply to the general, who continued to look on, quietly observing. "She is protecting her cousin. Jeff Thatcher killed the man. He got away from Tom Sawyer and is hiding out with his uncle. The provost marshal reported they were meeting regularly."

"My report made it clear that I *assumed* they were meeting," Sid corrected. "No one saw them together and I couldn't prove it. That is why I waited until I had those brochures to arrest Judge Thatcher. But those pamphlets weren't printed at the newspaper office. They came from—"

"Are you defending those traitors?" The colonel demanded. "You were the one who wrote, and I quote, 'the simple truth is the judge won't sign the oath of loyalty, which makes him disloyal at best."

Sid had no answer and wouldn't meet Becky's gaze.

Surprisingly, she couldn't muster the old feelings of resentment. Sid had pursued what he believed was the truth.

Alfred made a sound of irritation. "Isn't it *obvious* to everyone here that Becky is lying to cover for her relatives? And Tom Sawyer is protecting her."

She picked up the blackened tin box. "If that's the case, why would he turn this in?"

"Agent Sawyer delivered that to my hands," Sid stated. "He found it with Jeff Thatcher's help."

"Don't forget the part about the runaway slaves," Alfred said in a sarcastic tone. "Tom spun quite a story, but we trust what he says implicitly because he never lies. He also told us the judge is dead. Isn't that right, Becky?"

She had anticipated this question. "He assumed the judge was dead because he knows my father wouldn't allow me to return alone if he were able to stop me. Tom is not lying to protect me or my family."

"Ha!" Alfred burst out. "Now you're lying to protect him. Here's what I'll bet happened. Tom found out about Jeff and the judge and the fact that you're covering for them. Your cousin showed him to the island where they were hiding that stuff and made a deal with him. They both knew full well that if you were implicated in a plot involving your family, nothing would save you. Sawyer was in an impossible situation. He learned from Sid that I'd picked up the shipment and—" Alfred put his finger in the air. "Ah ha! Perfect solution! Tell Sid that Alfred did it."

He dropped his hand onto his knee and his lip lifted in a disgusted sneer. "He's hated me since we were kids. Let's be realistic. How could I single-handedly plan and execute all this activity from St. Louis? And why would I? Jeff has the motive. He's a rebel and a murderer. He has the connections. That nonsense about helping slaves escape is just what it sounds like. Nonsense."

The general rubbed a hand over his red beard, clearly relieved to have been given an explanation, all wrapped up and finished with a bow.

Becky couldn't keep her gaze from wandering to Alfred. His eyes gleamed with triumph. He hadn't reckoned on everything she would say, but he'd worked out his defense quick enough to dismiss her testimony as mad ravings or intentional dissembling.

"What about the messenger you mentioned?" Sid asked.

"More make-believe," Alfred scoffed.

No. She was drowning. Sid had thrown her a rope.

"The man Alfred killed called her *an old woman.* He declared she had betrayed them because she hadn't delivered the last message. After Mrs. Bent was murdered, Tom asked me if I had any knowledge of what Mrs. Bent might've been involved in."

"Did you?" Sid asked.

Becky trembled. In betraying Alfred, she betrayed herself. She would hang alongside him. No one would believe her to be an innocent dupe, or if they did, they would still condemn her. Tom never let danger stop him. If he'd taught her one thing, it was courage.

"Let me start from the beginning. A year ago, my friend, Anne McDermott, was imprisoned because of her husband's guerilla activities. *She* hadn't done anything, other than feed and tend to him when he was injured, what any woman would do for a man she loved. Her widowed mother, our neighbor, told me that an old friend of mine was a general's adjutant in St. Louis. She begged me to write to him to find out how Anne was getting along.

"Alfred and I began corresponding after that. He was the one to suggest sending notes from Anne to her mother inside the letters he posted to me. With the understanding that I wouldn't tell anyone because it would get him into trouble. I thought he was being kind. I don't know what the notes meant to that mercenary. But he killed the widow because she didn't have a message to give him."

Alfred had started shaking his head halfway through her explanation. "You may have been passing notes, but they weren't from me. I will say you have a remarkable imagination."

He had told her that he would deny it.

The general stepped closer to the desk. "Did anyone else know about this?"

She shook her head. "Not that I know of. I was aware that prisoners weren't allowed to send or receive mail, and it would get Alfred into trouble if anyone found out, so I kept mum. I didn't tell my father or my best friend Sally. I didn't tell Tom."

"You don't have one of these notes?

How she wished she had kept it. "I received one earlier on the day Tom arrived at our house, injured. I didn't have a chance to deliver it to the widow until a few days later. I found her dead. When I saw her there with her neck broken, I was in such a state of shock, I think I dropped it. But I don't know what happened to it."

"Convenient," Alfred drawled. He had his leg extended and sat in a sprawl, appearing at ease, giving the impression of being bored. His gaze held hers and dared her to continue with what was sure to be an impossible case to make without a shred of evidence.

Sid cleared his throat. He reached into his jacket and withdrew a folded piece of paper. "Is this the note you dropped?"

CHAPTER TWENTY-EIGHT

Patience had never been one of Tom's gifts. Waiting for Sid to act was worse than watching an inchworm attempt to win a footrace. Tom couldn't wait any longer. He had to get out of this jail, find out what had happened to Becky, and make sure Alfred couldn't harm her.

Over the past few hours, he'd chatted amiably with the guards and shared some card tricks. His attempt to escape would work better if they weren't annoyed with him.

He slid down the bars, groaning, and then toppled over to make it appear as if he'd passed out.

"What's wrong with him?" One of the other prisoners rolled him on his back. "Mister?"

Tom made a snarling sound. He bit the inside of his lip, cried out in real pain, and thrashed his head, flinging red spittle from his mouth.

The other prisoner backed away, alarmed. He waved to the guards. "Hey! This fella is havin' some sorta fit."

Tom thrashed, bowed his back, stiffened, rolled his eyes back in his head, and generally put on a grand impression of having a seizure. He had almost convinced himself by the time someone came to check on him.

The two guards approached the large iron door. One of them opened it while the other one held a gun on the prisoners to dissuade them from attempting escape. The guard who'd come after Tom grabbed him by his ankles and dragged him across the straw, out of the cell, and then locked the door.

Tom gasped and thrashed some more. The self-injury had produced an impressive flow. Blood ran down his cheeks and chin.

"What do we do with him?" said one guard to the other.

"He's the provost marshal's brother. Reckon we ought to call for a doc."

"Let's take him upstairs. We don't want him dying down here."

The guards grabbed Tom beneath his armpits and hoisted him up between them.

He remained limp, moaning and dripping blood.

When they reached the stairwell, he could wrestle one of them for a gun. Or it might work better if they took him upstairs and Sid thought he was dying.

CHAPTER TWENTY-NINE

The paper in Sid's hand might as well have been the Holy Grail, as far as Becky was concerned. "Where did you find it?" she asked.

"Beneath the widow's rocking chair," the provost marshal answered.

Alfred shifted forward and peered at the paper in Sid's hand as if he'd never seen it.

"Yes, that is the note I was going to give her." Becky glanced at the general, who had moved to the desk. His frown could mean many things. "I didn't think it was wrong."

"Funneling mail from prisoners to family members is a criminal act," the general stated. "Read it. What does it say?"

"Not much that I could tell." Sid held it close to the oil lamp and began to read: *Lately I have been sick with the ague. I wish I could get a bowl of your—* What the devil?"

He started and yanked the paper up. After a moment, he lowered it again. From her vantage point, Becky could see what had startled him. Faint marks had appeared when Sid lowered the paper close to the lamp.

"My God, look at that," he said, as the marks darkened. "I should've thought to check."

"Check what?" the colonel demanded.

"It's a message, in between the other lines. Invisible until activated by heat."

"That proves nothing," Alfred snapped. "She made this up and wrote that message with lemon juice. It's a common enough trick. She used it to distract you from what her father and cousin are up to."

Becky stared at him, dumbfounded. He hadn't veered from his story and he'd kept his cool. He lied better than Tom.

Sid held out the note to the general. "Based on what I can tell, this is a shorthand for troop movements. Numbers, places, dates... things only someone would know if they were privy to this kind of information. That person wouldn't be a rebel outlaw or a girl stuck in prison."

Quick as a flash, Alfred leaped from his chair, dragged Becky up against him, and put a gun to her head. "If any of you move an inch, I'll leave her brains spattered all over these walls."

Terror stiffened Becky's limbs. Her breath came in ragged gasps as he pulled her toward the door. The other men hadn't moved after their initial start of surprise. They might've expected this. She, of all people, should have been on guard.

"You won't get away, Captain Temple," the general said coolly. "Even if you manage to get past the soldiers guarding the door, which I sincerely doubt, we will hunt you down."

"I'm not hanging for something I didn't do," Alfred sneered. He gestured with the gun. "Call in the two men at the door."

Sid called them in.

No other soldiers were on the staircase. Would Alfred shoot the guards outside the front door?

He twisted her arm behind her with a painful grip. Holding

the gun pointed at her head, he forced her down the stairs. "You're going with me."

Becky struggled to maintain her composure and not panic. She winced with pain each time she came down awkwardly on her swollen ankle. "I can't help you, Alfred. I'll only be a burden."

"Move, you conniving bitch." He pushed her. "I ought to put a bullet through your head for betraying me. I would've saved you. All you had to do was keep your mouth shut."

"And let you pin this on my father and Jeff?"

"I had this planned out every step of the way until those two Sawyers fouled it up." Alfred shoved her off the last step. "I've loved you for years, and this is how you repay me?"

She would wait until they were out the door. He would have to get past more soldiers in the freight yard and on the docks. At some point, he would be distracted, then she would grab the gun. Wrestle it away or force him to kill her. She wasn't going anywhere with him ever again.

"You don't love me," she replied to his absurd claim. "You tricked me and lied to me."

"What do you think that useless cur Tom Sawyer has been doing all this time?"

"Stop!"

The shout came from the stone stairwell leading from the basement. Tom stumbled up out of the darkness with two soldiers on his heels. "Becky, run! Get away! Now!"

Alfred jerked the gun around and fired.

Tom fell against the stone wall and slid down.

Terror ripped a hole in her chest. "Oh God no! Tom—"

Alfred's arm cut off her cry and her airway. He pulled her up against him, using her as a shield while shooting at the two soldiers who'd been behind Tom.

"Can't breathe..." She frantically clawed at his arm as he hauled her out the door.

Another gunshot resounded.

In that split-second, Becky was sure he had put a bullet in her head and she was simply not yet aware she was dead. She prayed she would soon join Tom in the hereafter.

Alfred's chokehold around her neck loosened and fell away. She grabbed the door frame for support, sucking air in great gulps. Alfred turned and lifted his hand as if beseeching before he toppled down the wooden steps and landed sprawled on his back in the gravel.

The soldiers in the freight yard remained motionless. Not a sound came from inside the freight house. She stared with disbelief, half-expecting the fallen man to get up and come after her. But he remained where he was, unmoving, staring sightlessly into the dusky sky.

A few steps away stood a grim giant with wild hair and an unkempt beard. He hugged a bandage around his ribs with one hand and held a smoking gun in the other.

Jeff stepped over Alfred's prone form and stopped at the bottom of the steps leading up to the front door. The fatigue etched on his face altered his appearance, but his eyes, so like her father's, burned with intelligence and determination. "It's over."

CHAPTER THIRTY

Tom missed the excitement surrounding his death. After Alfred fired at him, everyone assumed he was a goner. Even he drew the same conclusion in the instant before he called out to draw Alfred's fire and give Becky a chance to run. Then he ruined a perfectly heroic demise by rolling over and groaning, beset with the worst headache he'd suffered in weeks.

His sacrifice, as she called it, didn't help her cause. The authorities had shown a modicum of decency by agreeing to let her and the judge remain under house arrest while the investigation plodded on while he was stuck in bed.

Although he'd assured her that he was much improved by the next day, she continued to hover over him, tenderly nursing him, at the same time scolding him for getting himself shot.

She sat on the edge of the bed and finished wrapping a fresh bandage around his head while he leaned forward to make it easier for her to reach him. "You'll have another scar to add to your collection," she pointed out. "But I'd say you're very lucky. The bullet only grazed you."

Her eyes grew bright.

He'd prefer her annoyance. That, he could handle. Her tears would set off a barrage of emotions he had no idea how to manage.

"I'm too hard-headed to kill," he remarked dryly.

Her tender pain-filled gaze flashed with anger. "You are too *fat-headed* to miss as a target. If Alfred hadn't been such a bad shot, I wouldn't be dressing your wounds. I'd be dressing you for a coffin."

She gathered up the bloody rags and dropped them in the bowl on the bedside table, clearly intending to leave. Perhaps going to tend to her father, who lay in the next room. She'd been nursing both of them and had to be exhausted.

Tom grasped her wrist before she could get away. "Becky, wait. I'm jesting. It's all I know to do when I can't think of what else to say. I am sorry for upsetting you. But I'm not sorry for what I did, and I'd do it again to save you."

She gazed down at him and her anger dissipated into a look of sadness that tweaked something in his chest. "You're impossible."

"And brave?"

"Foolishly so."

"Handsome and charming?"

A tear rolled down her cheek.

No, no...she wasn't supposed to cry, she was supposed to laugh.

He blinked when his eyes started to sting. If he started crying, he wouldn't be a bit of good to her. As it was, he hadn't done much more than lay around like an infant.

"Pesky headache," he muttered.

"You need to rest." Becky took a cup from the bedside table and offered it to him. "Drink this willow bark tea. It'll help with the pain."

She had a home remedy for just about everything except for lovesickness. Sadly, no one had discovered a cure for that.

He had run away from the malady seven years ago and had

lied to everyone, including himself, about the reasons. That he had wanted more out of life than Life was willing to allot him; and he feared if he stayed, he would miss his opportunities. The best opportunity he would ever get had been here all along.

Finally, he'd wised up. Too late. So had Becky. She could see through every smokescreen he put up. She couldn't possibly like what she saw, but her actions pointed to an unbelievable truth. She still cared for him despite his mistakes.

Tom accepted the cup and dutifully took a sip. He grimaced and vowed never to mention pain again while in her presence. "The taste is enough to make me forget about the headache."

Becky crossed her arms. "The worse it tastes, the better it works."

"Now you sound like Aunt Polly. She dosed me with one of her poisons when I complained about being too sick to go to school. After she turned her back, I gave it to the cat."

Amusement flickered in Becky's sideways glance. "Did the cat feel better?"

"Sure did look like it," he drawled. "Perked right up."

"Sadly, I don't have a cat for you to cure. Drink up."

At least he'd made her smile.

Sid's timely appearance at the open door saved Tom from having to drink the foul brew.

"Come in!" Tom called out enthusiastically.

When Becky turned to see who'd arrived, Tom slipped the cup back on the table.

Sid removed his hat with a slight smile. "Good to see you're awake and feeling better, Tom. Becky's good medicine must be working."

The remark drew her attention to Tom's feeble effort to distract her. "Tattletale," he muttered.

With a sweet smile, Becky picked up the cup and held it out. "All of it."

Tom heaved a resigned sigh, knowing it was time to raise the white flag. "Reckon I can put up with being poisoned if it means you'll tend me for a few more days."

He drained the cup and returned it to his triumphant nurse. "Sid, you really ought to try some of that tea," he rasped. "It cures bilious dispositions and bad manners."

His brother's smile faded. "Your disposition might need some improvement after what I have to tell you."

"Trust you to be the bearer of bad news," Tom remarked without humor.

Becky had gone from pale to ashen. "I wondered how long it would take..."

Tom reached for her hand. He would be with her every step of the way, and he would not stop until he'd secured freedom for her and her father.

Sid tapped his hat on his thigh. He did that when he was antsy. "First, Jeff won't face charges for shooting Captain Temple."

"That's good news," she pointed out.

"He *will* face charges for being involved in the plot to blow up Union boats."

Tom glared at his brother. "Jeff saved thousands of lives when he helped me find that bomb and bring it back. We can build a convincing argument to help him avoid the noose."

"We can try. But that's not all," Sid intoned.

"Well, go on, grim reaper."

"Becky is to be charged as an accessory."

Becky sat heavily on the side of the bed with a dazed look, while the pronouncement hit Tom with the force of a cannon.

"What?" He hollered. "Alfred damn near killed her. How could they be so stupid as to think she had anything to do with his scheming? I'm going over there now." He threw aside the covers and swung his bare legs over the bed.

She stopped him with her hand on his arm. "Tom, wait. I

expected this." Her eyes pleaded. "You don't know the whole story. I didn't tell you..."

She proceeded to inform him about an important detail she'd failed to mention, the notes she'd been passing to the widow, missives secretly tucked into Alfred's love letters. "I thought it was only a gesture of kindness for a lonely old lady. It turns out Alfred was using me to send secret messages to his contacts."

Tom steadied himself with his hands to keep from pitching off the bed as a wave of dizziness struck. It wasn't his injury that caught him so unprepared. It was the truth.

Becky had been the courier for a traitor.

"I found a note underneath the widow's rocking chair," Sid added. "Wasn't sure what it meant until I held it to the light and saw writing appear."

Dread coiled in Tom's belly, tightening it into a painful knot. He'd known something was amiss, but he hadn't anticipated how deeply entangled she was in the whole ugly mess. Didn't matter that she'd been used. The army would be looking for a scapegoat. Alfred was dead. They couldn't make a spectacle of him. They would go after those they could publicly hang.

Sid moved closer to the bed. He turned the hat brim in a way that suggested he was ill at ease. "I'm sorry, Tom."

"Not as sorry as I am." The dull ache behind Tom's eyes became a heavy throb. "I should've figured it out sooner."

Becky shook her head. "Figured what out, Tom? That I was Alfred's dupe? You didn't have all the information. As it was, you did put it together. The scheme. Alfred. Sid told me what you said to him after you found that bomb."

Tom released a dry laugh. "I also thought Sid was a traitor."

Sid didn't appear surprised. "I suspected the same of you. Alfred pitted us against each other so we wouldn't notice what he was up to. I've made more arrests. One of the men we brought in admitted to planting those brochures at the newspaper office. He was directed to do so by the agent Alfred hired and killed."

"Why did he set up the judge?"

Becky finally met Tom's eyes. "Alfred viewed me as a conquest. He wanted to control me and my father was in his way. The way I see it, Papa served as a convenient dupe."

"If Alfred expected he could control you, he didn't know you very well." As soon as the words left Tom's mouth, the irony struck him. In a sense, wasn't that what he'd tried to do? He had used her uncertain situation to coerce her into accepting his help so she would see him as a hero and want him back.

Aside from their political loyalties, he wasn't so different from Alfred. He'd been too arrogant to acknowledge his true nature. His motives were undeniably selfish. He wanted her respect, her affirmation, her love, without offering her true love in return. In the end, it shouldn't come as a surprise that she had so little faith in him.

"I'm thinking I don't know you all that well either," he admitted.

Tears filled her eyes. "I'm sorry I didn't tell you everything."

"Don't apologize. I've given you precious few reasons to trust me. I didn't tell you the truth about me, at least what I could recall. All this excitement dislodged a few more memories."

"Such as?"

"The reason I came back here. General Grant handed off the request from the Department of Missouri to my boss, Alan Pinkerton, and asked if one of his agents could go undercover to expose a potential plot. I requested the assignment."

Becky stared at her laced fingers. "Why?"

He wanted to say the reasons were complicated, but that wasn't the truth. "Because I wanted the opportunity to reconnect with you. I thought if I came back, rooted out the real traitors, and got to the truth, you would admire me."

Tom winced at how pathetic the admission sounded. He was no more worthy of her now than he was seven years ago.

Sid cleared his throat. "I'll leave you two alone."

"Wait." Tom held his hand up. "You need to stay long enough to hear this. I met with the general to discuss the facts of the case. Alfred was present. Rosecrans asked his aide to take me to Gratiot prison to question a female captive. One of the women I spoke to was Anne McDermott."

Becky's eyes widened. "What did she say?"

"Not much. She'd been in prison and sick for most of the past year, so I didn't suspect she was involved in anything. Before I left, she whispered to me to make sure you were safe. I thought her concern unusual, but I took it to heart. That was the reason I was on my way to your house, to check on you."

She eyed him, still uncertain, still afraid to believe him. "You weren't coming there to arrest my father?"

Tom took her hand and gently squeezed her slender palm to assure her. "No. I had no orders to arrest him."

Sid frowned. "The message from the general about bringing the judge to St. Louis?"

"I suspect Alfred arranged that. He was all too happy to use the judge's misfortune to create a distraction and shift the blame. He had his men plant those brochures and tell you where to look."

Sid shifted his stance, appearing discomfited, as he should be.

"Alfred fooled a general, a colonel, a provost marshal, and a spy," Tom pointed out. "Why not charge all of us as accessories? Why stop with an innocent woman who had every reason to trust him? They had more opportunities to figure out what he was doing! You know full well Becky didn't have any foreknowledge of what Alfred was up to—and I'll prove it."

"You need to stay out of it," Sid warned. "They already think you're compromised. Let me finish gathering the evidence."

"She'll be in jail by the time you manage to sort it out. I won't allow her to be made a scapegoat to cover the sins of two incompetent leaders." Tom adjusted the nightshirt and braced his hands on the side of the bed for leverage.

Want something done? Do it yourself. That was the creed he had lived by all his life, and it was no different now. It was up to him to save Becky from becoming a sacrificial lamb.

Becky held onto his arm. "You are in no condition to go off on a crusade. You heard the doctor. Two weeks in bed, minimum."

Tom snorted at the absurdity. "If I'm down for two weeks, it'll be because I'm dead."

The color drained from her face. She jerked to her feet with her apron fisted in her hands and a fearful expression. "Fine. Be a fool."

With that, she whirled on her heel and left the room.

"Wait! Becky!" Tom stood up. The floor tilted to the right. He grabbed the post at the foot of the bed to steady himself. "Did you feel that?" he asked Sid, hoping for an affirmative.

Instead, Sid folded his arms across his chest and offered an arched look of disapproval. "She's right. You're acting like an idiot."

The righteous heat centered in Tom's chest transformed into an embarrassed flush, spreading upward to his neck and face. How could either of them think he'd lie around in bed for weeks without doing anything? He was a man of action. Inaction drove him crazy. "Dammit, Sid. I can't let them lock her up. It's not right. Someone has to protect her."

"Seems to me she's been doing a fair job taking care of herself and her father for the past seven years. Without your help." Sid's wry tone implied the words were intended as a jab. But the truth behind them sank deep into Tom's soul.

His brother was right in saying that Becky didn't need him. Certainly not like she had before when she had depended on him for affection, advice, and adventure. In the years he'd been away, she had found her strength and all the courage she required. He had nothing left to give her.

Except for her freedom. He would find some way to give her that.

Tom hitched up his drawers and tightened the drawstring. "Would you hand me my clothes?"

Sid heaved a sigh, but went to the wardrobe and opened it, retrieved the uniform, and tossed Tom his shirt. "This isn't going to impress her."

Tom pulled the shirt over his head. He sat on the side of the bed and drew up his trousers then stood to tuck in the shirttails before he snapped the suspenders over his shoulders. "I'm not trying to impress her. I'm trying to keep her out of jail."

Sid held out Tom's coat. "Who's going to keep you out of trouble?"

Becky retreated down the stairs, fuming at Tom. No one had ever been able to make that aggravating man behave. Why should she have better luck at it? Fine, let him run off and collapse if he wouldn't stay in bed where he belonged.

She stopped halfway on a sharp sob. Who was she kidding? She wasn't waging war to keep Tom in bed. She fought her desire to hold onto him as long as she could until her poor choices caught up with her, and prison—or death—separated them forever. Time was running out. God had granted her a few more days. Sid had made it clear she would be lucky to gain a few more hours.

A hard knock sounded at the front door.

She rotated her sore, but improving, ankle before she went the rest of the way down the steps and adjusted the net holding her untidy hair.

Who would come to see her? She'd been marked as an outcast after word had spread through town about Alfred's traitorous death and her involvement in it. More likely the visitor was one of Sid's guards.

She opened the door to find Amy Lawrence standing on the front porch regarding her suspiciously from beneath a wide-brimmed bonnet.

"You aren't expecting me, I know."

True. She would be less surprised had a rabbit in a frock coat come calling. Becky shook off the momentary daze and opened the door wider. "Pardon my poor manners, come in."

Amy entered, casting wary glances around as if she expected someone to leap out at her. She wore the same patched and faded dress she'd had on the other day—her favorite or the only one she owned—and clutched a tapestry satchel in both hands.

"May I take your shawl and your, um, bag?"

"No. What I have to say won't take long."

Becky mused over the remark, which came across as a rude rebuff, except it likely wasn't meant that way. Amy didn't treat her enemies like friends. She wouldn't stab them in the back. She'd sink the knife into their chest.

So why had she come here?

Earlier, Tom had conveyed an astonishing revelation about Jeff taking on a role left empty by Amy's brother's death. As incredible as it was to hear that Jeff had been ferrying runaway slaves across the river, the explanation made sense.

How much did Amy know? If she was willing to confirm Jeff's story, it might save him from a firing squad.

At the sound of footsteps, Becky turned.

Tom had donned his uniform and was coming downstairs with Sid right behind him.

"Hello, Amy," he said, pleasantly.

Her expression transformed from tight and unfriendly to soft and concerned. "How are you feeling, Tom? I heard you were shot."

"Just a scratch." He put his hand on the bandage around his head and gave her a crooked smile, which made Becky want to throw up.

He was putting on an act, this time for Amy.

Would the two of them end up together? It was certainly possible. They'd been thick as thieves at times. Didn't she want Tom to be happy? Happy with anyone except Amy.

He stepped off the last riser and his gaze questioned Becky's chilly reception, her only defense against the warmth he stirred in her heart.

"Becky patched me up," he said, not breaking eye contact.

"Not for the first time, I hear." Amy had caught up on all the gossip.

"This makes the third time, I believe," Sid spoke as he descended the stairs behind Tom.

"And it's the last," Becky finished. "Surely you didn't come here to discuss Tom's penchant for getting himself hurt. May I offer you some coffee?"

"I'd love some," Sid replied.

He hadn't been invited. Neither had Tom. On the other hand, if Amy had something to confess, it would be good for other witnesses to hear it.

After settling her guests in the formal sitting room, Becky went into the kitchen, returning with four cups of coffee. She placed the tray on the low table in front of the crimson settee where Amy had taken a seat.

"Help yourselves," she offered.

Amy fiddled with the large bag at her feet.

Sid took a cup, murmured thanks then once again took up his spot near the door.

Tom made his way to the piano bench. He wasn't as well as he

279

claimed to be.

Becky balanced on the edge of a cushioned chair. "What brings you to my door?"

"The provost marshal stopped by my house yesterday. We had an interesting conversation." Amy sent a scathing look in Sid's direction. "He suggested I come over here and have a talk with you before making a formal statement."

Sid gave his full attention to sipping his coffee. He was up to something. Whether it was good or bad was hard to tell.

"A statement about what?" Becky asked.

"What I know about your cousin's activities."

"You were aware Jeff was helping slaves escape?"

"Not until Sid informed me. I confirmed the story with someone else. I can't tell you anything more."

Sid set his cup on the server. "You can speak plainly. Tom and I both know that Jim is involved. I'm not interested in arresting him or making trouble for either of you. We need to get the facts straight to find out who was involved in a plot to sabotage our fleet."

"I don't know anything about that."

"Tell Becky what you relayed to me."

Amy frowned, then continued. "Last year, Jim sent word that he'd met with a man who wanted to help us ferry people to freedom across the river."

"Jim?" Becky was having trouble following.

"Little Jim," Tom clarified.

"You wouldn't recognize him," Amy added, impatiently.

Becky caught on, finally. The man she'd met in church. "He wanted to take me to Tom."

"I don't think so." Tom leaned forward from his perch on the piano bench to address Amy. "Did you ever see him, this man Jim told you about?"

"No. He rendezvoused in the woods with the people he transported. Sometimes he left supplies on my porch. When he left notes with instructions, he signed the messages. *Little John*."

"That's Jeff!" Becky answered. Now it all made sense. Somehow, her cousin had connected with Jim, and they had worked together without Amy knowing it. And Jim had been trying to get her to follow him so he could lead her to Jeff.

"I don't understand," Amy said, clearly not believing her.

"When we were kids, it was a game we played," Tom explained. "Robin Hood and his Merry Men. Jeff was always bigger than the other boys. The role of *Little John* suited him. We swore each other to secrecy so no one else would know."

"Becky knew," Amy pointed out.

"She was the only girl we allowed to be part of our band."

The tightness in Becky's chest lessened. With those words, Tom reminded her of what she'd once meant to him. What she possibly still meant to him.

Did he love her?

She ought to wish he didn't. It would make it so much easier for him, and for her, to let go.

Amy unlatched the satchel. She withdrew a quilt. "This, I assume, belongs to you. I found it on my porch about a week ago."

Becky examined it. "Yes. This is one of the quilts our sewing circle made for the soldiers' hospital." She smoothed the quilt over her lap. "Each basket design was made by a different woman. Mine features lilacs."

Symbolic of first love. Did Tom remember bringing her bouquets of the fragrant flowers that he'd hooked from her mother's garden? His gaze told her he did.

"This design with the hawthorns is the one Mrs. Bent sewed. After we attached all the squares, the widow would finish the quilt and put on the trim. I'd send it north to the District of Missouri offices. To Alfred. Providing the quilts was another one of his ideas—"

Becky gasped. Why hadn't she thought of it earlier? This could be one of the missing links in the chain of evidence leading to Alfred.

"Does anyone have a pocketknife?" she asked.

"How about this?" Tom handed her a hunting knife.

Becky carefully opened a seam on the side of the hawthorn basket design and burrowed her fingers through the bunting. She felt something...a piece of paper.

"What is it?" Sid moved closer.

She unfolded it. "I don't know. Words, but...gibberish."

"Let me look," Tom offered.

She handed over the paper.

"It's written in Freemason's cipher." He handed the message to Sid. "I can translate it later. Did Jeff leave this quilt on Amy's porch?"

"I don't know," Amy said. "I didn't see him."

Becky filled in the missing pieces. "The judge must've left it for him at the old tree in the cemetery. I noticed the quilt was missing, but he wouldn't tell me what he'd done with it."

"We can ask him," Sid suggested.

"After he wakes up. I don't want to disturb him."

"If the judge and Jeff were co-conspirators, they wouldn't have given the quilt away," Tom pointed out. "They would've known better."

Exactly.

Amy stared at the spread on Becky's lap. "They could still use this as evidence against you. You knew about it."

Tom picked up the quilt and held it up. "No, she didn't. She figured it out like a good investigator. Why would Alfred use Mrs. Bent to pass along messages if he had Becky to do it? Why bother with another middleman?"

His defense appeared to convince Amy and soothed Becky's

soul. Tom believed in her innocence. He'd believed in her even when she hadn't put her faith in him.

She lowered her head so he wouldn't see the tears. Her crying bothered him, likely because he couldn't do anything about it. But she didn't expect him to solve her problems. She didn't expect anything. He'd done more than enough to help her and her family. It was time he moved on and found another adventure to occupy his active mind.

"Time to go."

She jerked her head up. "Go? Go where? You're supposed to be in bed."

"Huh. I can do something more useful than sleep." Tom clapped his hand on his brother's shoulder. "Right, Sid?"

"What?" Sid appeared not to understand.

"Becky's done her part. Now it's time for us to do ours."

CHAPTER THIRTY-ONE

Two weeks later

Becky stepped out the back door and set down a dish of table scraps. She missed seeing the stray, which had been a regular visitor before Tom showed up. The two wanderers were alike in that regard. They came and went as they pleased. The cat would show itself eventually, just as she was certain Tom would return. In the meantime, she remained under house arrest while she awaited word of her fate.

She had prepared herself for the worst.

After breakfast, she found the judge in his study, thumbing through a book. The scene brought tears to her eyes. He had been so sick when they'd brought him home. But under her care, he had healed and was now back to his old self.

"Are you busy?" she asked.

"Come in, my dear." The judge motioned for her to take a chair near the desk. "I've been looking over your mother's book on flowers."

"That's an interesting choice, given the severity of our situation." She was only half joking.

He responded with a smile. "Reflecting on the good things in life is better than brooding over bad circumstances one cannot change. Have you heard from Tom?"

"Not yet." She tried to smile. "I told him to leave so many times, perhaps he took my admonitions to heart."

"Do you believe that?" Kindness warmed her father's eyes.

"No. Tom said he would be back, and he will. I trust him to keep his word. Though I'm not so sure the news will be good, considering how long it's taken to hear anything."

The judge reached for his pipe, then took his time tamping down the tobacco and lighting it. Becky relaxed while he engaged in the ritual. These days, she found comfort in ordinary customs, which in the past she had borne with impatience or taken for granted.

He sent a cloud of smoke into the air as he leaned back in his chair. "I have a feeling that things will work out for the best."

"Do you?" She heaved a resigned sigh. "I wish I had your optimism. A military court won't believe I couldn't see through Alfred's schemes."

"Neither did anyone else, many of whom had a better line of vision to what he was up to."

That might be, but powerful men rarely took responsibility for failures.

"You were right in warning me against him. I wish I'd listened.

"I didn't warn you he was a traitor. I didn't see that coming."

"Even so, I fear my judgment is flawed."

"Don't be so hard on yourself. You have unique insight into people's needs and compassion compels you to try to meet them. Sometimes, your best intentions get you into trouble. Give yourself the same grace you extend to others."

How could she forgive herself?

"I was blind to Alfred's nature."

"You weren't blind. You looked past his flaws and decided he was your best chance at a respectable marriage so you could give your stubborn father a chance at a better life."

She didn't want her father to feel guilty about what, in the end, was her decision. "That's not why I agreed to marry—"

"Yes, it is." The judge set his pipe aside. "And I deeply regret putting you in that position. You are not responsible for saving me. But, as your father, I am responsible for protecting you, and I didn't do a very good job of it. I put my sense of honor above your safety."

"Stop apologizing for being an honorable man. I wouldn't have you behave any other way. I would've done the same thing."

He rested his hand on the book he'd been reading. "You know how much I loved your mother. But what you may not know is, at the time I met her, she had her pick of potential husbands with much better pedigrees. I wasn't wealthy or even a promising suitor. But she perceived something in me that I couldn't see in myself, and her faith gave me confidence."

"She adored you," Becky acknowledged. Her relationship, on the other hand... A wave of melancholy swept over her. She rubbed her finger along the cracked leather on the chair arm so her father wouldn't notice. "I'm afraid I was a disappointment to her."

"Look at me, Rebecca." His gaze shone with a certainty he normally reserved for the bench. "You are not and never were a disappointment to either of us. I will say, as our only living child, you carried a rather heavy load—all our hopes and dreams."

He came around to where she sat and drew her to her feet, then cupped her cheek tenderly. "When you love someone that much, you do everything you can to protect them. Sometimes walls become barriers. The important thing is, don't let fear become a prison. You are strong and courageous. Fight for what you want."

She hugged her father tight. "Papa, I love you."

"I love you, too, my dearest." After a moment, he released her and turned to the desk, picking up a sheaf of paper. "I'm writing to my cousins in Illinois to accept their invitation to visit, after we've settled things here, of course. You can accompany me if you'd like. But I would understand if a better offer comes along."

"Better offer?" She laughed without humor. "Such as a chance to visit Gratiot prison?"

"Let's not buy trouble," he chided, without smiling.

"If that's my fate, I'm prepared. I accept responsibility for what I've done, regardless of the reason. It could've ended worse than it did, and I played a part in it."

"Just be as prepared to accept mercy."

A knock sounded from the front hallway.

"I'll get it." Becky left the study to answer the door, more hopeful without a single reason. Her father's optimism must be catching.

Her good mood bloomed into pure joy. "Tom! Why look at you." He wore a crisp black suit with a gold brocade vest. He had gotten a haircut and a proper shave. "You do clean up nicely. But I must say, I'll miss the scruffy pirate."

He started when a black cat wound itself around his ankles.

"You've brought a friend, I see." She opened the door wider. "Come in."

The old stray padded inside. She scooped the cat up to pet it, and prevent the clever creature from running under the sofa. It took Tom another moment to enter, and he still hadn't said anything.

"You are very solemn." Becky tried not to show her nervousness.

Her father emerged from his study. "Ah! We have company."

"I'll put on a pot of tea," she said pleasantly.

"Wait!" Tom removed his hat. "I came to tell you. You're free."

His pronouncement struck her dumb. It was beyond her wildest hopes. When she found her voice, she stammered. "Th-thank you, I don't know what to…"

"We're still hammering out an arrangement for Jeff. He'll have to spend some time in prison, but he can avoid a death sentence if he's willing to plead guilty to lesser charges."

Far better than a firing squad.

"How did you do it?" She absently stroked the cat's head.

"Sid collected the facts and put them together, I built a case and talked with the President."

Her hand stilled. "The President? As in, Lincoln?"

Tom gave a slight nod. "I explained everything. He signed two pardons. One for you, and one for your father."

Astonishing.

"Why would he do that?"

"Because he understands mercy as well as justice."

There was that word. *Mercy.* Her father had urged her to be prepared to accept it. Had he known this was coming?

He smiled slightly and shrugged. "As I said, hope for the best."

Becky couldn't take it all in. She had to keep busy or she would burst into tears and then start dancing, and they would think she'd lost her mind.

"Did you just get back to town?" she asked Tom. "You must be tired. Hungry. Come into the kitchen and I'll find something for you to eat."

"You and Tom have a nice visit. I believe I will enjoy my freedom with a walk into town." Her father took his hat off the hall tree. As he passed, he leaned in and whispered in her ear. "Go easy on him."

What did he think she was going to do? Beat Tom with a frying pan for giving them the most precious gift in the world.

She went to the kitchen with Tom trailing along behind her. After she'd put the cat outside, she turned up the stove to put on a pot of water for tea.

Tom had pulled off a miracle or pulled some strings. She couldn't imagine how.

"There's more to this story. Why would the President do you this favor? And don't tell me it wasn't a favor. I know better."

Tom took a seat at the table. "It might have something to do with the help I provided a few years ago in thwarting an assassination plot."

"Good heavens." She spooned fragrant tea into a teapot. "That would make you a hero."

"If anyone else knew about it." He put his finger to his lips.

Poor Tom. He'd done something astounding and couldn't tell anyone!

His earlier news sank in, and the weight she'd been carrying without even realizing it lifted. She put her hands to her chest. "I'm free."

A smile pulled at Tom's lips. "As a bird."

"What about you?"

"I'm free, too."

Indeed. He wasn't in uniform. She hadn't considered the possible reason earlier. "You aren't going back to the army?"

"I was never in the army."

"The uniform?"

"A disguise. I worked for Pinkerton as an agent, then for Grant, as a spy."

"You aren't returning to your job?"

He didn't answer her right away. "That depends."

"On what?"

"On whether my partner wants to go with me."

"Your partner?"

"Yep. You've met her. She's smart, resourceful, good at

disguises, quick on her feet, luckier than a cat with nine lives, she saved my life at least two times, and..." He became solemn. "She gave me another chance to get it right. I couldn't possibly go off without her."

Becky stood in front of the stove transfixed by the notion that she could be reborn as the person Tom described. Or had she been that person all along?

For years she'd tried to fit the mold society deemed appropriate. If nothing else, the past tumultuous weeks had proved she could never be satisfied with a man who would try to shape her into an image of womanly perfection. Tom, God love him, didn't care a crumb about molds. He delighted in breaking them.

"You need a partner. Is that what you're saying?"

"I'm saying I love you." He folded his arms on the table and started tapping his finger. Nervous, though he didn't need to be.

Did she love him? Lord, yes. Did she need him? Not in the way most women needed a man. She didn't need to be rescued or promoted to a pedestal. As he'd pointed out, she was *free as a bird*, which meant her heart was also free. Fear no longer tethered it. She could spread her wings and let love take her where it would.

Even birds needed a place to rest and raise a family.

"If your partner got tired of wandering around and wished to settle down, would you be willing to do so?"

"I'm willing to do whatever makes her happy. Because that will make me happy."

The pot of water on the stove started to sing.

Becky went to pour the tea. Her hands shook. Imagine, Tom, willing to build a nest for her sake. She wouldn't clip his wings. If they did eventually land in one place, he would always be on the lookout for a new adventure because that's who he was, and it was one of the many things she loved about him. She loved the man who wanted to explore the world and at the same time, save it.

"You don't have to answer right away. I'll understand if you want to think about it. I've got quite a bit to do around here. File reports, help Sid with his paperwork…" Tom fiddled with a napkin on the table and tried not to look disappointed.

She fought a smile. Her father had advised her to go easy on him, and to give herself the same grace she would give Tom. If she got it wrong, if she messed up, or if he messed up, she would forgive both of them and go on.

Seven years ago, she hadn't been ready for the kind of marriage she would have with this extraordinary man. But now, having discovered her strength as a woman, she was prepared. More than prepared, she was eager.

She went to the fireplace and picked up a knob that had once adorned an andiron. The old brass had a patina from age and wear. She set it on the table in front of him.

He stared at it with incomprehension. "What is that?"

"Something you gave me a long time ago."

As a boy, he had gifted her with his precious treasure to win back her favor after hurting her feelings.

His forehead wrinkled with incomprehension. "But you gave it back to me."

"Yes, sadly, I did. Something I regretted immediately. It sat on your aunt's fireplace for years until I worked up the nerve to ask her for it. She didn't say a thing, didn't ask why I'd want it, just wrapped it up in a newspaper and gave it to me. It's been with me ever since. Whenever I looked at it, I was comforted. It also made my heart hurt because it brought to mind how much I'd lost."

Tom's fingers curled around the brass knob. "I've never stopped loving you."

"No. I stopped loving you." Becky quickly finished the thought before he misunderstood. "Or I thought I did until you fell back into my life. Since then, I've discovered I hadn't lost my love for you at all. I'd only given it back for a time."

Tom pushed the bench away and came around the table. He

dragged her into his arms for a kiss that lifted her toes several inches off the ground. Abruptly, he left her on her feet, dazed. Then he went down on one knee and took her hand.

"Put me out of my misery. Marry me."

Leave it to Tom to offer a proposal and make it sound like he was dying.

"With that kind of offer, how can I turn you away?"

The smile he gave her deepened the dimple in his cheek. "You can't. This is one stray you won't get rid of."

The End

ALSO BY E.E. BURKE

The New Adventures

Tom Sawyer Returns

Taming Huck Finn

Steam! Romance and Rails Series

Her Bodyguard

Kate's Outlaw

A Dangerous Passion

Fugitive Hearts

The Bride Train Series

Valentine's Rose

Patrick's Charm

Tempting Prudence

Seducing Susannah

American Mail-Order Brides

Victoria Bride of Kansas

Santa's Mail-Order Bride

The Brides of Noelle

Twelve Days of Christmas Mail-Order Brides

Jolie, A Valentine's Day Bride

The Drum (Twelve Days of Christmas Mail-Order Brides)

ABOUT THE AUTHOR

E.E. Burke is a bestselling author of historical fiction and romances that combine her unique blend of wit and warmth. Her books have been nominated for numerous national and regional awards, including Booksellers' Best, National Readers' Choice and Kindle Best Book. She was also a finalist in the RWA's prestigious Golden Heart® contest. Over the years, she's been a disc jockey, a journalist and an advertising executive, before finally getting around to living the dream--writing stories readers can get lost in.

Find out more about her books at her website: www. eeburke.com.

TAMING HUCK FINN

CHAPTER ONE

"What you layin' in there for, mister?"

A child's voice disturbed Huck's sleep. He screwed his eyes tightly shut, willing his mind to return to dreams of pleasanter things than inquisitive children.

Something struck the bottom of his boot, and Huck jerked awake, his head connecting with a crack against the inside of the hogshead barrel. "Ow! Blame it."

He gingerly touched a rising lump, grimacing at the painful reminder of where he'd ended up after a bout of celebrating his recovery and imminent return to the pilothouse. The abandoned barrel had appeared to be the most convenient place to await the next packet steaming up the Missouri River. Sobriety declared it a bad idea

Curling around, he squinted at the opening, past his legs, to where daylight outlined the figure of a child. Huck shut his eyes hopeful it was just a dream. When he opened them again, the boy had bent to peer inside the barrel. Gap-toothed smile, snub nose, merry eyes that held the promise of mischief...

"Tom?" Huck rasped. No, couldn't possibly be. Tom was full grown with his own children.

The boy giggled. "I'm Tad."

Who? Huck rubbed his stinging eyes. He must've gotten hold of some bad brew like the Fire Rod his old man used to swig by the jug full. That stuff made Pap see crazier things than a boy who wasn't there.

The spitting image of Tom laughed again. "Uncle Huck?"

Uncle?

Huck shook his head to clear it. By God, he'd swear off whiskey forever if it brought on these strange imaginings, and it had to be his imagination. Huck Finn weren't nobody's uncle.

He backed out of the barrel, grumbling. It wasn't just his head that ached, now his stomach joined in, churning in objection to the rank odors washed up by the river.

Surprisingly, the child didn't run away.

Huck scowled to warn him off. "Here now. Don't you got nothin' better to do than comb a body?"

The boy—couldn't be more'n seven or eight—just grinned at him. From beneath the brim of a straw hat, his brown eyes gleamed with anything but repentance. Not Tom, but he could've passed for the younger version with that sorrel coloring and cocky stance.

The oddness of the moment rendered Huck speechless. While he'd been out of head with a fever, he had dreamt of Tom and their pirate gang and the murderous Injun Joe. This pint-sized rascal showing up could be a sign.

"Pardon us for disturbing you, sir. Young Thaddeus meant no offense."

Huck hadn't even noticed the man standing off to one side, a whiskered gent with a stovepipe hat and trim black coat. Had to be an undertaker or a lawyer. Neither boded well.

The man tipped his hat. "We're looking for Mr. Finn. One of the gentlemen in the freight office said we might find him down by the river."

Huck scratched his head. He didn't owe anybody money, and far as he could tell, he was still among the living. Maybe it was *another* Mr. Finn they were seeking. He scanned the wharf expectantly. The only other folks out this early were dock workers and morning crews, most of whom he knew. None of them would answer to the name Finn.

"Reckon you mean me." He stuck out his hand, reluctantly.

"I knew it!" Tad squealed, throwing his arms around Huck's middle, sending him staggering back, nearly toppling him over the big barrel.

He tugged at spindly arms as strong as braided hemp while his unhappy stomach flip-flopped and sweat popped out on his forehead. This had to be prank, but he couldn't think clear enough to work out who'd be in on it and why.

At last, he pried the boy loose and set him at arm's length, and kept a wary eye on the him while addressing his keeper. "Who's looking for me?"

The gentleman dipped his chin in a little bow. "Ambrose Dubois, attorney for the late Mrs. Douglas."

"The *late* Mrs. Douglas?" Huck echoed. A cold shiver passed through him, same as when he'd been shot by that gang of thieving jackals. Only this time, it wasn't bullets that stunned him. The sweet lady who'd taken him in years ago, dead. He barely had time to register the wave of grief when the lawyer continued.

"I'm handling matters related to her will. You have been assigned as guardian for her orphaned grandson, your nephew, Thaddeus Douglas..."

Guardian? Nephew?

Huck groped behind him for the barrel's rounded edge before

his legs gave way. "Here now, what's this about the widow dying and making me this boy's—" He shook his head. No, there had to be some mistake. "You got it wrong. I've never seen this child before."

The lawyer kept on like he hadn't heard. "His father, Captain Douglas, was killed during the war, and his mother passed some years back. Mrs. Douglas, his grandmother, had care of him until her death. She named you as guardian and next of kin."

Huck's mind got clear real quick. Whether this was a simple misunderstanding or an elaborate prank, he was in no mood to play along. It was time to send this gentleman and his sidekick on their way. "Well, now I'm *dead* sure you got it wrong. I'm no kin to Widow Douglas."

"Is that so?" The lawyer cocked his head in a gesture that reminded Huck of a bird examining a bit of string. "According to papers filed fifteen years ago, Mrs. Douglas adopted you."

Try as he might, Huck couldn't wrap his mind around what this lawyer was telling him. Adopted by the Widow Douglas? How was that possible? Well, she *had* claimed she was set to raise him up after his pap had died, and there weren't ever a shortage of prim ladies wanting to civilize him. He reckoned she had given up on him after he ran off. That must've been about the time she made her move.

He drew in a deep breath and slowly released it. He had been Widow Douglas's son all these years and never knew it. His whole life might've been different.

No. He wouldn't have stayed even if he'd known.

"Mr. Finn, you are legally this boy's uncle, and now, his guardian," the lawyer pronounced.

Huck opened his mouth, but all that came out was one word that stuck like a bone in his craw. "Guardian?"

"Yes, that's right," the lawyer continued in a tone that implied he was dealing with a simpleton. "It means you have full responsibility for Thaddeus's care and education, and will be expected to act in his best interests until he is of age. That is, unless you sign over guardianship to someone else."

"No!" The boy shot off like a bullet from a gun but missed his mark when Huck dodged to one side. "You won't give me up, will you, Uncle Huck? There ain't no perversions in that will what'll let you do that."

"Provisions, you mean, and I don't know a thing about this will." Huck sidestepped another pass and put his hand out to keep the boy from hugging him again.

He hadn't gotten this much affection since letting in an old cat from out of the cold to sleep at the foot of his bed. Stray cats he could manage. Stray boys were another matter altogether.

Mr. Dubois stepped in and scooped the child away. "Mind your manners, Thaddeus. You will make a better impression on your uncle if you use them."

This calmed the little imp right fast. He stood Sunday-school still with his hat clutched in his hands. Why hadn't the widow asked this lawyer to be the guardian? He seemed right handy at it. Besides, the boy looked respectable and well brought up, even young as he was. The last thing he needed was the influence of a restless wanderer who didn't put stock in what society deemed necessary.

"What about his other family?"

Dubois shook his head. "No other family has spoken for him."

Huck met the child's anxious gaze and felt a tug on his heart. He understood that alone feeling. It wasn't something a boy outgrew like shoes and britches. Even if he could sympathize, that didn't make him a fit guardian. "Why did the widow reckon I could take care of this boy?"

The lawyer looked pleased he'd asked. "Mr. Sawyer received a letter from you several months back, and he shared it with Mrs. Douglas. They were under the impression you had a good job and had settled down."

Huck bent and retrieved his hat from the ground to hide the shine on his face. How could a little harmless exaggeration have landed him in such a predicament?

He wasn't much for writing and had only penned the letter to Tom because of a strong urge to reconnect after coming so close to death. He'd filled the pages with memories of their youthful adventures, plus a little bragging thrown in about his "luck" in the gold fields. He hadn't mentioned being robbed and nearly killed, or that his injuries had kept him land-locked for so long he had to seek temporary employment. Rather, he'd played up his good fortune at finding work managing the freight yard. A job he quit yesterday so he could get back on the river doing what he loved best.

"They ought to know better than to take what I wrote as gospel."

Dubois frowned. "You lied?"

"It was mostly true, with a few stretchers. Truth always sounds better when it's decorated up, like this here hat." Huck rubbed his thumb over the beaded band. "If I'd known the widow was thinking of sending me this boy, I would've wrote I was broke and near dead. That was true as well, just at a different time."

Keeping his gaze lowered, Huck preoccupied himself with brushing dirt off the sleeve of his old buckskin coat. He'd planned on cleaning up before he started searching for a pilot's position. But if he put on like he was a bum, maybe this man would go back to St. Petersburg and find the child a proper family.

His stomach let loose with a rumbling growl.

Tad's eyes widened.

Dubois cleared his throat. "Mr. Finn, perhaps we could go

somewhere more comfortable and discuss this further. May I buy you breakfast?"

It would be downright rude to refuse, and he had to eat. Once he'd filled his stomach, his mind would work better and he could figure out how to get rid of these two. Then he'd find a private spot where he could properly mourn the Widow Douglas. He couldn't see how taking him in all those years ago had done her much good. Even so, she had put her heart into it, and he was grateful even if he hadn't ever showed it.

He secured his hat on his head and motioned for the two to follow. "There's a boarding house up on Commercial Street. Mae serves a fine breakfast."

Gravel crunched beneath their feet as they trod up the path to a road that led into town.

The levee was ominously quiet, with a few lonesome freight piles scattered about, along with barrels and wood flats stacked up at the head of the dock. Fewer big boats crowded the landing than when he'd first arrived on the edge of the frontier, a shave-tail with no money, no prospects, and not enough sense to care about either.

He cast a wistful glance over his shoulder at the sprawling Missouri River, swollen so high its brown water consumed the lower half of the wharf. The current ran like a racehorse, bearing along leafy limbs, broken branches, and even whole trunks that served as temporary rafts for the birds that rode them with the unblinking nerve of keelboat men.

A shrill sound pierced the air. Not the melodic chords unique to each steamboat but a railroad whistle that 'most gave him the fantods every time he heard it. Each day, railroad crews laid more track westward across unspoiled lands. Soon, the trains would follow, bringing with them society folk intent on taming the uncivilized.

Huck lengthened his stride with renewed determination. They

could build all the railroads they wanted and send a hundred orphans his way, and it still wouldn't change him. He'd escaped civilizing before and he could do it again. Nobody was going to tame Huck Finn.

~

Read the rest of *Taming Huck Finn*.
On sale now at all major online retailers.

www.ingramcontent.com/pod-product-compliance
Lightning Source LLC
Chambersburg PA
CBHW060402260626
47160CB00006B/2406